PORTERGEIST

PORTERGEIST

Steve Porter

www.blkdogpublishing.com

ACKNOWLEDGEMENTS

I would like to express my thanks to:

My father, who tried very hard.
Anja and Kai, for putting up with me throughout the
development of this work.
Janet, for her encouragement.
My editor, Carol Trow, for 'getting it' and helping it become.

DAVID

"Words are flowing endlessly like rain into a paper cup. They slither wildly, as they slip away, across the universe."

Across the Universe, John Lennon

W hen I died, I noticed several changes. My breathing stopped, my skin was pale, I'd collapsed on the pavement, and from the look on my brother Michael's face, I must have smelt something awful.

The crinkled lines at the top of Michael's nose made him look terrified. It scared me.

He was trying to pull free the lace of his ill-fitting shoe from the broken edges of the pavement slabs. So he could escape, maybe? Hide from that Hawker Hurricane above from taking him over completely. Michael never had been able to take much in the way of loudness.

Poor boy.

I wanted to help him, as any older brother should, even if I was only older by a minute. I tried to go to him, but I felt no longer connected to my body on the pavement, nor in fact moving at all.

1

The Hurricane soared.

Maybe this was the cause of my starting to rise. It felt like I was being pulled by the drag of the Hurricane's engine's that were forming a great fiery wake in the above clouds.

Maybe, Thelma would be able to explain it, later. Thelma, I just knew from Michael's smile, before a light that started to shine through from a small gap in the clouds, would be the only one who could ever really understand any of this.

I found myself being drawn to this light, as the Hurricane disappeared behind these clouds. I tried to resist, so as not to leave Michael, but I found I had no strength and was overcome. Then it all broke down in me.

I didn't know why, or what, just couldn't understand it, and pretty soon I was leaning over Michael, like I was a part of this phony war, as Father called it, and was about to do something really terrible.

'You just left me to...!'

From the pavement, Michael let out a piercing scream, like his shoe was pinching him again. Either that, or he was terrified.

I was sorry.

'Michael, it's only me!'

He was still staring at my body on the pavement, the lines at the top of his nose deepening, but more, it seemed, in puzzlement than fear, like he knew something was very wrong, but couldn't quite make out what.

It was a game, I decided. Him sulking, rejecting the very parting he had a hand in causing. It must have been. Mine, needing him just as much, but to join me, rescue me from all that he had caused and otherwise lay before me.

I had been telling Michael of the importance of a need for such an adventure since we were seven, a year before, following our visits to the Gaumont at Chatham, to see *Flash Gordon* for the umpteenth time. But, as Mother had said at the time, a bit too critically, I though, it wasn't Michael's fault that he had always been a little slow on the uptake.

Michael freed his shoe. I could just about see it from the distance. He turned and took a few steps in the direction of the bike-shed of our Abbey Road house in Gillingham.

'Michael?'

He couldn't hear me. That would be it. I found myself wanting him to know about why, but the call of the light, my light, like from father's stars – he was a famous astronomer – was pulling me upwards, forwards and stronger, until I was flying, actually flying, like the Hurricane before. Or, maybe I was in a space ship, because that would have been so much more in keeping with my need for an adventure, to set me free me from all present peril, with my fraternal twin brother's help.

But he still hadn't noticed.

I reasoned that, as Michael had seen in *Flash Gordon* at Saturday morning pictures, the emperor Ming never cried at the loss of anyone, so neither would he. That would be it. That would explain his reluctance, his retreating need for, what would it be this time? A stalk of pampas grass. A flick of his quiff, Whatever, it took to soothe his not so obvious sadness at our apparent parting.

'Michael, I'm calling to you.'

He would have known, of course, that for ignoring me he would have to be punished. We had, after all, promised never to be separated back at the Gaumont and what we promised was always sacred and if broken, well, it would deserve punishment. In adventures, you always do.

Michael sulked his way towards the bike-shed, turning back every now and then to look at my body on the pavement.

At least he gave me that.

Too right!

Yes, he seemed so desperate. I needed him to be desperate. He was my twin-brother, and I did really want to help him. It was my job as the eldest, even if it was only by a minute.

'You can do it, Michael,' I urged. 'You can come with me too. Save me!'

He looked to the sky, to the clouds that were forming as though to obscure any meaning and a thunderclap explosion, like God, or something, blowing up the engines of the hurricane or space ship, right there in front of us, signalling for me to bring this burgeoning adventure to a start.

I let go the elastic of my sling and all my fears, hopes and determination to be realised, shot out, up and away to blind all in this eye from whatever was being conjured there to be my fate, having been left alone on the pavement by Michael, for evermore, with nothing but a pale red, bulbous, distended belly.

'Your turn now, Michael.'

He tripped.

As the clouds swallowed my determination to make it all right again, Mother came out to the pavement, with the others. At first fussing, ordering Michael to find my father who, apparently, was off for some fun with his secretary in Hailsham, again. But Michael hesitated, as Mr. Widdecombe, our neighbour and trusted Sea-Scout leader, picked up the body from the pavement and hurried it inside. My body! My house! And the clouds above were then gathering into what looked like – well, Babel.

A swarthy doctor appeared. I sought to find out why. The doctor was trying to minister to Mother's desperation at what was being rather ominously described as my death.

Death? No, I wouldn't have it.

The adventure to be called, asked for us both and it was so very important to adhere to its call.

There was so much wailing.

And were Michael not to keep, our brave, new adventure, alive, drag him back to what he needed, just as much as I, then he was to be so punished.

'Feel the guilt, Michael.'

He was cowering in the corner of the living room, opposite Mother. Her head dropped in depression.

Nothing.

The pull to the fiery wake was increasing, a rocket, perhaps, screaming down the length of our back garden, with some fat boy, as Michael used to see me – astride the rocket's engine-casing, shouting. 'Crikey, the world has become all so different.'

It was so confusing. I found it hard to get Michael, or me, to remember it all fully.

Beep! Beep! Beep! Beep!

It was the beginning of the main feature.

GREATEST SCOOP in Motion Picture History.

Coming to the screen.

Roar through space aboard the rocket ship!

Shoot through the stratosphere at bullet speed.

Amazing.

Breathtaking.

Hold on to your seats tightly, because here comes the new beginning of a whole new kind of existence.

Michael, looked up from his seat at the front stopped playing with the swizzley bits at the end of his chocolate sweet wrapper, but on seeing the picture of Buster Crabbe, he immediately fell back into his usual, protesting sulk.

Despite my telling Michael otherwise, he was determined that late in nineteen forty-three, there was no spacecraft, and no fiery wake screaming down the garden of Abbey Road for him.

At eleven, he was far too grown-up for this. He was far too intelligent for *Flash* to be anything less than silly. He was only present at the Chatham Gaumont, Saturday morning pictures because Mother wanted the house to herself, so she could clean.

We would see about that!

There was a nasty storm, over the Atlantic, in which a transcontinental plane was being thrown all over the place, its wicker seats tipping over – a design fault that would have annoyed Michael very much.

They could have at least fixed them down with clothes pegs, a bit of plastic upholstery, perhaps.

But the tossing of me and that annoying Mona Freeman - that got Michael's attention – Miss Subways of New York, America, as Michael had found in a copy of the *New Yorker*. Soon to become a star!

'Really?' asked Michael. He flicked his quiff again, whilst playing with his shiny chocolate sweet wrappers.

The tossing of us all about the wooden fuselage, I hoped, would encourage him, perhaps, to call out, gather up his courage and come and rescue us both?

Michael was searching instead through the Gaumont weekly programme for an accompanying picture of Mona. She was a bobby-soxer, apparently.

I had to try differently, I realized.

Mr Widdecombe, our neighbour, was a mad scientist, which wasn't a very good name, I decided, and so it was Dr Zarkov instead, that opened the doors to the space ship.

'We have to save everyone from the approach of the comet hurtling toward everything we ever truly believed in,' he said.

Absolutely!

'Controlled, probably, by none other than Emperor Ming.'

Heavens!

'Only Vortun, with the stumpy big toes, can help!'

A glimmer of recognition from Michael's slightly raised eyebrows. His signature frown.

Come on, Michael. You can do it!

He twitched, a little, in defiance, as others had described.

So I had to have him in the screen, with me, right into Dr Zarkov's ship. It was so futuristic, black, white and grey interior, Bakelite plastic casing. Hundreds of valves and super conductive flashing lightbulbs, almost blinding us.

'Shall we begin?' I had Dr Zarkov say.

Michael appeared quite mesmerized by all the lightbulbs. He didn't seem to mind.

'Five,' I picked up Dr Zarkov's cue. 'Four! Three!'

Michael lifted each of his fingers in count down with me.

I was satisfied to have his recognition and help. A chance for us to make the difference needed to save both of our worlds.

Dead, my arse!

Zarkov, meanwhile, flicked switches, blew with an earnest hope on the candle powered lightbulbs. Then, the boom. Lift off. Up, up and away. As quick as the flash of Gordon's costume, we were speeding through the stratosphere, faster than a string-pulled tin can with a chemistry set flame.

Michael was more interested in Mona, though. The noise of her calling out from the screen was too much for him to resist.

So after a bit of noise control about this and our, crash landing on the rocky barren desert, he looked up again at Babel before him. Some Lion men, with wings, appeared from behind one of the rocks, wielding their tiny black and white tiny, swords.

Michael leant forward at Mona's every intake of breath

before being beaten back with each swish of a tiny sword, as the Lion men took threatening and treacherous steps towards our brave party.

Michael was sulking again.

But with the touch of a button on one of the soldier's belts and we were instantly transported to Prince Vortun's pit of despondency.

'Deathly, it is, Michael.'

He tutted.

Evidently, he thought this had crossed the extra line and was extra special ridiculous.

'How can the adventure we have shared for so long be extra special ridiculous?'

I had to show him.

'Michael, I mean, Vortun, quick, your laser gun.'

He didn't have a laser gun. He did have a stalk of pampas grass, shaped like a bird's beak, that he was flailing about, as though wanting to tickle Mona, or was that just his imagination, or mine?

It wasn't working. It was time to ramp things up a little to draw him in. Michael really needed the drama. He always did like a good drama, responding always with his characteristic, *Uhms and Ahhs.*

Ming, back in his command centre, in Babel, was ordering Captain Brian, our older brother, to swing a massive dehumanizer contraption, thingy, in the general direction of me.

That got his attention.

'Uhm, Uhm. Stop it! He came back. 'I couldn't get to Father on time to save you, because my bicycle had a puncture! And why do you persist in portraying me like this, when you know...

'Shsh, Mister,' said a girl from the row in front of us. And when a girl gave orders to Michael, well, he had to obey!

It was back to the chocolate sweet wrappers, another little hyperventilation in his seat.

'Halt!' shouted Ming, mercilessly, from the screen, his all-conquering gaze now fully trained on the new Prince of Vortun with the stumpy toes and quite a collection of shiny chocolate sweet wrappers.

'You wished to save your brother from the total annihilation of his world, but you had a puncture?'

Mona Freeman laughed, her bobby socks dancing in agreement of this.

I looked at Michael. He seemed utterly devastated at Mona's dismissal of him.

Dr Zarkov was looking at one of his waterproofed maps, just like those he had fashioned before for rainy-day trips in a dinghy, out to Sheerness.

'The prince deserves all you can give, Ming.' I told him. I told them all. 'He is like you always said, locked into his own world, hiding behind his oddness, never there for any of us, not even one bit affected by what he caused back at the pavement of Gillingham.'

He was about to shake and fit one of his protests at this. I could see this building in his expanding pupils.

So I raced over to the doors at the edge of the pit, pulled down on the secure bolt with the strength of Flash. I broke off the handle and the doors flew open. The pressure of the gushing water that was quickly threatening Michael's scratching of his stumpy toes, as though too bored, he was giving up on all this.

'David,' he said. 'Leave me, alone.' His eyes returned to their sulking stare. 'This is all far too silly, I am not like this at all, even for you!'

How could it be that he could give up on an adventure this exciting, not want to play like we used to. How could he leave me like this?

I had to think it through, carefully, because this Flash thing was not exactly working as I'd expected.

The credits rolled. The cliffhanger failed, but not me. I was not going to fail.

Monday, eighth of October, nineteen forty-six. There was a change of adventure. There had to be, with the other not working out.

Michael was in the Abbey Road living room, alone, with me not invited.

'This is the BBC. And now...'

I had to force it somehow.

'Well, you can stop all that calling me Sir, Snowy. It's been years since...'

Because for Michael to believe in this new adventure, he needed someone to be in charge.

'Oh, lumme! After five years in the war and another one after that, foiling devious plots against not being able to grow up, Commander Barton.'

I'd done it once before. Why not again?

Of course, with the programming having become more sophisticated, and Michael getting older and more discerning about what he would listen to, it had to be more exciting, to get him to actively participate, maybe enough to discover what had happened to his teeth-rotting desire for chocolate.

Hush, man. Did you hear that?'

The Devil's Gallop intro music to Barton, next, preparing us for the new adventure.

'Can't say that I did, Sir.'

I was to be the commander, of course, the nation's special agent of hope. He, as Snowy, my right-hand man would indeed be a fellow of great bravery. Self-assured and confident of always doing the right thing, just like all little brothers should.

But he was staring into nothing again, as was sometimes the way with him.

'Snap out of it man!'

All Snowy had to do was believe in himself, again, as capable of living the new, cold war adventure, that I had been learning about recently from his readings of the wind, and become the superhero that I really needed him to be.

'You mean, the Americans, Sir?' His hand reached down to his abdomen, pulled up his shirt and he scratched.

'Indeed, I do, my good man,' I said, happy to have him with me again. We have to restore the nation's energy from the threat of what the Russians are treacherously trying to bring about.'

But Michael was playing with the cat, Tingle, that Mother had got Michael to replace me.

How could she?

'Yes, Snowy, the Russians. I hear they have developed some

sort of strange curtain and I hear Mars Bars give out a whole lot of energy to stand against this curtain?'

Frowning murderously, then, I could see it in Michael's eyebrows, about me, probably, as was his usual wont.

So I had to take his focus, entirely. A crackling underfoot as I set *orf*. And Michael was with me, I had it, following the nation's most accomplished special agent on his bicycle on a great search for a Mars Bar. His quiff flying, as his head bent low over the handlebars. "Yes, you can, Michael, you can do it, bring sense back to your existence and help me foil the Russians plan."

Michael didn't react. He seemed much more interested in examining the scab, caused by the sharp edge of Patricia Grimshaw's set-square, the week before. He prodded, poked.

'Michael, my man. We have to get a move on!'

As we arrived just outside Woolworths, I had it, we could see the expected terrible sign being put up in the shop window.

'Snowy, look. We have to do something.'

Michael was still picking at his scab. 'What do you want from me?' he said.

So I showed him. Two men, looking stern enough to be Russians, or at least I thought So were watching over the tall man fixing the sign on the window, nodding, as the usually cheery, but now forlorn, sales staff, were tearing out coupons from ration books of those in the queue.

I showed Michael the sign, as clear as the reflective water in the picture of Babel back at home.

"Chocolate sweet rations are now reduced to 6oz", it read, "by order of the Ministry of Food."

'You can't do this,' I said, expecting Michael to hurry towards them with great urgency. But Michael didn't seem in the slightest bit concerned

So it was up to me. 'Stop this,' I said, rushing over to them, 'By all that is decent and fair to the children of this country, you must stop this now.'

The men turned. 'Ve are only doing as ordered by your sozialist leaders.'

'By our socialist leaders?' I exclaimed. 'In the land of Barton, Melton Mowbrays, and *The Daily Telegraph*?'

Michael shrugged, as though he really didn't care.

So I had to show him. I had to do something to bring Michael back. I took off my Homburg, shot the lead Russian a characteristically penetrating, steely-eyed stare, enough to mesmerize him with a good dose of British resolve, as Michael, I was surprised to then witness, started to mooch toward the signs, to the great cheers and singing of all the children waiting patiently in line.

'We shall overcome,' they sang.

The store manager arrived then, to great derision from the assembled, saying something about how such attitudes on the radio, these days, were completely unfit for children, just after all the horrors of war and all. And that we, or I, as Barton, was having a deeply harmful effect on the young, of which Michael was no longer.

'I think, David,' he said, tossing aside his copy of the *Radio Times,* with the latest picture of Mona Freeman staring back at me, 'uhm, that you really should stop all this nonsense, leave me alone and uhm, that you should really learn to grow up.'

As he sat back, probably to relax from his exertions and hold back another attack of hyperventilation, our mother came in to the living room and glanced at the picture of Mona.

'You know, Michael,' she said. 'I really think you should leave the girls alone and snap out of all those silly ideas you have about David that get into in your head. Shall we hear the news, instead.' She leant forwards to the wireless to change the station. 'I hear that nice Mr. Bevan's is going to be on, now there's a man that you should listen to, that is much more likely to cure us of all our ills.'

The news started and I was alone again.

We continued to battle like this throughout the late forties. Sometimes, I was American and he Benjamin Britten., Other times, he, when not in charge of the wireless, would count up his pocket money, carefully.

Because Father, having taken off with all the rest of the caring only for his comets of doom and Auntie Eileen. He got published for it too, in a Yale paper and became quite rich and famous for it. Well, famous at any rate, with his book, 'The Night Sky.'

'But Michael, you are my brother to save me.'

'You are a child.'

I wanted to find a way to get Mona to sort it out, but there was no chance of that, now that she had become a film star.

'What was that about Mona?'

'Oh, didn't you know, Michael. She is now called "That Brennan Girl." I think she's on at the ABC, which is a bit too posh for you.'

Michael tried to go see her, but they wouldn't let him into the cinema with Patricia Grimshaw. His trousers smelt too badly. And with Mother taking over the radio to hear Mr Bevan, he had to build his own crystal radio set so he could listen in peace to his music on the BBC Third Programme – when there was space between documentaries, rather than any of my childish adventures.

RAF Church Fenton, November 1951. I was still with Michael, barely. Had a look in, at least, every now and then.

He was standing a little off from the Watch Tower in line of sight of a couple of Gloster Meteors and some of the older Mosquitoes.

'Beautiful, aren't they?'

'Sir?'

'AC1, Porter 5103890, is it?'

'No, Sir I'm an AC2 Plonk, Colour blind and stumpy-toed. My purpose is to bash the spuds, but I think the Mosquito should have had the same engines.'

The station Chaplain turned to Michael.

'Well, tell me, Plonk. Have you ever taken the Lord Jesus into your heart?'

It wasn't the type of adventure I had first imagined, but it was a start.

'Your turn, Michael!'

Michael's call-up had come in the middle of his studies, Mechanical Engineering, deferred, as was allowed, which was very kind of them, he thought.

Entry, kit, swearing in and square bashing at Bridgnorth, choice of trade, RTDF radio, rejected. Posted to Fenton, for the spud basher vacancy, but alSo apparently, because Michael had an appreciation for the jet-propelled.

'You can come back to me in one of those,' I said.

'No,' said Michael, 'I cannot.'

The Chaplain, nodded, as much to Michael as to the Pilot Officer approaching the Meteor.

'Spot of bother with the DFDS – needs one of you chaps to fix the bugger.'

Michael was being allowed to board, to look at the torn-out radio dial, or what was behind it.

The Chaplain, from the ground, waved.

Chatter: FC 4512, on approach.

'Up, man, up,' this was me, in Michael, and as I pulled back on the joy and the Meteor lifted into a forty-five percent ascent, heading straight into the fiery wake.

'What about my other duties,' said Michael. 'Flight 34 will be expecting me soon.'

The Meteor climbed past the city of clouds to forty-four thousand feet.

Control: 'Calling FC4512. You are close to exceeding your surface ceiling.'

Who cared? It was all so exciting!

Michael, also tinkering with the wires at the back.

'It would be very wise for you to accept your brother back into your heart again.'

There was too much static.

'And his name shall be call-ed, David,' I said.

Looking down at the clouds, Michael set about testing each of the wires with an electric screwdriver, he just happened to have in his top pocket, to clear up the static.

'Beware the false God of the anabaptist,' said a new vision as she flew past in a wispy acrobatic manoeuvre coming straight in from out of the sun.

Could it be? Was it actually the Thelma?

Michael downed his screwdriver. 'Will you shut up, David, especially about Thelma. She doesn't even have a concept yet.

It made no sense to him. None of it made any sense, at all.

But the meteor shook, as a stone shot out of a slingshot would have at the highest point of its elliptical curved trajectory.

The pressure increased.

'Down FC4512. Down,' barked the orders from a concerned command on the DFDS.

Michael twiddled his nose as I pushed forward on the throttle. The Meteor descended into safety as I allowed Michael to secure the radio dial properly in its dark, fibre-glass casing.

'My other duties await,' said Michael, climbing out of the Meteor, waving goodbye and when firmly on the ground by the tower again, saluting the Chaplain.

His arm around Michael's shoulders.

'You didn't answer my question, Plonk.'

The Chaplain looked most put out at this.

'Sir,' replied Michael, with due, earnest respect. 'I heard his word, his warning about the anabaptist methodists and my heart was indeed joy filled.'

The Chaplain smiled.

'You know Plonk, I actually believe you. You are not like the others, chasing all the WAAFS, for unclean temporary fulfilment.'

'Scared of them, Sir.'

'As it should be, my man. Well, I hope to see you on Sunday for your baptism!'

Michael, stood at ease, even though he hadn't been given permission.

'Right, you are, sir!'

That was when Michael realised the adventure of the good Lord entering his heart.

They'd met in fifty-seven. She wasn't as pretty as *that Brennan Girl*, with her gimpy, bucked front teeth, her swell of curly hair and a mousiness, derived from years of desire for revenge and a penchant for patricide.

They'd met at a church dance, shortly after Michael had de-mobbed from the RAF.

'Oh, you,' said Hannah

'No, you, dear.'

'He he. Do you mean it?'

It was the first time ever Michael had been called 'dear' and he was quite excited about it, what with Hannah's availability and later introduction of salad-cream to his otherwise restrained palate, it was indeed a recipe for what he was certain was to be a true love.

But Michael had no right to it.

I had to hatch another plan I realized and the past, I always found, offered the best solution in this regard, especially if one's future was in any kind of doubt, as mine most certainly was.

So I was all over Michael then, like before, pressing into him a Skylon shaped beak, even if it would mean he would let out a terrible scream.

'Michael, it's me, David. Don't leave me for the buck-toothed one. It will come to no good, I tell you. No good at all!'

But he already had me dispatched and was courting *that* Hannah in the park.

I tried the radio, again to thwart this. *The Goon Show,* but no-one could ever understand what they were on about.

And when Hannah graced his digs with a fine Melton Mowbray, and a rather limp lettuce leaf, the grave threat to our future bond was sealed.

With a stalk of pampas grass, she did it, playing him so well. Knighting him, as her deliverer, in giggle – the first man she'd met who wouldn't shout back.

Why must you demean me, like this, David?

And in the corner of the living room of the couple's soon-to-be-shared digs, a wondrous moving-picture box appeared called a television, that would have a far greater degree of influence on the future than any radio, comic, film, or made-up voice ever could.

It was all linked, apparently, to a prophecy about a light hidden behind Babel, connected to a sacred pact, made all that time ago, at the Gaumont, rather than the posh ABC!

'I really like walking with you, Hannah.'

'Well, of course you do,' Hannah said back, 'and you are, if you don't mind my saying, very lucky to know me.'

'I shall love you, of course' said Michael.

Which, despite everything, again threatened to leave me alone, without so much as a hurricane, mosquito, or Meteor, by the fiery wake of our Abbey Road back garden, to get Michael to face up to what he'd been and gone and done.

We would see about that!

MICHAEL

I always say that if someone has the right to ask a question, the person answering always has the right to say no.

I must confess that I sometimes wished I'd said no a bit more to Hannah.

But then, where would I have been with the children? How could they understand? And could I have really let David die all over again?

It was nineteen sixty. Father peered at me in his usual accusing way, from behind the front pew of St Leonard's, his eyebrows bouncing, as a man from father's television was admiring a huge telescope and the commentary. 'I think, Patrick, he is now almost totally obscured.'

Hannah squeezed my hand. I had to focus on what was happening on this day we had both wanted and for so long.

There was laughter. It was taking over. Then this Patrick, Patrick Morgan, maybe, for everything was so confused and yet also genius. At least that was how my colleagues, sighing in exasperation, as I entered each and every room, would describe the problem. I couldn't possibly comment.

'Indeed, all the indications are that the Russians, and you have to take your hat off to them, are now making such immense progress that almost anything can happen.'

I had to ignore David. Father was expecting.

The Minister guided my gaze back to the purpose of the gathering with his own eyes.

Poor man had only started last month and apparently, he was a scientist before his ordination.

"Do you Michael Porter, take Hannah Price?"

I checked the watch I'd stolen from David, looked back at Hannah's hopeful, expectant, stare.

As father had once described the ghost craters, on the outer slopes of the Moon, I could see the same in her eyes.

'Michael?'

David was back, showing me the effects on my life if I allowed this wedding to go ahead, as catastrophic as his imaginary sputnik, three warheads were on a passion to start something preposterous.

'Michael, please!'

I stiffened, looked into Hannah's eyes, with all the defiance I needed to help me pull it off.

'I do!'

I looked to the congregation, willing waves of well-wishes for our future from the assembled and a cold draught blew down the aisle, as Mother buried her head in her black shawl, like she'd already worked out what was going to happen.

From the ensuing scream in my head, I dropped the ring. The best man, a friend of Hannah's, I didn't really know him, caught it, as David's loudest scream, like the beginning of Mussorgsky's, *Night on Bald Mountain*, at the Royal Albert Hall concert I'd recently attended, sounded, and Father's accusing eyes, piercing me, Mother, sobbing, in a far from good way, and Hannah, Hannah, pleading with me from utter desperation.

I took the ring. I followed the Minister's lead and placed this on Hannah's finger, as she did mine, quickly.

The Minister switched to use the older *Book of Common Prayer* ceremony to seal the union, his words raced, to my own embattled adventure with David, staring all the evil that could ever come from such a heavy guilt.

'Do you take?'

Hannah did. And somehow, I did as well and then I found myself walking back down the aisle with my new wife, Hannah.

I found Mother looking up at me with bloodshot eyes and Father, clutching at Auntie Eileen's hand, as though his hand was a vice.

I remembered what she'd said, back then when she'd first started out with Father.

'Because, "No Man can ever be an island", Michael, she'd said, '"entire of itself", as it has been for you and for so long.'

I had realized she was quoting, but I didn't know who, or what, precisely.

David thought he did.

'"Therefore, never send to know", Michael,' he finished off, '"for whom the bell tolls", because, if you're not very careful, and who knows, it might have already, I haven't quite decided yet, but it could, Michael, as you, yourself, have determined, by denying me. Yes, Michael, do not be surprised if it decides to toll for thee!'

2 December, 1962, 14.32, Stewart John, 10lb 8oz.

I needed to put away all the silliness of David. I was a father now. I needed a responsible future! Not a three-button wool navy blazer with straight flapped pockets, and a single vent.

How did David even know about tailoring terminology? I didn't at his age.

On the Fergusson television. I should have known.

'Templar,' he said, trying to introduce himself.

It was too much. I needed a distraction. David too, and urgently. Something to throw David off.

And as luck would have it, there was an opportunity, lying suitably there, right in front of me. Small, needy, gawping.

So I picked up little Stewart from his carry-cot, drew and held him close. He didn't yet know the importance of geometric shapes. He wasn't able to hold back. So when the dribble ran down my tank-top, that was bought for me by Hannah, it was better to ignore, than... because how could anyone resent such a small child?

It was as good a time as any to make my pledge. 'I shall try to love you,' I said to little Stewart, wiping his drool from my tank-top. 'I will do my best and God-willing, you too shall have all you ever deserve and want.'

'Michael?'

Hannah was down from her rest, ready to inspect the shopping. I did resent how she made me do that!

It was all laid out neatly on the kitchen worktop for her, as she had ordered.

She checked off each item. 'Cornflakes, eggs. Marzipan for your Battenburg. Very good. But pilchards, Michael? When I specifically asked you for baby food! You will have to go back. Do you never listen to me?'

Stewart was turning some sort of colour in the face.

I failed to see why Hannah always felt she had to adopt such a critical tone and I tried to explain.

'They didn't have any baby food at the Wavy Line dear. And pilchards were always accepted as well enough for us, when we were small.'

Hannah rolled her eyes.

Did she not think I could see this? Did she even care enough to wonder? She had been so spoilt. All those opinions about acceptable eating behaviours.

David was laughing, or for a moment it very much sounded like him.

The telly, again.

Then Stewart was sick. There was quite a force to it. This time all over my shirt that had to be changed, so I offered Stewart out with my vomit-stained sleeves, but would Hannah help?

She was taking her time about it.

'Maybe, when you change,' she said, finally, taking Stewart from me, 'you can have a wash, too.' She nuzzled Stewart up against her chest. That was rare.

This was the thing with Hannah. There was hardly ever any love. I had drained her of it all, or so she'd said. She could be really quite cruel, sometimes.

But it was the ladder in her Debenham's tights that I resented the most. It wasn't so much that they were so expensive, as the haphazard nature of the tear.

'Such as Templar likes, probably,' said David.

But Hannah was still in the kitchen and would have been able to hear. So instead, I tried to put this and David right out of my mind.

His continued laughter, though, at Hannah's remonstrations of my recent shopping was becoming increasingly hard to ignore.

'I honestly don't get you, sometimes,' continued Hannah. 'Pilchards in place of your own child's needed baby food?'

'Stop it, David.' There, I'd said it.

No response from Hannah.

'She doesn't seem to want to notice,' he said. 'Why do you even give her the time of day?'

The cheek!

Because it was my job to get Hannah to notice. It was my job to be more like that Templar fellow. Suave, well dressed and full of responsible action. And 'which is more, you'll be a man my son'. That was what she wanted, That, was what women like Hannah always wanted, I had by then entirely come to realize.

But did anyone really care what I wanted?

'To come to the light with me.'

With Stewart now down and bedded, I gave him a look, pursuant to his achieving all his dreams and put on a Symphonic poem – because I needed it. Stewart wasn't gawping any longer. Just content. But not Liszt. Never Liszt. This moment required nothing less than Delius.

I suppose I could have loved Hannah more, were she receptive to the attention I'd tried to show her. But since she'd come home from the hospital, she had pushed me aside and spent most of her time shouting at me.

'Michael, stop that. Leave me alone.'

So I did and was blamed for that too.

She was sitting at her place behind the sewing machine, ready, no doubt, to run off her version of a new three-button wool navy blazer.

Sometimes, one has to allow one's circumstances an element of hope.

Little Stewart, with his arms dancing along in the background to Mahler's fifth.

She looked as though she were deep in thought, perhaps contemplating the delights of the new Moulinex she'd demanded the previous week.

'Michael?' she asked.

'Yes, dear.'

'Why is it that you always make me so depressed?'

Again?

Tears, lots of them.

How was I supposed to answer when she was like that, and what did she want of me? I had already taken two weeks off work, sacrificing my supervision of the test build of Concorde's oscillating separator.

'She needs you to leave her,' said David, 'either that, or suffer that heavy-set plant pot on her head, so you will be forced to get me to work out who did it. Can you not see, she is no good for you, Michael? She rejects what you have to offer. She even rejects your pilchards.'

I decided not to let David get to me and so started to think about all the excitement Stewart was going to behold under my guidance. The line of sight of architraves, as they disappeared into their perfect right angles, the thrill he was going to get when his hand touched upon Tingle Two's fur. A performance of *that* Prokofiev, even with a wolf, but this time, hopefully not intent on breaking up my union with Hannah to deny me the chance to live a future.

The ascent of David on my much-imagined staircase was about to begin.

'You, really are quite good at inducing a depression, Michael, aren't you?!'

I was Stoic. Calm. How would Mr Widdecombe have handled this?

Tingle Two came in for some attention – the first of that name having died from a rather nasty flea-infection. The vet, apparently, from the look of my greyed tank-top of the time, under mother's care, had taken pity on me and given me a replacement for free.

Now, there was a kindly, good man. He'd obviously found God early in life.

'Bloody mangy animal,' Hannah said. 'Needs putting down.'

I had come to learn that when it came to Tingle Two, Hannah could become quite prone to jealousy. It was one of the nasty sides of relationships with women. Mine anyway.

But it was when Mother arrived that things really started to turn bad.

Past statues of Flash Gordon, Bunter, Barton and Churchill, I tried to get David to ascend, but often he only wanted to play his games.

The sound of the door knocker.

Hannah rushed to it and as she opened the door.

'Not the spawn of Satan!'

Where most mothers-in-law would do anything to pour love onto a babe in arms, Mother, carrying a bunch of near dead asphodels, 'for the flower pot, I bought you', she said, had a whole other set of ideas as to the needs of small children.

'Why don't you leave it all to me, dear?' Mother chimed in. 'After all, raising a child, as you know I know, if he is anything like Michael here, is like trying to vomit without having a mouth!'

I could see Hannah's blood rising in her face. I had to step in and say something.

'Mother,' I said. 'Must you?'

'You have to let children cry a little,' she returned.

'Dr Spock,' countered Hannah.

Whatever that was supposed to mean?

I gave Stewart his pilchards anyway, some of the sauce, at least. He kept looking at a play bucket to the right of his cot. Shiny. I grabbed it and gave it to him to play with.

'How is Stewart supposed to understand the world if he is not even allowed to feel?'

Stewart looked like he was inspecting the bucket's fine lines.

'He needs schedules, discipline...'

'...and no affection, at all?' Hannah warred back.

'No, Hannah,' said Mother. 'I certainly will not leave. I have only just arrived.'

I didn't want to, but Hannah had said the words, and anyway, as I was instructed in the excellent *How to Be a Husband in the Modern World.* 'If the wife is so distressed then the husband is advised to go find her a little present to show her just how much he cares.'

I reached for my gaberdine mac.

'Not you, stupid!'

But Mother was giving me her look.

So I mounted the saddle, and after adjusting the Sturmey-Archer three-cog gears to first, for safety's sake – it was, after all, a particularly cold and slippery-iced day – I set off.

The journey was not unlike another I'd once made to my father in Hailsham. A sports car roared past me on the Upper Richmond Road.

'Show off!'

I was too annoyed and needed to think on something entirely different.

I thought about when I took the short cut across the lakes to Hailsham, where my father and Eileen then lived, as I remembered each tree on which David and I had once played and swung and thrown paper planes at each other.

It was not where I wanted my thoughts to go.

So I remembered, instead, a quality purveyor of bubble bath in the late Victorian stretch of shops on the imposing Streatham High Road.

Bubble bath had always soothed Hannah, when troubled, and had often got me back into the love that we were supposed to feel. somehow, for each other.

Through the forest of doubt, as David and I used to call it, with the original Tingle jumping, reminding me how, at the time, she was my only friend.

'No, Michael.' David again. 'I am your only friend?'

The Streatham High Road was a carnival of stupidity, with all the floats inching along, blocking me. The Streatham Film Society was the worst, adverts for the latest films, someone dressed up as Mona Freeman, a travesty, and Wilfrid Brambell at the end with a cup. Ridiculous man.

Through the open fields of heather, I needed just to shut David up. But when making it to the tree from which David and I had once gazed at the night stars with Father, a man pushed me. I hope it was an accident and I fell, landing on the pavement with a thud to rival any plant-pot crashing down on the head of one's newly appointed wife.

No! David. No! No! No!

At the time, with Auntie Eileen opening the door. 'Emergency. It's David. He is writhing on pavement, near home. Abbey Road. He looks very ill and is clutching at his tummy with a queer look in his almost expanding pupils.'

'Well, you'd better come in, then.'

Father lifted his annoyed, bristling eyebrows, from his book 'How long ago?' he asked.

The plastic bag containing an expensive bottle of bubble-bath hanging from my handlebars, had swung up and hit me in the face.

'A whole hour! Why, didn't you come by your bicycle, you stupid boy?'

It was so uncalled for.

Hannah's brother emerged from the crowd.

'That's where you are. Hannah called me from a telephone box in Sunbury. Given all the time you were taking, she was scared, frightened that you might have listened again to your voices and abandoned her.'

'But I wouldn't do that,' I protested. 'Hannah is my wife; the mother of my child and I am very much pleased with her.'

'That's good,' said Gerald, 'because if you don't get a proper perspective on your life and marriage to my older sister, then I'm afraid I'm going to have to take your aspirations and show you exactly what the meaning of life truly is.'

In my mind, I raised a flower pot. A great big and heavy flower pot. It was not for Hannah.

I got in Gerald's car, anyway. It was the same sports car from earlier. We strapped my bicycle to the roof rack, with a length of some old light cord that Gerald just happened to have lying about in his boot.

When we got back home, Hannah was addressing Stewart, as though he could understand her. 'You are going to be my best boy,' she was saying. 'Yes, you are. You are going to be the one that makes everything work out, despite your daft father.'

Charming!

'I will show you how. I will show you how to be my best boy.'
Gerald pushed the door open

'He's back, Hannah.'

'Take her,' said Hannah, pushing Mother forward. 'Take this awful woman away from me.'

Gerald grabbed a hold of her.

'I say. Michael, are you going to let him handle me like this.' Hannah had her stare on at me.

'But your wife doesn't know what she is doing, she is going to ruin the poor child's life.'

Mother's cries were summoning me to make a stand, defend her, as they always did, but Hannah's stare and the look in Gerald's eye, just like it was in the playground all those years ago.

'You want to do something about it?'

They were both right. I did need to do something about it, so I stood up straight, placed my hands upon my awkwardly positioned hips.

'Mother,' I asserted in her general direction. 'In this, you are not being very helpful – at all.'

As Mother left with Gerald, I handed Hannah the bottle of bubble bath and Hannah was grateful for my stand.

'You mustn't ever leave like that without even a word,' she pleaded. 'You must never, ever leave me again, dear!'

That was what she said.

She took herself off up the stairs and started to run the bath. I could hear the gurgles of Stewart, for his wanted coochy-coo, or whatever it was that he sought. It was the shiny bucket again.

I gave it back to him and twiddled his nose.

It seemed to work, for a bit, at least, until Reginald Bosanquet, came on the television, proud, determined and ready to conduct an interview with a new and up-and-coming star, except it was an imposter.

'I know no man can be an island, but this is all really becoming very tiresome.'

It was not so much about the influence of Mr. Templar on the world, as the struggle that Hannah and I always had when trying to understand one another. We found such difficulty in recognizing where all our dissonance came from.

'Michael,' said Hannah appearing in the doorway, 'what you did to me. I mean, I'm looking in the mirror and I'm huge.'

'I thought that was what you wanted, dear.'

I changed the channel.

The heavy-set plant pot, as shown on screen, pushed by the wife murderer that Templar had been trying to foil in that stupid television programme, crashed down onto the patio of what must have been the set where the programme was being shot.

Whilst at the same time, I didn't see, so I don't know how David did it, but a shiny bucket hurtled past my right eye and landed right in the face of Hannah.

'Hannah are you alright?'

Stewart was giggling, along with David, or it might have just been David, I wasn't sure.

Hannah seemed more shocked than anything. That her own best boy...

'It wasn't intentional.' I tried to comfort her, dabbing at the cut on her cheek with my handkerchief.

Hannah was distraught.

'Of course, it wasn't,' she screamed. 'He's a baby, it was because you weren't supervising him. What kind of father do you think you are?'

March 10, 1964, Midnight. Douglas Philip, 10lb 13oz.

He was absolutely enormous and when I picked him up, the wrinkled image left in the sheets from all his thrashing was like a depiction of God's very wrath.

Even though the sheets were all scrunched up, the image was unmistakable. Douglas looked just like David. Or, one of David's photos, when he was a child, at least. The same face, eyes, nose and that glint is his imagined eye as we fiddled with our toy bi-planes.

It was a repeat of when Stewart was first born when Hannah got into a similar stupor and took to her bed and David played his games. Different, though, this time. It was not so much post-natal depression, like with Stewart, as sheer exhaustion, and –

dare I confess it – a pure and unadulterated fear, bordering on Job's terror of the almighty!

What came from this, though, was a new kind of connection between Hannah and me. She crumpled at the sight, or any mention of her father and my knowing, from experience by then, exactly how to deal with things.

I thought it best to run Hannah a bath when she got home. She did seem to like them.

So I was given a second chance at being a father. The endless washing of nappies. My having to calm Douglas from the incessant screaming, trying to poke apple sauce into a mouth that just wouldn't open. Not to mention the fixing of the clothes pegs when they would break to amuse him. Thank the Lord that Stewart was never so troublesome.

After a while, though. Quite a long while, actually, I made sure of that, so I could not be accused as not having any patience

'Hannah, will you get out of that bath and help? What kind of mother, are you?'

It was a bit risky, turning the tables, like that, but required. Douglas was turning out to be an impossibly difficult child.

'Boo!' He was surprised at this, Douglas, at me, and looked straight up, it seemed, with so much yearning. It was a stare such as I had never seen, even from David when he was on the pavement. A stare of death, or one that heralded the building of a new world, making everything up again in ways that he might, even, one day, understand.

I caught sight of a discarded postcard to Hannah from Edna Bone, from next door. They were best chums, given that I didn't have any of my own to introduce Hannah to, or so she said.

The front picture of this postcard showed a picture of a baby sat in a feeder chair, strapped to a cow and sucking life through a tube that was attached to one of the cow's udders. It really was very strange.

'The surrealists,' as Auntie Eileen had often told me on my visits to her back then on my bicycle, 'were very strange about babies too.'

'Really, Auntie?' I had feigned my interest at the time, amazed at the size of her Eccles cake.

'Oh, yes, dear. Do you know they used to make postcards of babies in such peculiar settings, so as to provide inspiration for their art.'

This postcard was one of them.

I looked again, then at Douglas, then at the card again and it was uncanny, but then most babies looked the same.

Hannah was far from happy when she came down.

'You dare speak to me in that tone of voice, Michael! Well, I'll show you,' and she picked up Douglas, stared right back at him, as though there was a contest between them. Douglas's eyes were agape; Hannah fighting back an attack of blinking.

I didn't have much time for the surrealists but I did enjoy a picture with an excellent command of perspective, all those straight lines to look for, imagine the artist creating his work with, such as, and this was surely the stuff of David, or I wouldn't put it past him, right there in the *Radio Times*, an advert for a reproduction print of the 'The Music Lesson', by Vermeer, and all for the cost of a stamp, if I were prepared to cut out the vouchers and send them off.

Well, I did.

'Good, just as I want,' but this new David game had started to puzzle me.

Hannah held out against Douglas, far longer than I expected, but it wasn't a good thing to let Hannah know when I was aware of her losing anything, so I said nothing as she put him back in his cot and made my way to the kitchen to make a cup of tea. It was not a very good cup.

About a week later, I received notification that the Vermeer as ready. It would look good in the music room by the side of the record cabinet.

'I'm off, dear.'

'No, you're bloody well not.'

'I think you will find that I am. It is time that you earned your keep around here.'

The rising of her chest, and the running of her sentimental tears again, but as it was written in *How to Be a Husband in the Modern World*, a challenge such as this to break one's ailing wife out of her predicament was very often just the ticket, or what the Doctor ordered, which was good, now that we didn't have to pay for it, was a sort of social prescription.

I had coined a phrase.

To Westbourne Park, I had planned the journey long. The first part, through North Feltham, past the hardware shop, where I could pick up some more springs for the clothes pegs. More strength was needed with which to secure the fatter nappies.

When I got there, a metal bucket, in which a baby was sat, a marketing gimmick photograph as placed by Q, from that latest film about that Bond chap, but the realism of that stare, like before, and it was a good likeness too, was quite mesmerizing.

I was not going to allow myself to be so unhinged.

With the replacement springs secure in my saddlebag, it was into the Staines Road where I encountered a debilitating cold to fight against.

At Hounslow, High Street, in the display window of British Home Stores, another rendition of Douglas's stare, with him perched on top of some bicycle handlebars, a reasonable enough image, were it not for the telephone call between him and Rosa Klebb.

'The call of the bell, goes ding, ding, ding.'

It was the cold playing tricks with my mind, or that was what I thought, until underneath the picture, I saw the words, 'He stares because he loves and seeks to understand you in his bold new world.'

At Shepherd's Bush, Douglas was depicted, as though talking into the Lektor cypher machine, with wires coming out of his ears to Rosa, or Hannah, spreading all her hatred.

I had to call on the bible. *Be sober-minded; be watchful. Your adversary the devil prowls around like a roaring lion, seeking someone to devour.* Peter could always be more relied upon than David.

I arrived at the correct address. It was a record shop. Christian. Good. I gave the man my ticket, his beard, very disconcerting, and he gave me the reproduction print.

'I like the perspective,' I said.

'There are many,' he returned, and then, 'But you really

must mind how you go with them. You wouldn't want to be led astray, now.'

On the way back, the sun came out. There were no speeches from David to be worried about. Just the traffic of emotions affecting my overview of the road all the way back to Feltham.

I stopped off for some proper baby food in the Co-op too. The cherry on the top, I thought.

Hannah would be so pleased.

I found her parents had arrived, on a whim.

Hannah sat far away on the other side of the room.

'No, dear, said Cressida,' we don't get angry.'

I took the tube casing from off my shoulder and handed this to Hannah.

'A version of 'The Music Lesson' that you like, dear.' I explained.

Ralph was peering through his glasses with obvious interest, as Douglas's stare at me intensified.

Hannah opened the tube, took out the print, unrolled.

'What's this?' she said, throwing this on the sofa.

And there laid out like a different version of the wrath of God, was a completely different picture.

'That's not *The Music Lesson*, that's Bruegel, that is,' said Ralph. 'The Elder. *Tower of Babel.* How could you do this to me, Michael?'

Cressida was shaking her head.

How could I what? It was the bearded one in the shop that had made a mistake, but what was the significance of this particular picture, that I had never set eyes upon before.

I was as perplexed as when at the RAF entrance examination, they tried to convince me that red was not the same colour as sand.

As Cressida set to comforting Hannah, moving to the place next to her on the sofa, Ralph took me aside.

'Some tea, I think, Michael.'

But as I left, Stewart's bucket seemed to be causing Douglas distress. I had to collect Douglas, leaving Stewart to take it all in, but Douglas did start to settle when I placed him on the kitchen sideboard with a direct line of sight to me.

'How's work?' asked Ralph. 'While we wait for that ancient kettle of yours.'

'Fine,' I said. 'My oscillator, got approval from the director.'

I reached for the used tea bags in the plastic cups, but given it was Ralph, I thought again and it was out with the wedding present tea-set.

'I see.'

'But with a reduction in the oscillator's vibration speed, I wasn't happy. It just wouldn't do.'

Edward arranged the bottle of milk and the sugar, whilst I shook the four cups into position, four inches from the edge, to be safe.

'Yes, it's for that new plane isn't it, superseding something, or whatever.'

'Supersonic, Concorde they call it, but I don't hold out much confidence with the reduction.'

The kettle rattle had reached full force and with the steam coming out of its spout, the grand revelation was expected.

'You have it with, I presume?'

The tea-bags slowly infused.

I ignored him, this latest game I did not understand. But like with the red wine with the fish, it should have told me something.

'Hannah can get a little obsessed,' said Edward, 'as you probably well know.'

'Do I, Ralph? No, I don't think that I do.'

I poured, thinking it best to be the Daddy in my own house.

'Oh, yes,' continued Ralph, 'when Hannah was a child, she was often getting obsessed with things, such as how and when her anger was to be expressed. She spoke to her mother about it all the time. You see, she didn't like me much in those days, had me down as some left-leaning woman-hater, or so she would tell Sheila, and she wanted to get back at me.'

'Ralph, Michael, how are you getting on with the tea? Do you have lemon?'

I didn't, but I wasn't going to deal with that then, with Edward in full communication.

'A light shall break forth amongst them that sit in darkness, as the fulness of my gospel,' but this was David. Or, was it?

I didn't have the time to find out.

'Hannah was obsessed with that God of hers,' said Ralph, 'as though he could have done anything to help her? But we don't talk about it, which is where, I think, you made your mistake, Michael.'

He picked up the two cups allocated to him, made his way through the doors, me following with mine and Douglas, sat upon my forearm, like he was straddling the back of a cow.

Hannah was studying the picture laid out before her.

'You just don't understand me, Michael? You never have.'

She was pointing to the clouds and then withdrawing her finger quickly, as though she feared being burnt by it.

'Whatever is the matter?' I asked of her, placing both of our teas very firmly on the flat wooden surfaces of either arm rest and then Douglas back next to Stewart. Two peas in a pod, except for the stare of one.

'Don't you know me at all?' Hannah continued.

Douglas was a gawp, as Stewart studied his bucket and possibly his options.

'How can I like that which attempts to defy God's own will?'

Cressida turned to Ralph. Ralph turned to Cressida. They each nodded to each other.

'Yes, Michael, well, thank you for the tea, but we are due for a brass-rubbing session at the old church in Staines. They heat up the pies for an entrance precisely at three o'clock.'

'Defy God's will?!' I asked Hannah.

'Yes,' she said, 'make good all that divides us.'

'What do you mean?'

Ralph and Cressida left in a hurry.

Hannah turned back to the painting and then pointed at all the ant-like figures portrayed.

'What they are trying to do, Michael. Such a creation, so as to subvert God's will, reach beyond the clouds so as to challenge and take over, maybe even govern heaven!'

'But, as I understand, this picture is about creation,' I said. 'The creation of a bold new world. A new set of voices, whole new languages too.'

Hannah turned, looked straight at me.

'Wait for it,' said David, and I could feel it in him, just how very pleased with himself and all he was about to achieve.

'Or, ways of being,' continued Hannah, 'in which we are to be separated, in word, mind, and deed. The builders building, as the few women that join them, support, unable to create in their own right.'

I looked at her and tried my very best to understand what she was saying.

'But it was a different time, Hannah.'

The sound of the front door slamming.

'Really?' she asked. 'Are things so different? Do not your voices, your departures, seek a dampening of my will in our creation here, our family and how it will all crumble from your refusal to include me, your complete inability to understand?'

'Understand what, Hannah?' I asked.

This was certainly not the woman that I had married.

'Michael,' she said, 'as you know, I have little enough confidence in this marriage, especially after I saw the red in your eyes on our wedding night. The same red as I saw with my own father, when I crumpled and so when you left me, I thought,' and tears started to well in her eyes... 'Well, I thought that you'd abandoned me for that David of yours again.'

Hannah held out her hand, as though wanting something. I let her. It didn't matter what she wanted, because I knew she wanted it from a different man, one that loved her dearly, for giving to him a family, even with a cat named Tingle Two.

And this man would have to be on his own brave new adventure to understand how he could possibly pull any of this off, despite the voices of Babel?

David wasn't laughing at me anymore.

'You listen to me now Michael and mark my words well. There are many flickering lights at the pictures. You have to choose wisely, which one to follow.'

But it wasn't so much what I saw that affected me, then, as what I heard from Hannah about what was coming next.

'Michael,' she said.

'Yes, dear.'

'Have a bath!'

I wanted the heavy-set plant pot back, but there wasn't one present. I wanted the babies from my journey to scream God's wrath of revenge at Hannah. I wanted to run, hide, anything to get my own back for Hannah's betrayal of me in this bold new world, as created by Douglas's great gawping stare.

But this was Hannah, the woman I had married and I knew that in this, at least, my silences about all that was going on inside my head were justified.

A cow jumped over the moon.

2.25am 22 September 1965, Polly Diane, 8lb 6oz.

Oh, heavens, a girl!

David's central theme of the beautiful will always turn evil, so obviously taken from the latest *Dr Who* episode – there was nothing else on – might have been easy enough to counter, if I could have found a decent enough article in the *Radio Times*.

'We shall call her Polly,' said Hannah, 'in hope that she will be able to find her glad game, against all your silences, dear.'

My silences? 'Oh, right you are, dear.'

I'd learnt long before that it was far easier to go with Hannah in these things.

Yes, I was a little angry about it.

'Don't you think she is beautiful?'

But only internally.

It was what I'd learnt to be a catch me question, if I said one thing, my world would fall in, if, I said another, perhaps... but then I remembered.

'She's got your smile.' It was a line from '*How to Be a Husband in the Modern World.*' It had worked before.

Hannah didn't react. She made her way upstairs, leaving me to deal with David's usual manipulations of the television.

There was nothing on the Radio; I'd checked. And neither did the *Radio Times*, unusually, have any interesting article from which to draw any defence. But I did have my diary to work with. Something, anything to protect me from allowing David to take over again.

I picked up my pen.

"Woke 7.30. Rose 8.15. Cool start, still tired from last night at hospital. Polly, out. Promise of clouds. Hannah too snarky today. Tax refund letter came. All of £12 8s 14d. Not what I'd calculated. Quick letter to London Electricity, asking if they could accept part-payments."

But then. I must have missed it, with the calculator going into scientific mode.

'They are from the planet Skara, twelfth planet from the sun,' said David, but it wasn't, it was William Hartnell, from the doctor he was playing, that for once, in this ridiculous adventure David was trying to draw me into, wasn't swarthy.

'You don't belong here', he said, as though directly to me, but I defended with my memory of Hartnell being so much better in *The Mouse That Roared*.

'Michael,' came Hannah's call from upstairs. 'Have you got any milk left over from the boys. Polly's hurting me, now.'

I put down my pen and diary, made my way to the feeding station in the corner of the living room, picked up a partially used bottle – the boys were alright in their caged pens, opposite – and hurried upstairs to source of the distraction.

'She doesn't like me,' said Hannah, when I got there. 'She hates me.'

'Who?'

'Polly, she won't latch on. Probably thinks I'm poisonous.'

'Now, Hannah,' I said. 'We've talked about this.'

'Did we, when?'

Maybe, it was with David. Well, I meant to.

I gave Hannah the bottle, who just had to tease little Polly's lips before she took in the teat and started to drain it.

'I hope you washed it of the poison you have given me and will probably want to pass on to Polly too, such as you are.'

'Hannah?'

'It's why you mustn't surrender to her,' said David, as the leader of the pathetic Daleks. His only real experience of this of course, being Mother. 'Or die!'

'Oh, do be quiet, David!

I returned to my diary, downstairs.

It was all very well, Hannah's hurt from Polly's suck, whilst I, with my own purpose of how to be a good husband and father, drawn out by the constant piercing of Hannah's barbs, needing to turn me into the monster I could never be.

'She is woman and she hates you, as she needs you to hate her, so you can leave her and come back to me.'

Ignore. Deny, Defy. Denounce.

What had I done to deserve this, Lord? Answered by Paster Mead's sermon, if I was prepared to read between lines. It was an affliction, temporary, Hannah would get over it and I wasn't to react. Never let her know how I really felt.

I found my place again in the black-leather swivel chair. The boys were quiet enough.

"Washed kitchen floor. A huge amount of washing-up. Exhorted to give money to the Reynolds. They had to pay to fix the lawn mower that I broke on some stones, last week. Three shillings was all I had."

As for David: 'The Dalek's were not always So child,' said Hartnell. 'Mutated from within, like a hurt turned in itself, along with a few helpful pills, of course.'

It was why I had to hide the pills from Hannah.

Then, the boys started up. One of them, both of them. It didn't matter, they both sounded in the same pitch with their incessant wailing.

'Deal with them Michael, will you?' It was Hannah, from upstairs. 'And come and get Polly too. My wound from her tear of me has started to bleed again and this time it's running all over the sheets!'

I did as her dalek bid.

As I made my way again to the door, Hartnell, or David, revealed Davros to be the leader of the Daleks and quite capable... It was like she was deranged from all the bitterness of his being, or not.

'Well, if you continue to refuse to come to me!'

If only Hannah had allowed the babysitter to stay, instead of accusing me of my unhealthy urgency towards her, whilst trying to repair her own tights, I might have actually had some help and none of it would have ever happened.

'Crippling you with her selfishness. Crippling you and your family and then blaming you. Why don't you ever stand up for yourself, Michael?'

Baby Polly was quite calm in my arms as I left Hannah there. She wasn't the epitome of fears instilled in both of us, as the various voices of David was trying to make out. How could a little a babe in arms be the source of a plot to have me leave, for him, and so fail in my duties towards my family?

Tingle Two entered the living room with me, allowed me to stroke her and the boys, as I looked deep into Polly's eyes and found no sign of Hannah – good.

Dr Who had ended, replaced by *Thunderbirds*, for the children, but it had a very engaging theme tune and the eyebrows on the puppets, that were very imaginative, I thought, were just like Father's.

'No, David. I won't. Here, now, for the sake of my very own anti-adventure, Thunderbirds, are not going anywhere.'

'Coward,' pronounced David.

My diary.

"Pastor Mead told me last night at evensong that it was mine and Hannah's turn to clean the Church. But the cow was flying over the moon again.'

I only hoped God would understand.

I placed the diary back in the bureau. I had made enough entries and with the family asleep, I was about to catch up with indexing my record collection, whilst trying to avoid the annoying sputtering of the new Servowarm heating system. It took practically a whole new mortgage, that did.

'Polly needs you to be a real man!'

It was a fight David wanted, like the old days. But I was tired and I didn't have the time, or energy. I was a husband and parent, with a job to hold down, bills to pay and to ensure enough bubble bath to smooth the way to what my own parents never managed, just as Hannah's hadn't either.

'You as the mutated, with your family corrupted by your guilt at leaving me, like that.'

With last month's purchases correctly indexed and my Seagull four twin-lens, put back in its case – how could I have been so without the required attention – I concentrated on my work. The fibreglass sandwich honeycomb blast shield that I had been put on to designing for Concorde, at work, was thought to have possibly had an effect of the near fatal failure of the first fuel stack to ignite.

'And from his guilt set in motion his turning.'

Quite how they thought this possible, with the two systems being unrelated, was beyond even Engineer Director Leiter, at my new workplace, but the Americans, like Hannah had to be, were always right about such things, and I had to prove how this was the case, even though it wasn't, just to ensure our contract negotiations about joining the new Apollo programme.

'Don't leave us again in your silences.'

'He was ready then.'

'Exterminate. Exterminate.'

Stewart's screaming was the loudest, enough to bring about an obliteration of everything, until Hannah made it up to him.

'Oh, my poor, best poppet. Did your nasty Daddy's neglect of you cause you to cry?'

'Dada,' said Douglas.

Polly, rolling in her cage pen, a light green evil expression leaking from the sides of her Woolworths bargain cotton wool facing nappy.

'Michael!'

Maybe if I'd secured the safety-pins better, with some of those fixed clothes pegs?

William Hartnell again, in *Carry On Sergeant.*

'And no more skylarking, right?'

What the hell did he know about what I did at work and my drawing up of Concorde's state secret project specifications.

'From your duty to me, Michael.'

'Michael,' continued Hannah, 'I am trying to have a conversation with you.'

I bent down to attend to Polly, carefully unpinned her as it dawned on me that David might actually have a point. Were the skylarking to have been just a little to the left instead, the fastening bolts might be strong enough to prevent a little shearing. It was going in the report to the Director.

Baby Polly's expression had the look of all the confusion you would expect from Babel.

Oh, heavens, the church. I had forgotten to attend to my duties at the church!

I tuned to Hannah

'I'm just off to Manor Lane, dear. I will be about an hour.'

'You, are not leaving again, are you?'

What else could I do? Even if I were to be able to seek forgiveness from Paster Mead, there was no way I could succeed in escaping God!

David, again. 'So turn your bike into a spaceship and come find me. We can adventure the cosmos together, sort it all out.'

But if the answer didn't lie with Hannah's tights, or any other representation of the glad game she so liked to play, stealing every penny we had, forcing us to have pork pies, instead of the much cheaper liver, onions and bacon everyone knew should be served in the modern age.

'Yes, Michael, that's right,' said David. 'And So we must stick together. Not have anything to do with any of them.' Soo my bicycle was intended unto God!

'No, David,' I had to return. 'In this we are far from together. For this is Polly, my daughter and she has a right, like her mother, whom I love, I think. Yes, I do. I must, given that I married her.'

And then David took over again, with a rather appealing suggestion, to seek out, new ways of being, of life, new civilizations. To boldly go, where no man, or imaginative, I grant you, ghost-boy, has ever gone before.

4.07am, 10th November 1966, Elle Frances.

Captain's Logarithm, Star age, new adventure, the future. But which future? The kind where David would finally be allowed to coax me into his more exciting escapade. Or the kind where the *Sent Surprise*, at Dark Sand Alert, would distract me from the sadness about the challenged birth of Elle, having to suffer a lack of oxygen to a much-altered brain?

A challenge of a far greater magnitude than anyone had ever encountered before? It was like with the 0.987 variance in the stress load factor in the engines of Concorde.

Four play-missiles were shooting across the universe towards the *Sent Surprise!*

This wasn't what was on the television.

'Do we have recognition, Commander Leiter?'

'Yes, Sir! Max-factor six.'

Shup shup. Captain Dave, the only true hero, strode onto the bridge and over to the black leather swivel-chair I sat on in the middle of the sitting room. He looked young and pale, as he kicked me out of it, so much so that I almost didn't recognize him. If only I had been able to see the colour of his shirt, so I could see him coming.

'Missile spread, Commander Leiter?'

'Yes, sir,' I said. But Lieutenant Polly took over. 'But at less than the speed of light, and with hardly any destructive yield, it's as though an unidentified alien species threw us all out of a pram. Either that or someone refused to spend on the taxi-fare, when your wife first presented, causing a dangerous increase in her blood-pressure and all those problems for the one to come.'

The captain turned to Yeowoman Elle, at Comms. 'Anything on the DFDS?'

'No sir. All 'feerence clear.'

'Course of the missiles?'

'It would appear,' said Tactical Officer Stewart, 'that they aim at us, Sir!'

I was taken over by a desire to purge all vestigial emotions and guilt for not having the money for the taxi, into my most favoured Vulcan ritual, whilst listening to a rather sparky Strauss.

'Prepare laser banks, one and two.'

I leant forward into the longed-for punishment of my future.

'Mr Douglas, get a fix on the point of origin of the explosive yield bombs, and earn your right to your death-scream, will you?'

'Aye, sir.'

A pause, as Mr Douglas worked his beeping console.

'They come from the brightest comet in the galaxy, via the

new house near Sunbury, Sir, number twenty-six. Sorry, it can't be, the newly installed electrostatic speakers, sir. There is too much crackled interference.'

For the first time in a long time, I acknowledged my anxiety, looked to my watch and drew it all out.

'The destructive yield bombs, Captain,' I said. 'They're on a collision course with your very existence, Sir. Ours too.'

'Ready lasers.'

Yeowoman Elle tapped her earpiece at her station. 'Capin, I'm get a tress call. Sounds... Yeah. Is chillen cry – one 'ticlar.'

The doors *shup, shupped* again.

A swarthy doctor type, recently promoted to third-in-command, who was not entirely unknown to me, as the Freeman, and a buck-toothed nurse named Hannah, entered the *Sent Surprise* bridge.

'Do you not hear her, Michael?'

'Fire!'

The destructive bombs vessels were obliterated. No more lack of oxygen to the brain, existence for Elle.

'It would have been kinder to have paid the taxi fare,' said the captain.

But Elle was still at the Comms station. Was this a game. Was any of it real?

'Mr Douglas, alter course to where they all came from and let's find out.'

'Aye sir.'

'Space contortion factor four, Commander. Leiter.'

'Contortion factor four, it is, Sir.'

'Capin, we gets message that Crypto Linguifing not to unnerstand, me.'

Yeowoman Elle seemed so upset.

The captain looked as though he expected me to offer help. Why would I seek to help my nemesis?

'I confirm the yeowoman's analysis, Captain. These are not messages from any language that you can understand.'

'I would be obliged, Commander.' I looked at Yeowoman Elle, who nodded, in telepathic agreement.

'They appear to be communications of a pre-digital age.'

The Chief Engineer, a wonky-eyed, elderly soothsayer by the name of Widdecombe-Ming, held on to the rail, in fear for his pilchard-shaped crystals.

'They canny be emotional equations, can they?' the Engineer asked.

I shook my head, 'The concept may fit into your fantasies, Engineer, but as you should well know, such a concept, at least in this reality, is entirely beyond the dreams of Babel.'

Shup, shup. Hannah's arms folded in a cradling fashion.

Convinced of a correlation between the arm-folding of my wife, and the entry of a mangy cat onto the bridge, I opened my mouth to speak.

'Don't you bully my nurse,' started the good doctor, with a thoroughly unnecessary protectionism towards Hannah's pills and the children, 'you grass-colour, blooded, pathetic...'

'Silence,' urged the captain. 'We are not going to reach anywhere if we argue like this.'

There was something, but it was becoming harder and harder to understand.

'I am simply pointing out the baseless hope of the engineer's position, Captain.'

'Can you play back the children's cry,' asked Hannah, who, staring at her daughter at the Comms Station, seemed to be very surprised, but was yet on to something huge.

Yeowoman Elle first looked at me then at the good captain.

A pause, some beeping from another console. The cat stepped on a bleeping erase button.

'Is strange,' said the Yeowoman. 'Nuffink on sensors, but did hear something. 'onest.'

I was beside myself.

The doctor, 'Didn't we just blow any hope of them surviving emotionally to smithereens?'

'Unless like on our previous mission,' I said, 'we are dealing with a completely different type of sentient lifeforce here, such as has not been seen since that Gordon show.'

The captain turned again, this time looking concerned. 'Is something wrong, Commander?'

'You ask *him*?' The doctor couldn't contain himself any

longer. Are you mad? 'I mean, it's not as though our quiffy friend here is completely with us here with his dish running away with the spoon.'

'Enough!'

I held up my hands in defeat. There was just too much for my liking, too much noise, too many memories and emotions, beyond understanding. I was overwhelmed with the guilt over for not getting Hannah to the hospital in time.

'Mr. Stewart,' I said. 'Can you repeat what you said earlier about the comet?'

'The brightest in the galaxy, sir.'

A deep sand-alert beep. Alarmed, the cat jumped off the console. Then, on the viewscreen...

'Captain!'

A pork-pie-shaped Hailsham Warbird decloaked with great threat on the screen.

'Absorber screens, Mr. Stewart. Immediate screens, now!'

'Sir,' said Yeowoman Elle, 'they is *manding* we open us elicratic municators!'

'Tune it in, better. Tune it in.'

At first all we saw was a silhouette, with a pair of heavy-set, bushy eyebrows. I knew exactly who he was.

'It wasn't my fault,' I said, trying to protect myself.

'What did you say, Commander? Do you know anything about this?'

I hung my head.

'Yes, sir. I am So sorry, but as you might recognize, Captain, our new adversary, coming into focus, is our very own father.'

A woman was by his side, holding a near perfect eccles cake.

'Michael,' she shouted, urgently. 'Get out of there, get away. You have to get away, now.'

'And our Auntie Thelma, I mean Eileen,' I said, with an embarrassed smile at Yeowoman Elle.

The Doctor looked me up and down, waving his hand in irritation: 'Have you not taken any of the pills I gave you?'

'Michael,' our adversary on the other ship did not even introduce himself. 'You know why I am here.' He snapped his fingers. 'Eileen. Load the destructive yield bombs. Shield-penetrating and catastrophic.'

The captain gestured for Yeowoman Elle to cut communications, but she was too slow.

'You have to end this, Michael,' said Auntie Eileen. 'You have your own family to consider now. It's not your fault and it never was.'

The captain looked at me.

'Explanation, Commander?'

As our father pulled Auntie Eileen's finger towards the bright, yellow laser button on the screen, I heard the soft gurgling laughs of little children, four of them actually, and they seemed very familiar.

'Destructive yield bombs, again,' said Tactical Officer Stewart, 'and coming right at us, Captain!'

'Class?'

'Shield penetrating and catastrophic, Sir.'

On the screen, Auntie Eileen was being escorted, under guard, to our father's star-mapped living room.

'Captain,' said father, holding up his hands, confidently, but not in any kind of surrender.

The captain nodded, as though he knew this was expected.

It was not fair. Not fair at all. So with great concentration, I willed the destructive yield bombs to turn. Slowly, they bent back in on themselves until they pointed at the Hailsham Warbird and were aimed at our bushy-eyebrowed father.

'Beam her to the *Sent Surprise*,' I ordered.

'Who?' asked the captain.

'Who do you think?'

At the destructive yield bombs, he looked, as they sped away from the *Sent surprise,* under the control of his esteemed brother, me, whilst, at the same time also hurtling towards his total annihilation.

'That's right, Michael,' shouted Auntie Eileen. 'You don't need him anymore, Michael. You need a woman who understands you and your family. You need your Hannah to help you overcome what you have caused for Elle by not giving Hannah the taxi fare.'

As the destructive yield bombs hit, a blurry image appeared

in front of me. A small boy lay holding a bulbous abdomen first on a pavement, then in a mouldy-green shed, by some pampas grass and laurel leaves, in the garden of number twenty-six.

I wiped my eyes, knowing only when I'd done So I could become. I would bring together logic, emotions, history and death to become the real man I was supposed to be.

I looked at my watch, checking to see if it was all still OK.

The ship's cat seemed impressed. She rubbed up against my legs, like she too had finally avoided her enemy. Hannah stared her own powerful destructive yield at her.

'Get that mangy, flea-infested thing away. I don't want anything infecting our children, like that brother of yours has infected you.'

Tingle Two slunk off.

'Oh, and Michael, dear,' she continued, 'yes, it is and very much all your fault that you are the man that you are and that all the terrible things you are doing to our children, well, you really should be very ashamed of yourself!'

But the Good Lord had me in his sights then again, as in closing the show, the eerie theme tune announced him.

I took great comfort from his grace and presence, his ability to forgive and forget, unlike some, or one, formerly mousy wife, in particular.

Hannah picked up my bible, turned her gaze towards the reproduction Babel City picture I'd once bought, by mistake, trying a different perspective this time.

She was my wife!

'Come, Michael,' she said. 'Is it not time to let go? Let us just ignore, confuse the meaning of him, so no-one will understand him anymore – so that you won't ever have to put up with him again.'

I took her hand and together we knelt.

'Oh, Lord, we beseech thee that the false light be replaced by your own, in our covenant to put asunder all this Babel intended confusion.'

And with the guile of a fearsome Domesday machine, at the end of a fiery wake, David was beamed into Douglas.

'Like a light that refused to understand the dark?' asked

Reginald Bosanquet from ITV.

It was. But was it real?

Was I really, as Hannah had once asked, mad?

It didn't matter anymore. It was time to put an end to it all and so with the full force of imagination, I willed it all into a little black box in my mind.

I shut the lid tight.

'Now, go to sleep, will you,' said Hannah, by my side in our bed, 'and don't get any more of your ideas.'

I didn't.

David had already got away with far too much.

They proceeded with Concorde, anyway.

Madness, utter madness.

But it was of the really juvenile and stupid kind that could never have been mine.

Steve Porter

DOUGLAS

When she received the note summoning me to the headmaster's office, my teacher Miss Dobson's expression demanded discipline. The sort of discipline any around the houses, overly imaginative seven-year-old should reasonably expect. Her stern bobbed hair complemented her crimson dress, mirroring the severity of the situation at hand.

'Take him, then!'

The caretaker, bearing the note, looked at me. He beckoned with a rugged finger, and I followed him out of the door.

I checked the time on Daddy's watch; twenty seconds after one, twenty-three am, the twenty-ninth of July, nineteen seventy-one. He'd told me once that the watch used to be in a crocodile.

With my insole supports hurting, I hobbled along the corridor after him, the outside world hidden from view by the muddy handprints on the thick windows.

Naughty, I thought. *Very bad!*

The corridor walls were cheery, gloss-yellow on the lower half and crimson red above. It was just like rhubarb and custard.

I'd eaten too much pudding.

We arrived outside the headmaster of the Oriel Infant and Junior School's office. The caretaker delicately knocked.

'Come in.'

Nervous, I was pushed inside.

'Ah, young Douglas!'

Mr Singleton, the Headmaster, got up from behind his big desk and approached me. I found him unexpectedly unthreatening, in a brown pin-striped suit and orange tie. He bent down slowly, with a smile, and handed me an envelope with 'Mrs H Porter' written neatly on the front.

'Would you be kind enough to give this letter to your mother?'

Why did he pick me? I didn't want to be shouted at again by Mummy. Stewart was the eldest and best.

I was relieved that this summons wasn't about the boy who had recently appeared in the mouldy green shed in the back garden at home. He scared me more than Stewart or even the threat of Peter Pan's crocodile.

'Run along, now.'

The boy in the mouldy-green shed agreed.

I should have been scared, and I knew also that I needed to be very careful.

Later, after school, I found Polly reading in the black leather swivel chair in the lounge. Was she trying to get her head around a Janet and Gerald book, or was it that Shed Boy? I couldn't understand why he would be in Polly's book. And what was it with those tank tops and nineteen-forties trousers, anyway?

Mummy had collected the post.

'Mummy likes letters,' I told Polly. At least, I thought she did. I was always curious to know what Mummy really liked. She had such a deceptive smile.

'What's a deceptive?'

'Mummy gets hand-written letters from the headmaster,' I tried to explain to Polly. 'Daddy's are usually printed, which means they are bills.'

This made Daddy's face scrunch up, as bad as a melted Curly Wurly.

We got a Curley Wurly once a year on our birthdays, so it was hard to remember what they looked like.

But printed letters weren't good.

From the headmaster. We would just have to wait to see.

'Anyway, we need to learn more from TV about how to get rid of Mummy!' I continued, with Polly nodding. 'Learn from the light!'

Maybe it was from Crackerjack!

Mummy looked up. 'What did you say?'

'It wasn't me. I never said it.'

'Well, stop it, anyway!'

Polly still had her head in her reading book. Mummy's reproach was followed then by a smile of anticipation. Like she was about to get her own rhubarb and custard, with an extra portion, too. Her lips curled upwards as she read her letter.

'Michael, they've offered me the job!'

Daddy peered over the top of his *Radio Times* with a long face just like the dog of His Master's Voice fame.

'Leave me alone.'

To help Daddy, I wiped a particularly gruesome bogey over the open page of Polly's reading book.

'Da-a-addy!'

Polly always called for Daddy to see if he could make things alright, but he never did. Polly had to learn that Daddy would never give us the slightest attention unless it was from one of his spectacular sneezes.

'You have to make him feel the guilt of having left me,' snapped Shed Boy, as he liked me to call him, 'to help your Daddy take his journey to the light.'

Oh!

'After you make your mummy up and up and leave and go, of course.'

Mummy was busy creating Peter Pan on her Singer Sewing Machine, or the costumes for her production of it at least. Green felt, silk sashes, popper pockets and sparkly sequins all over the crimson bobble hat.

She had her creative defence against all that would befall her, and Daddy had his. All that was missing, according to Shed Boy, was a means to get Daddy to the light so he may do his penance.

'My dearest poppet, Stewart,' said Mummy. 'You're so

talented. Such a star and a born actor. You are going to be such a one.'

And then Tink, from one of Polly's better books, appeared on the Telly, darting about like and looking a bit like Elle in her fairy costume, who threw some imaginary pixie dust and mumbled something about being late.

Polly had as many fears and fantasies as me, but none were as strong as Daddy's faith.

'And after fourteen days and fourteen nights,' monotoned the Vicar from the Telly whilst Daddy twiddled with his nose.

It had recently become Daddy's favourite programme. *Songs of Praise*, with Richard Baker.

Shed Boy would have none of this and was beckoning me to do something, but he didn't know what, as my brother Stewart cringed at Mummy's measuring of him for that crimson bobble hat so he could claim his destiny.

'From the small parish of Tickencote, we come to you.'

I wished I had a destiny other than being drawn into the call of Shed Boy in the mouldy green shed.

If anyone knew Daddy didn't care, it was Mummy because she was going to be a teacher so she could teach people exactly how to love her. Someone? Anyone? That was how it was, according to Shed Boy?

'Michael, did you hear me?'

Polly threw my latest snot glob back at me. It landed right in my eye.

Well-deserved, I supposed, but slimy. I made my way off to the kitchen sink to wash it out.

Daddy said Mummy's new job meant a celebration dinner. Mummy smiled. She looked very proud.

Daddy had to make one of his salads. Pilchards or pork pies, with salad cream, of course. Limp lettuce, ham, squares of cheese, and exactly quarter-inch tomato slices. Battenburg cake was for afters, for sure.

'Such guilt is not of David's making.'

'What's that, Douglas?' asked Mummy. 'What isn't of whose making, dear?'

I didn't respond because there was beetroot on the plate. I didn't like beetroot! Same as the red in the blood of Polly and Elle's hedgehogs. They used to rescue them to make them glad. And there were crocodiles.

'No, Douglas,' said Shed Boy. 'God be in your head and in your understanding, like your daft father,' then he laughed. 'For the sake of everyone's future, if you don't help me, get him away from your mother and into the light.'

Tingle Two brought a wounded bird in from the garden, its crimson blood dripping slowly from its abdomen. It made such a mess.

It was like a great babel of nonsense I really wanted to burst.

'The mysterious,' said Shed Boy, 'is not an adventure.'

So I left the kitchen for the mouldy green shed, carrying the dead bird by its wing to give flight to my latest idea, I had just thought of.

Babel was a place in a picture in Daddy's music room. I liked it. Maybe, because it hung lopsided.

None of the others, at first, not even Polly, knew about Uncle David as a Shed Boy, as he liked to be called. The others had never seen him in the shed like I had. It was because the first time I saw him, Daddy had pulled me away and given me a freshly cut sliver of Mars Bar to shut me up.

I didn't ask Daddy why I had seen a pale-looking boy with a cat sitting on his bloated belly as though waiting for a putrid wound to open and weep streams of hedgehog or crocodile blood. At the time, the promise of a delicious quarter-inch sliver of Mars Bar had seemed so much more important.

Maybe there weren't any birds in the picture in the music room because Tingle Two had killed them.

It made sense.

I was the epitome of all evil when I was found picking my knee scab in Manor Lane Church, or so Daddy said.

He sent me off to pray for my forgiveness by the bibles in the entrance hall.

Cold there.

'Dear God,' I started. 'My Discoverer's workbook says you have a will and a purpose. We all have one, apparently, which means me, too, I think. What is it, then? I mean beyond what I am supposed to believe about the coming of this Thelma, which it says in my Discoverer's workbook is my will to do. But Stewart always tells me to do what he wants.

Is this what you want of me? Or should I listen to Mummy's screams about all my failings? Or Daddy, if he ever said anything other than about his planes and the costs of his woe betide me's.

I know what a woe is. Who doesn't, but how can you be a tide? Perhaps, you can help me out there, God. I am a child, after all, and I really do suffer.

Yes, I know brothers are supposed to help each other out. But you see, God, I can't. Stewart is always better than me at everything. Like with Daddy, who wants us all to come unto You when you're never even at Manor Lane, or are you?

Maybe to play football, even Subbuteo? Is that it? Stewart seems to think so. And Mummy says that's all rubbish, claptrap and against God, which is You, isn't it, as I thought we had established? They do say there can be only one.

Oh, and is Daddy the archangel by your side, like the one in my Discoverer's Club workbook, flying up to the light? Won't you tell me because Polly wants to know too and keeps on and on about how she will rescue me from it if it ever has the gall to come and get me?

I hope it doesn't get me another scab.'

I thought I was done then when the vision entered my heart. My purpose was to find the meaning of rubbish, claptrap, but Daddy's frown from the seat reminded me.

"Oh, yes. Sorry, God. Amen!"

We were on holiday at Mablethorpe. I was trying to figure out why Daddy would hardly respond to anything, except money.

My grandfather tried to explain, Grandmother with him, patting her carefully sculpted hair-bun at the time. 'When your Daddy gets into his sulky, it's just intolerable.'

Shed Boy took over the challenge. 'With your grandfather's clump, clump, clump, upstairs to your Mummy when she was a child, and your Mummy seeing the same intolerable in your Daddy, it isn't any wonder that Mummy seeks to smite your Daddy, force him into one of his sulks, so she can berate him even more.'

'It's like he's a melancholic,' continued Grandfather.

If there had been a telly there, I would have asked to switch it on, but there wasn't, so I picked up a handful of custard-coloured sand and threw it at Daddy's back, with some of it flying into the light of the sun. Was that how to do it? How to get to the light. It would catch Daddy's attention, any rate.

'There flies the Tinkerbell dust, Daddy,' I said, 'showing you the way to freedom of your own Never Never land.'

Shed Boy was very pleased at that.

Daddy got up in a hurry, stomped his stumpy toes into the sand. And when brushing himself free of the sand and with everyone laughing, his watch flew off behind a sand dune.

'My watch, my watch, how can I make it alright again without my watch?'

'Why are you all laughing?' asked Grandfather looking at Grandmother, as Mummy looked at me and looking very worried too and then she shook her head.

Grandmother patted the bun at the top of her hair, trying very hard to smile away all the tension.

Mummy handed Daddy the watch.

'Michael, you really do need to stop encouraging him!'

Grandfather was about to stand up, but Grandmother, probably to stop him from interfering when Mummy had her say, as he did often like to do and often, hurried over to give him a peanut butter sandwich.

'And anyway, Michael,' continued Mummy, changing the subject, 'I've been thinking, with my new job, I can buy the children clothes now, and we can afford for you to have a bath more than once a month!'

She was very clear and decided about this.

Daddy sat down in the sand again, suitably subdued, scratching his head as though searching for simpler times, the safety of his escape from the pavement, perhaps?

'Michael, I'm here.'

Grandfather took out his teeth and licked them free of all peanut butter.

'Daddy,' I said, 'what adventure would you really like to go on with your watch?'

I didn't want to say it to him, but sometimes I knew I just wasn't in charge.

Daddy just looked to the sand and sighed.

A flame was dancing about from a giant candle on the telly, behind the credits of *Songs of Praise*, and Daddy cocked me the same all-telling look he had when we were at Tesco's, and all the other times, when Mummy didn't trust anything I said, or did.

Daddy was my hero, then. He did speak back to Mummy. He did defend me.

'You are hardly being nice to him, dear.'

And Polly got out her foam sponge model of her Skylark from her toy bag, bouncing this in the air, as though heading straight into the light, with my hand swooping practice moves of passing through the Babel clouds. But how could a balloon fixed to a Skylark sponge ever take anyone to the light?

"It's the will of God,' said Shed Boy, 'how you should reform your mind if what was said in prophecy about the light was true. You just got to get on with it and make believe.'

That was hard to do then with all the babel of us singing *Abide with Me*, along with the Telly, against the background clatter of Mummy's sewing machine.

'You see,' said Shed Boy, 'your mother always ruins it. You will just have to work out how to send her away quickly.'

Polly offered me her Skylark sponge, but when I didn't want it, she started to cry at the rejection and put it away.

It was just after tea time when I told Daddy. 'If you stop worrying so much,' I said to him, 'then you might even be able to get rid of your dirty dandruff.'

I had heard this when standing outside the school staff room. Though Daddy's dirty dandruff had something to do with Shed Boy's punishment of him, for leaving him when he was Uncle David, I was sure.

The flickering pixels on the telly, like pixie dust, was showing me the way 'to the light, stupid,' or so Shed Boy was telling me, and I was supposed to tell Daddy this, and what to do, when the time was right.

'Why?

I didn't want to.

So it was off to the shed instead, where Tingle Two, crocodile-like, squeezed through the gap in the window by Daddy's bicycle for her tea, first to licky-lick Shed Boy's, bright red, but not yet burst, abdomen, then her tentative paw swipe at the front wheel of Daddy's bicycle, causing a puncture.

It was about this time, I realised that I wasn't always in charge, and I mustn't pass any of this, or David on to the others.

It was time for Roobarb and Custard on the telly, but it was spelt wrong! See, Mummy, I was too capable of learning. Not so different. When we sat on the carpet, I tried to allow the strange theme tune to drown out more of Mummy's screaming as I tried to absorb myself into the show.

Roobarb and Custard were a little like Shed Boy and Polly, with their fantastic schemes that were never really thought through properly.

Whoever thought things through? It was always so much better to let it happen, I always found.

But then Grandmother turned up in the house with Grandfather's mixed terrier, Bembo, named after a typeface, apparently, what with Grandfather having his links to the printing industry.

The little dog laughed to see such fun.

I heard them in the kitchen.

'If you want to keep Hannah as your wife, Michael,' she said, 'then you are going to have to man up and grow a pair.'

Grow a pair of what?

Polly didn't know, either.

And Roobarb, spelt wrong, by then, had got all his fellow cartoon characters under the big fluffy-Babel cloud on the telly and had them agree on their own will and language.

To help Daddy see that it wasn't his fault he'd lost his twin, that it was all mine for not being worthy enough. I wanted to tell David that Daddy had just been too late to save him on the pavement because of his puncture, and desperately needed another brother, or similar, didn't he?

Shed Boy disagreed. To him, Custard's only purpose, like with my Daddy, was to run away from it all and for that, he needed to be stopped, even rescued from this in an adventure.

I heard Bembo yapping in the kitchen. It seemed that he was in agreement.

Tingle Two stole in, looking very sorry for herself, with a tuft of her mangey coat missing and blood dripping from her head and leg wounds.

It was all Shed Boy's fault, I was sure.

'The answer, my dear boy, is in the light,' he said. 'The answer is always in the light.'

It was Mummy's first day as a new teacher at my school. Miranda, or Little Miss Clever Case, would learn everything from her. Miranda was the daughter of our school lollipop lady, who worked for the Police. Ooh, err.

As Miranda had it, the Butler boys first benefitted from Mummy's teaching. They were both in the children's home, because they like to pull up the girls' netball skirts.

Mummy would later explain they were a right pair of council house kids.

Miranda didn't like that.

'Well then,' asked Mummy, as if to prove her point, 'what's the number on the top of the paper clock, with the chocolate arrows pointing out to the light from the centre of the circle?'

Miranda was bent over, looking backwards through her legs.

'Well?' asked Mummy, again.

'Twelfth,' Terrene Pothecary answered,

And I tried to point out his error by shooting my hand up.

But Mummy ignored me.

'Jimmy Butler,' Mummy said, turning to a real council house kid, 'can you tell me what this is?'

Jimmy's response was immediate.

'Free Miss, that's a free.'

And Mummy nodded. 'Well done, Jimmy, that's nearly right. Now class, after me, let's all say, Th, like in the word throne that the Queen sits on and used to receive all the debutantes. Does everyone know who the Queen is? Good! Th, followed by Ree, as in three.'

But Miranda, now sitting down properly on her chair, was not the type to give up so easily. She showed us all.

'Miss. Miss!

'Yes, Miranda?'

'One minute past three-o'-clock,' she said, 'pointing towards the light,' in a pronouncement of absolute, certain, finality.

But it wasn't that final because what Miranda also said was that 'teachers like you aren't supposed to shake their heads when kids get it so wrong.'

I got up from my own chair, hurried to Miranda to claim my essential part in the developing drama.

'Don't you talk to my mother like that! Don't you know what she has to put up with at home?'

Mummy smiled. Polly smiled, too, at first.

Shed Boy shouted.

'Just get on with the adventure to the light, won't you, you daft ha'p'orth.'

The next day, the other Butler boy, Sam, was in the deaf unit, a class that my Mummy had a lot of interest in of late. They were deaf but not dumb, like Mummy had always been to my needs. Not her fault. Not Daddy's either, really. Stewart was the eldest, best, and deserved, and that would all change when she saw how good I was, like I had been for Daddy.

Maybe they were all selectively hearing like me, a beneficial skill when you needed to avoid nasty, adventure-seeking Shed Boys, who were trying to corrupt with all the false light promise of what they had to offer.

Mummy was telling Daddy, 'Mrs Brown, the deaf teacher, has almost as many merits on her staff appraisal as there are the terrible instances of class 2b's noisy cake munching in assembly.'

Daddy would have never understood this because he would have been trying so hard, of course, to be the archangel Michael, ready for the light, I imagined again, in his prayer. And the hedgehog that Polly and Elle had recently rescued from its hibernation wouldn't have been very happy either to have Tingle Two attacking it in revenge for Bembo's earlier mauling.

But the light that I thought Daddy was supposed to already have as an archangel, in my mind, had then become a little obscured by the wings of a dove that Mummy and Elle used to sing about up the stairwell.

'Fly, Up,' sang Elle.

'Save him.' This from Polly, with her own snot and tears dropping from her nostrils.

Her hedgehog was dead. Mummy had finished it off.

'It was a kindness, dear.'

When I got home for tea, I heard Mummy tell Daddy. 'It really is quite normal, Michael. Selective hearing is common in young children. Acting out the distress is a psychological necessity when a child feels they aren't good enough for their parents.'

Maybe it was because some parents were not good enough for their children.

'That's it,' said Shed Boy, 'think bravely, and what are you going to call your superhero?'

But it wasn't their fault. It never was. There was another, always another. And what was I supposed to do about it?

Daddy, in a rare moment of engagement then, looking up from his *Radio Times*, said, 'I think the subterfuge has a Russian flavour and is really quite clever. I wonder why I've never thought of being deaf when it came to David?'

As Daddy atishood, the flecks of his dirty dandruff shot out from his quiff faster than a punch from Dean Savory, the most badassed school bully ever.

Mummy slipped into her place behind the sewing machine and prepared to create all the costumes for the latest school production. She kept looking me up and down. Maybe she was going to make me a Captain Lollop costume so I could run away to the light in with Daddy.

With the advice of Mr. Singleton, Mummy had adopted

Pelmanism to sort me out. It was the solution to what Mr. Singleton called my grasshopper mind, lack of system, and far too active an imagination. Baden Powell had used it, apparently, all the time, according to Patrick Moore on the telly.

But it wasn't this that led to my not being chosen to be a crocodile in Mummy's production, with a clock in a bulbous belly, like an ominous ticking time-bomb.

'Could you just not be Peter Pan to help your father and find the light?' asked Shed Boy.

'Absolutely not,' I told him. 'I was to be Captain Lollop to sort out all the shenanigans.'

It was then, for my cheek, that I was ordered by Mummy to stand in the corner and write down all the senses I noticed: sights, sounds, smells. 'Look at the cards carefully, Douglas, remember the cards, see the birdy?'

Polly said not to do it.

'Dead!'

And, 'Oh, my. Now what is this, I wonder?' She was pointing to my switched off hearing aid.

'Babel!'

'And this?'

It was a bobble hat and not for me.

'I want to be in your play, too,' I said. 'Everyone else is in your play.'

'Have you ever considered calm reflection about your choices in life?'

But I wasn't as calm or as divvy-spaz, like Elle, as those who would have me beaten again in the playground for my grasshopper mind. Mummy never liked that term. It wasn't for children of would-be debutantes, apparently.

'Hannah,' Mrs Brown said when I presented myself after playtime, all bloody about the ears. 'I really think you have done the right thing for Douglas. His joining the deaf unit will really be best for him.'

Then, heavens be praised, I heard Daddy from inside the mouldy-green shed. Shed Boy had me switch off the hearing aid, so I could hear.

He was in the garden with God, of course, Mummy and a

pair of shears. Shed Boy, at the time, had been teaching me some despicable things to do with Stewart's Action Man.

'You mean, you want him disabled? He's deceiving you, Hannah! He's minging it up. Don't you see? To make you think it's all my fault!'

Hang him by the neck, with the speech cord, till he is dead, dead, dead, like Auntie Eileen!

'Just cut that out,' said Mummy. 'It is all your fault for never playing with him. Even when he dresses up as Captain Lollop to battle against all those inadequacies of yours.'

I flipped open the beige box and spoke into it like Star Trek on the Telly.

'Flash to Zarkov. Cut all communication!'

Then I went into the music room and stared at the light in the Babel picture again. Polly held my hand tight and close.

It was eleven forty-three and thirty-four seconds on the twenty-first of June, nineteen seventy-two. There had been a brutal game of British Bulldog over my trying to tell Terrence Pothecary, 'Three free's do not make a twelfth on the chocolate pointing clock, but most certainly, four doth.' It was written down like that in my Discoverer's Workbook, and that was as certain as the word of Job's fearsome almighty.

'Is he dumb as well as deaf?' asked Terrence.

I didn't do very well in that game of British Bulldog. Not that Stewart would help or do anything about it. In fact, he was right up there with Terrence Pothecary in the front of the pack, or so they shouted.

I had sort of adopted the role, by then. If no-one wanted anything to do with me, then how could I pass anything about Shed Boy on?

'Oh, stop with all your daft whining,' protested Shed Boy. 'You just need a superhero to recognise you enough to dispose of your silly mother and take your father into the light.'

In bed, with the lights off, I was trying to work out why things were as they were. Shed Boy had convinced me, by then, it was the start of my turning, that Mummy, for making me do

Pelmanism and not letting me be in her play, was a 'debutante tart', or so Shed Boy said, though Daddy aid it was really Princess Margaret, and Mummy had a mental illness, or that was what Auntie Belinda and Daddy had worked out. I wondered what a mental illness was, it didn't sound good.

Indeed, we should all stand by Daddy, even if naughty Mummy said she was the one that needed help. We should allow Daddy to become the archangel in the that light he should have always been.

Stewart turned over in his bed on the far side of the room.

And Pastor Mead, from Manor Lane Church treated Daddy like a guilty lackey, just like David did me, making Daddy clean the church from top to bottom and back again to feel better about himself.

It was Mummy who had told Pastor Mead of Daddy's sin of forcing her to agree to Stewart's baptism, but not me and the girls, before Pastor Mead got his hands on Daddy and had his wicked, anabaptist way with him.

'Douglas,' said Stewart. 'Shut up, will you!'

Because Pastor Mead was the one who had convinced Daddy, in a manner most persuasive, in accordance with the coming of Thelma, as it clearly said in our Discoverer's Workbook, not to baptize the rest of the children until we were old enough to understand what being mentally ill was all about.

'Douglas, will you please just shut the fuck up!'

I did, but I thought still that Daddy needed a better friend in God than that. I felt sorry for him. I wanted to give him some help from the awfulness he felt about the puncture, his dirty dandruff and his stumpy toes.

So despite Shed Boy's express wishes, earlier given to me in the mouldy-green shed – 'Don't you even think you can stop the crocodile, if you don't get him to me in the light', I started to organize an 'It's-Not-Your-Fault-Your-Brother-Is-Dead' party.

The sewing machine had finished with its sequins. Music had been written. Lines had been simplified for the children and it was only a matter of time before the greatest show in Christendom was to take over the whole of the Oriel Infants and

Juniors School with more sequins and glitter than in Tinkerbell's much hoped-for palace.

It was Stewart in the end in lead role.

Well, he would get it, wouldn't he?

Baptised, weren't he!

'No, Douglas,' Mummy said. 'Crocodiles are far too scary for the little ones and Captain Hook will frighten them *orf*.'

Tick, tock, tick...

Then she took up her position next to Mrs. Mumford, pulling out from her handbag and looking at the bottles of Dr Freeman's lovely little helpers.

Mogadon, Valium, Paracetamol.

Was she asking if I should make use of them, what with my abject failure to succeed in Pelmanism?

'Well, yes, I know, Millicent, Douglas has always had a rich imagination, but do you think ... I mean should I, or at least have him see someone?'

The truth was, Shed Boy still couldn't believe that in my plan, if I had one and it could ever be realized, all Mummy and Daddy had had together would vanish.

We were in the grounds of Manor Lane Church, about to start playtime and Stewart was ready. We had discussed all about it, David and I, and I had to agree that it made no sense that my not being baptized was enough for Mummy to scream evil at me and for me to adopt the role of a divvy spaz.

Stewart started the party that I had then abandoned planning for him to take over. He was the eldest, as Shed Boy took pleasure in reminding me.

I was to represent the divvy spaz, deaf unit that I was destined for, and Stewart the rest of the Oriel school.

'It's the most extraordinary scenario you could have dreamt up. Ice-cool Porter, charging down the left field and they're all over the place. Porter pauses, checking to left, his right leg swinging back and you can see it's going to be a corker, but wait, the divvy spaz with his abdominal pain, and vomiting, as the crocodile bomb in its belly was about to blow us all to smithereens. Oh, this is terrible. Just terrible!'

'Join me, Daddy' I started shouting. 'If you can't find the reason to get rid of her, then just leave her, so we can be together again on the way to the light and fiery wake.'

Daddy from the side with a cup of tea and a slice of Battenburg looked like a person wanting to vomit, but without having a mouth.

Polly nodded, pulling me away from the sight. It was not right that a cub scout that had failed his Pelmanism trials should ever have to see such a sight. What would Akela say?

Hannah now, appearing from nowhere with her teeth, ready for the tick of the time bomb in a crocodile's belly, for me, as David, the cause of her husband's ignoring of her. She was shaking her head again.

'And to think that I, as the granddaughter of an Admiral, have to put up with all this!'

She was with Mrs Mumford then, a little closer than anyone would have expected for two teachers in school play, trying to teach about love between a would-be debutante and an Akela.

'Millicent, on your lips, there's a little piece of that lemon drizzle, you like.'

The kiss between them was enough of a reason for Daddy to leave, or be sent away, a betrayal that could be the start of the emotional death of a whole family, almost as dastardly as the black-suited one on the new cartoon on the TV, called *The Wacky Races*, because it was time then for an alternative to the pantomime reckoning being prepared, to confirm the full extent of all the conflicting babel around.

No one was at all bothered about the dead bird story in the deaf unit the next day, even though I signed it – well, finger spelt it.

'Douglas, look at me.'

Mrs. Brown was holding my head in her hands, mouthing it to me. 'You are here with me now, at Oriel. So will you put in your hearing aid, look to the light, and play your recorder.'

I would have preferred the later school assembly to start with a recorder, though on Top of the Pops, it was played by a long-haired lover in a kilt that flapped about more than Daddy's quiff.

'Watch out for the Devil,' said Shed Boy.

'Shut up,' I told him.

Mr. Singleton wasn't too impressed at having his assembly interrupted in this way.

'I'll be your long-haired lover from Liverpool, indeed,' I heard him say. 'What kind of country is this turning into?'

Tick, tock, tick. And the audience were assembled, the curtains rustling and then David reminded me I could play the recorder and clarinet. Not as well as Stewart, but then he couldn't play a fanfare anywhere near as well as me.

'It takes a certain quality of squeak,' I answered Shed Boy, as much as myself.

He had no choice but to agree.

The curtains started to open; children ran onto the stage. I was on the floor with all the recorders in front of the stage, looking urgently for Mrs. Boulting's cue from the piano.

Stewart strode onto the stage, dressed in green and with a crimson bobble-hat, entered the make-shift Wendy Darling House tent.

The notes from Mrs. Boulting, jumped like some of Daddy's negative integers, neither increasing, nor decreasing, as I imagined them flying through his head in the back row with his nose twiddle, to remind him of the selfish depression he was supposed to have for his choices in life, but were never his fault.

Couldn't be. He was ill, always ill with his depressive flu.

'Now, Douglas,' said Mummy.

Was this all that my mummy could expect of me, my destiny as she had once screamed upon me to justify why she could never love anyone at all.

And 'Two, three. Six-time. Ready now, steady Patience, boy,' Mrs. Boulting was steely-eyed about it. ''Now, Douglas!

Tock. I played my much-practiced clarinet squeak.

But it didn't take any of us into the light.

It was just like in that Babel picture, where there was never any action, just a still, presenting a whole lot of confusion of voices and intentions, like with Roobarb and Custard in the clouds, and was that really the Thelma, or Tinkerbell in the rain?

Well, I had to ask myself, because it was in the nature of my grasshopper mind, was this will of the archangel, or me? Had I caused the sixty paracetamols to disappear into our Mummy's stomach the day after the performance?

'Your father has begun to sense the truth,' said Shed Boy, taking up his position on a makeshift pulpit of talking over the lawn mower bin in the mouldy-green shed, 'and you should to. You see, Douglas, not everything is as cosy in your parent's marriage as the purchase of some aphrodisiac Noddy bubble-bath could solve.'

'But why?' I asked, in all innocence.

Shed Boy began, 'I am sent to help you understand how one day a woman, thy mother, took respite from her husband and all ye little ones that were not good enough. Especially that evil, deaf one, as wouldst a hedgehog take flight from a flea-bitten cat named Tingle Two. And how she travailed with a running away haste unto the House of her Mansfield's neighbours after. And for her sin of baptizing Stewart before, and having tasted the sour paracetamol, sixty, as a result, this being a part of her planned her escape from it all. From you, Douglas, for your squeak and not measuring up to your Pelmanism trials. And how the Mansfield, was representative of the Governing Authorities, an Inspector of the moral authority of Police, took her unto his authority and house for a short time, whilst searching for the key to his new Cortina and whenst found, bundled the quivering, guilty, wreck of thy mother into the back seat and then off, down the newly-built A316 to the place of healing of the Yea, verily afflicted mad mental place, named St Bernard's.'

'Why he talk strange?' asked Elle.

'And once arrived at this place of healing. Thy mummy had wept and was pale and pink. The healer's helper, with thy good Dr Freeman at her side, upon recognizing this voluntarily contrived admission, cast open the large doors, gazed upon this crocodile-buck-teethed woman and with all the power of her medicines, let the will of God claim her, as it should you.

Indeed.

Yea, and the beds about thy mummy were cold framed, the lunatics there before her, afflicted with much wailing and a gibber and with the wind of fear that bleweth in. And to comprehendeth what a mental illness was, thy mummy was placed into a wheeled chair with the grey-suited porter hastening her down the long corridors, to the Godless, white-tiled theatre, that was never made for Flash Gordon, Barton, or Bond.

'By the blood of the hedgehog,' I asked, 'is this really truth?'

'"Welcometh unto ye, said the swarthy healer,' said Shed boy, continuing, 'holding a rubbery funnel with a serpent-like tube trailing from it, whilst thy mummy's eyes screamed penitence for her selfishness over who was to be in Peter Pan. But before the penitence could travel and break free from thy mummy's lips, the end of the serpent-tube was stuffedest into thy mummy's still bitter-tasting mouth and throat, and the swarthy healer plungethed the snake down further and further into the very depths of her sin. Thenst, water was poured into the funnel, and more So without the chance for thy mummy to glug. The gaggeth reflex having been taken away already by the heinous procedure of the plunge down further.'

'Sounds 'orrible,' said Shed Boy, laughing. 'See what you did, by your deafness to her needs.'

'Thy mummy retched against the ministrations of her swarthy healer. Her body rising and falling and rising further still until she could taketh no more. Thenst, like the rushing of a river when the wind bloweth a tornado, the waters and the paracetamols did rise up, forcing the tube out. And thy mother gushethed her stomach for twenty full minutes until red-faced and empty, she was knackeredeth. She slumpethed back into the bed, with not a thought for all she had left behind, her husband, her children, or her future evermore as a person to be loved or ever trusted, anymore.'

It was a bit like the man in a parachute, but then it wasn't. The man was from the Doctor Who. Flouncy clothed, always so fast with his jibber-jabber and he was in my head.

'So what's your real name, then?' I asked.

Which was a bit bold of me, even if I say so myself.

'I am come from the beginning,' he said, 'and I am come from the end too.'

'In the middle,' I said, 'like me and Polly,' and she couldn't believe about Thelma being real, either, So why should I believe that Daddy was St Michael by the gates, all the way up in space to get too on her sponge.

Earlier, Stewart and me had met a real man with a parachute, or was it a cassock, in a car park by a new building, by the divvy-spaz school up Nallhead Road?

He wore black and was without any tie.

'You a God-botherer?' asked Stewart

I could never connect to Stewart when he behaved like that.

The man smiled widely extended his hand to us both, like adults do.

'Peter Morgan,' he said. 'I am the Vicar here at St Richard's and you are most welcome.'

This, the Church of St Richard's, not Michael, with its triangular concrete beams, rising like a wigwam into the sky to pop any nasty Roobarb and Custard cloud, or any Babel that would come about again from my Discoverer's Workbook.

Shed Boy, said: 'You are going to get into trouble for that. You mark my words.'

I said back to him. 'You haven't the first idea what you're talking about.'

Mr Morgan, the Vicar, took us into the Church and Stewart asked him. 'What's that?', he said, pointing to the table with the gleaming silver legs. Vicar Morgan seemed very pleased with this. 'What do you think you see?'

'Altar?' said Stewart.

'Yes, but an altar to whom?'

A bit of a stupid question, I thought, considering he was supposed to be the Vicar.

'Jesus,' said Stewart.

'Oh, so you know, then?'

'Look, mate, I ain't fick, like!'

Vicar Morgan nodded. 'No, indeed, I can certainly see that.'

But the thing was, how could Dad be an archangel, by the gates all the way up in space, that St Richard's didn't have anyway – just a car park that you couldn't ride your skateboard on, because there were too many stones, which was not very Christian. In fact, some might say it was really quite mean.

So I decided to change things between the pages of my Workbook, I cooked up my very own game plan.

Mummy would respect a Vicar's wife as a replacement friend for Mrs Mumford, to bring Mummy back, like, and then, we could avoid going to the light.

Polly agreed that it was more acceptable than Mum's lemon drizzle evils with the Deputy Head, who in revealing her desires after the Peter Pan production, had revealed how much of a 'debutant tart' Mummy had become.

'Hear, hear!'

But Shed Boy wasn't supposed to be here with me in this and nor was Polly's spongy space ship.

'If you want a pilot, signal then to Jesus,' that was to be my part of the plan. That was what was real, or so Polly had told me.

'Oh, I see!'

But Shed Boy *was* there in the pages I was writing. I couldn't get him out and he said that I didn't need any pilot, or at least not one called Jesus. I had him, to guide me and take me to the light, from whom, as it happened, Jesus had descended, apparently, if the name David had anything to do with it. They had said so at St Richard's. And this knowledge fried my brain for at least three months.

Polly was simply amazed at the new voice, this writing had given me, or I'd developed.

Indeed, the Morgans welcomed us all to this church with the triangular concrete beams, pointing to the light and the gates.

And sometimes, instead of playing bash up your sister in the living room at home, we got to go there, play table-tennis, eat gingerbread biscuits and drink lots of squash.

We also coloured in bible-stories and could ask the shocked, adult God-botherers questions inspired by the contents of Daddy's diary and the underwear section of the Grattan's catalogue.

'What exactly are bollocks?'

Stewart didn't care what he asked.

I showed more respect. This was Church. And Polly had told me what the Magaluf expected us all in Church.

'So tell me about the archangel Michael,' I asked, Vicar Morgan, over a game of ping pong, in the church hall, using bibles as bats. 'He's my dad!'

Shed Boy beamed like the North star at that. 'Wonderful,' he sang. 'Counsellor. The Mighty God. The everlasting...

And Mr. Morgan could hardly contain himself. His jaw was wide-open, his eyes pierced into me like he was looking for something special.

'Yes, and he's a King, don't you know? King David and he wrote prophecies, as well as all them psalms, or so Polly says.'

Mr. Morgan started to look very impressed – for a little bit.

'Yes, well that's all just as well, but I am very sure that your father isn't really the archangel, Michael.'

He would get back to me, though, when he had consulted Mrs Morgan about the future pastoral guidance of us all. Which I thought was very good and proper of him, actually.

Polly agreed with me.

We legged it home, like we did every day, for our tea. When getting there, we gorged on jam from dessert spoons, sugar sandwiches and, if we were feeling brave and adventurous and stood on Polly's cut-haired Sindy doll, we could operate the controls to make burnt butter-toast – who needed any of Dad's out of date tins of pilchards?

After, I would disappear into the mouldy-green shed, to work things out some more in between the pages of my Discoverer's Workbook and to pray, well commune, at least, with Shed Boy.

'And have you thought anymore about how you are going to bring your father to me?' he asked.

To which I didn't want to answer, really.

We had all just lost Mum and with Dad and his latest depressive flu, he was in danger of leaving – Hull – too. And would this be any good for him, for us, or was this just to please the awful plan of the selfish Shed Boy?

It was easy to blame Elle. Shed Boy had learnt things were always obvious with Elle, the chocolate dribble which oozed – good word that – from the side of her mouth, the smell of urine. But it wasn't Elle who gave the game away, really. It was me.

According to Mr Morgan, Mrs Morgan had spotted me chomping in the back seats of St Richard's, munching on bonbons and Mars Bars bought with the collection money from the gypsy caravan shop at the top of Nallhead Road.

'Yes, I see him.'

Mrs Morgan went straight off to tell her holy husband, who would be really disappointed, Polly had warned when we handed over the money.

Vicar Morgan would have already known, of course, because one of the house mothers from the Cygnets – the children's home we went to after school, before Elle caked the washing machines in shit and got us all banned – also went to St Richard's and already knew us for the terrible children that we really were. We just couldn't be trusted.

The mouldy-green shed wasn't a good place to pray, I knew, and especially not with the image of a dead boy with a bloated stomach, against all that was supposed to be right.

'Suffer the little children to come ... Bread, body ...'

'Shut up!' I said. 'You are false, not like Polly's Magaluf. It's very cold in your shed.'

But I wasn't heard and then I couldn't do anything, anyway, because a woman of a totally different faith came to the house and I was called back in.

She had painted fingernails and swishing clothes. Not so much a Christian, or Good Samaritan, or so Shed Boy said, as she was a devotee of the most ominous order of Hounslow Child Psychiatry, or that's what I interpreted her badge to say.

She was actually a – sound it out now – he-ri-ti-cal – one of those do-gooding, bloody social workers and her name was Mrs Grigg. She had so much difficulty comprehending the way of things, like ...

'Is the child just rude, or can he just not hear me?'

'You leave him alone,' said Polly.

Shed Boy couldn't work her out at all.

'Can you draw for me,' she would ask, 'what happens when your Mummy and Daddy might have cross words, or talk about Heavy set plant pots?'

I tried my own version of Babel, first, so easy to draw, I first thought, sort out a means of understanding, and then Action Man hanging from a crucifix, just like Auntie Eileen, as I thought she would like that. A depiction of Captain Lollop, derived from my imagination, entirely, which was just disgraceful. Didn't work at all.

Elle's response was so much more honest.

'My knicks get wet.'

For Shed Boy, though, such questions were a waste of time and so he had me read from and tell her about Daddy's diary.

'That's the real book of truth,' he said. He was trying to be a little more friendly, since he realized the effects on me of his causing Mummy's departure with my screeching clarinet squeak.

Which is how I learnt that Daddy would pedal up to see this Mrs. Grigg and Mummy at Group, three times a good, God-fearing week.

'What is Group?' asked Shed Boy.

As Dad had explained in his diary, Mummy had accused him in Group of being very tight, as could be seen by the threadbare carpets at number twenty-six, the overgrown garden and yet the beautifully painted, pristine outside. He had been told to maintain it that way by the builder.

And all our clothes and toothbrushes, apparently, as said at this group, were bought by Mum from the charity shop, after pawning her engagement ring for want of an allowance to bring us up and wasn't that enough of a reason to put him in Polly's sponge ship?

At one point in the group, 'Nah, you must be lying,' the steely-eyed chap, who looked a bit like Dick Barton, had said, from his position next to Daddy. 'No one ever buys toothbrushes from a Charity shop.'

But Mum, or so Dad's diary told, had explained back to him, that he, our dad, just wasn't capable of understanding the love that she thought she deserved, was entitled to and had a right to expect.

'Pot calling kettle, or what?' said Auntie Brenda, who was amazed at the diary, and she had some pretty big pots too, probably big enough for dunking one's feet in, I had to concede to Polly.

'I agree,' said Shed Boy. 'She wouldn't know how to recognize love, even if it did decide to come her way.'

Polly and I wanted to find out more of the circumstances, concerning the death of Dad's brother – which was very morbid – as Dad had apparently explained in group was always the cause of all things.

I am not dead!' said Shed Boy.

Mrs. Grigg, in response, whilst looking at Polly's Skylark sponge on the carpet, said that this dead brother complex might be worth looking into.

'And even if you do end up taking Jesus into your heart, Douglas,' continued Shed Boy, 'you must believe in me, that I am the only one that can offer the destiny that you seek to bring a happy family again.

But that was Polly's job.

The next Sunday, Vicar Morgan had the four of us line up in height-order in the vestry. It was the will of God, 'or Thelma, if you read it in Greek,' or so the Mr. Biggs the Church Warden, a friend of Inspector Mansfield, had, said, with much authority.

'Your Thelma be done on earth as it is by the light.'

We laughed.

Shed Boy, too.

Vicar Morgan gave Mr Biggs a shut-up look, before he turned to us.

'Now, then,' he said, 'do you remember Stewart and Douglas, when we first met and had our little chat about the archangel?'

'Yeah, what of it?'

Stewart was already on the defensive.

'Shsh,' said Polly, with the same respect she would always

and should show for a man in cassocked-cloth that looked so like a parachute.

'Well, St Michael was an archangel,' he continued, taking out his bible, which he opened to a page and started to read out. 'And blah, de blah de blah, the Devil.'

'The Devil?' I exclaimed.

'Yes, but who, or what is the Devil? asked Vicar Morgan.

'Tingle, our pestilential?' said Polly.

Shed Boy gave me the words to use, but I had my own voice to get into.

'It's not Dad's fault,' I said quickly. 'And he doesn't deserve to go into the stars, or the light on a ship to find the gates.'

'They tasted nice, the sweets,' said Elle. 'It was Stewart and Douglas wot done it.'

Mr. Biggs smiled from ear to ear, like a laughing Policeman.

'It's because we was hungry,' said Polly. 'We's always hungry, like that.'

After a long 'Hmm', Vicar Morgan said. 'I tell you what, do you all want to come to dinner with me after church, every week, so we can taste the goodness of the ever-forgiving Lord and saviour together?'

All four of us jumped up.

'Really, course, Mr. Morgan, guvnor, vicar and all. Sorry and all for the nicking!'

Tickencote, Lincolnshire. Another church.

This bit Polly didn't know. Too private, like it was not supposed to be revealed.

I wanted to do the brass rubbings that my grandfather was always on about. Tickencote Church had a Norman in it, named Thiry, but Shed Boy had called him T, for some reason. Something to do with the light and a gate.

When we got there, Stewart wanted to ride up and down the footpath on his new and certainly not dangerous skateboard he'd managed to convince Grandfather to buy him.

I got one too with a scary crocodile design, or was it a hedgehog, and smaller wheels and holes in the axles, where gravel could get inside and make some atrocious noises.

I had my paper ready, cobblers' wax and Sellotape all ready for the rubbing.

'The Normans,' said Grandfather, 'came to the country, after the great comet.'

'Like an archangel?' I asked.

Can't remember who said what then, cos I was hurrying to the part of the floor where the T Norman, was. I unrolled the paper. Grandfather helped, handed me the Sellotape in bits and I stuck it to the four corners and the side.

'And that one?' I asked.

It was a woman, also in the slab of stone.

'That's Dough,' said Shed Boy, and then in Grandfather's voice, 'the second of three in the trinity to reform open minds.'

It was then that Stewart crashed through the door, on his skateboard.

'You tell him nothing,' he said, and as was normal when this ever came up, I found it hard to breathe, and was catching every laboured breath.

Having delivered his line, Stewart then left.

'Gotta learn a backwards flip.'

Grandfather pulled me towards him.

'Look at me,' he said.

I couldn't, I was too much shaking.

'Look into my eyes, boy. Good and now take some long, deep breaths.'

After I calmed, Grandfather wanted to know all about what had happened to me at school, and why it was that I needed to get to the light with my dad.

I thought about it as I returned to my brass rubbing.

'It's like when Mummy screams,' I said.

'Your mother screams?' asked Grandfather, on his knees beside me, as though praying to the archangel.

T's face drew me back, the eyes looking up to the stained-glass window of the fiery wake leading all the way to Babel.

Grandfather was looking up at it too.

'It's, the last supper. But why are you so interested in that?' he asked.

'I am the one that reminds her,' I said. 'I that knows the

Shed Boy and I will be much the worse for it, maybe even worse than with Stewart and Dean Savory pissing all over me, like he tried to do to Daddy, when Daddy was in the bath with Mummy, which is why she had to go away and we had to go to The Cygnets, number three after school for our own last supper.'

'The Cygnets?'

'Yes, Grandfather, the first Children's home we went to, with Auntie Annie Mumford in charge.'

'Oh, yes,' said Grandfather. 'We were really very sorry about that. So Stewart tried to piss on you?'

'I'm not sure anymore. He might have wanted to.'

We finished the shoulders of T and moved down to his armour about his chest.

'So is T your archangel?' I asked, relieved that I hadn't told him anything I wasn't supposed to.

We were all there.

'Since I returned, and your mother's latest departure and all your stealing,' Daddy said. He looked at me first, then at Elle. Polly and Stewart did not give him the courtesy.

Shed Boy, through my eyes, looked up and down at the dirty curtains, like he'd exactly guessed what couldn't happen next.

'Since, your mother's latest departure,' he said, 'you know, I have been finding things rather hard.'

'I know Daddy,' sang Elle, 'don't cry.'

'I'm not,' said Daddy, then shaking himself down from his dandruff on the black-leather swivel-chair in the middle of the sitting room

'You see, I can't cope anymore, with all four of you.'

Tingle Three jumped onto Dad's lap, presumably, so she could enjoy the extreme dire of what we all expected to explode from Dad's not to be trusted anymore mouth.

I didn't hear it all, on account of Polly and Elle's crying.

'Well,' said Dad. 'They will be here in ten minutes.'

Stewart and Polly had left the room by then, but on coming back in, they were carrying bags stuffed with all kinds of things.

Polly had my school bag, filled with pants rather than her knickers, which was really not very nice of her. I noticed also she had swiped my action man and I had quite got used to that one with its 'Dig in, don't tell nothing more, or a mortar attack!'

Stewart handed Elle her Adidas bag, with a very obvious bottle of Noddy bubble-bath poking out.

It was supposed to be because I had a better connection with Elle, Dad said.

Mrs Grigg, said to us, one day, by the big tree in the grounds of St Bernard's of the Mentals, that St Richard's wasn't really our church. Neither was Manor Lane. She said St George's was our church, as it was the nearest to us. 'It was a sort of mini cathedral,' she'd explained. 'Evangelical, but not Pentecostal, and the Reverend Kibble was in charge there, an early advocate against women vicars and all.'

'Yeah, as well as being Dad's therapist,' I said.

It was in Dad's diary.

And the Reverend Kibble, I learnt from listening into a conversation in the vestry that day I went to see if St George's had better praying-potential than the mouldy-green shed, had very little patience for our dad's situation.

To the Reverend Kibble, it did not matter whether or not Dad thought himself a failed dad, or Mum had blamed him for a completely shitty, cat-ridden existence, or even if it was all the fault of his dead brother, David. Who, or what, in the name of the good Lord above, did Dad think he was doing?

'Oh,' said Dad. 'Oh, oh, oh!'

A simmering, silent anger filled Reverend Kibble's vestry, then, my own voice had it. All sinister and struggling for a way out. Much like it was, after, in the living room, when the candles lit the living room because that bloody Mr Heath had stolen all the electricity and replaced this with candles.

Polly had explained it all.

In Uncle Mick's Robin Reliant, we got taken, maybe even launched there. At least as far as Shed Boy was concerned. The polyester sail I imagined on the roof, from Brentford Nylons, strengthened by the blanket on the top, billowing all the way up the A316 towards the place of the damned!

'Where are we?' I asked as we drove through the huge gates.
'It's a home,' said Auntie Brenda.

It was huge, like the hospital Mummy was in, but with the cross on the top of the door, it didn't look like any hospital.

We got out of the Robin Reliant, Auntie Brenda took hold of Elle's hand and walked us both across the tarmac towards the big door. I looked as Elle took her hand from Auntie Brenda. Elle turned to look at Dad, but I pulled her onwards. I wasn't going to look back. I wasn't going to say goodbye.

'Will they let us watch Roobarb and Custard?' asked Elle.
'I don't know,' I answered.

Dad rang the doorbell and pretty soon the big door opened. There stood a fat woman wearing a hat that looked like it was made on Blue Peter.

'Hello. You must be the Porter two.'

I looked up at her, Elle curtsied, or tried to, but the fat one didn't see, because she'd turned her head.

A young woman stood behind.

'Won't you come and welcome the new inmates.'

The big door slammed behind us.

The young woman came, introduced herself as Carmen and started to explain the house rules.

'Our father's will,' she said, 'is what we believe here. He knows what is best and we are all a part of His plan. Even if it appears different sometimes to the new children amongst us.' She showed us into a big hall and then on to dormitories – one for the boys' and one for the girls'

There had been gates, but it was not Babel and there was no great light, either.

The dormitories were sparse. A bed sheet, cotton, cover, eiderdown and bedside cabinet.

I put my bag on my bed. Another child came running over to try and take Elle's bag. We stood to attention.

Piss trickled down Elle's leg.

I didn't know what to do, how to help her.

After saying goodnight to the young woman, in the big hall, I learnt Elle wasn't going to the girls' dormitories. I saw her being frog-marched towards...

'Stop that,' said the fat woman to a crimped-haired boy. 'Will you leave the new girl alone, this instant!'

Shed Boy was laughing.

I had nothing to say to him and my Discoverer's Workbook had been left at home, anyway.

What Stewart did not want me to tell Grandfather in that Tickencote Church.

'Ah, come in, dear boy, come in,' said Mr. Fergusson. 'Well, you might wonder why I have asked you here to my office and the truth is, what with your mother being away, for so long now, I wanted to know how things were going at home.'

I didn't know if I was to sit or not, so I stood, just like it was when I had been called to see Mr. Singleton.

Polly would have understood.

'I do my homework, Sir, when Tingle Three hasn't done a toilet on the table.'

Mr. Fergusson leant forward, smiling.

'Yes, I am sure that you do, but you can relax, Douglas. You are not in any trouble.'

He smiled again. I felt bad about telling on the cat like that. Wasn't her fault!

'Changing the subject, So tell me, does your father ever secretly take your sisters into the bath?'

The question of Mr. Fergusson was far too easy.

'Oh, no. My dad's far too smelly. They would never go.'

'So he does ask your sisters to go to with him?'

'Not really.'

It felt like he was playing a trick.

'Oh, I see,' said Mr. Fergusson, 'and I wonder if you know what sex is?'

That was an easy question to answer too.

What?

Shed Boy was just as fascinated.

'It's about when a man loves a woman very much, innit, and he gets out his Noddy...'

Mr. Fergusson's eyes rolled a little and he smiled again.

'Quite! And have you seen any sex in your house. I mean, does your father love your sisters in that way, Polly, or you, perhaps? Have you ever seen an erection, I mean, have you ever seen your father's penis?'

I wasn't sure if this was a trick anymore. I wasn't sure what this was about, at all.

'Yes, when we were small and I had to sleep with Daddy in the same bed, because Grandma only had two bedrooms.'

'I see. Well, well done, boy.' Then he checked himself, went all serious. 'So you did sleep with your Daddy then?'

'You didn't, did you?' asked Shed Boy.

I had to tell Mr. Fergusson the truth. He was a teacher. 'No, I didn't, because Daddy wouldn't let me sleep, Sir, because of his loud snoring.'

'He didn't do anything then?' I couldn't hear properly if this was Shed Boy or Mr. Fergusson?

'Yes, I just told you,' I said, 'he snored!'

At our weekend visits back home, Stewart and Polly would tell me how they needed it all to change.

'I've got no one to play football with.'

For Polly: 'And I have less clothes to iron and less washing-up to do, but I do miss you, terribly. It's so quiet when you two are not around.'

I smiled. I missed them too.

Elle told me Polly had been crying for four days.

'But I learnt song,' said Elle. 'Is by robots on the television and sing it very well.'

Dad was off quite a lot of the time, trying to make it up with Reverend Kibble.

"No, I do care for them, Maurice, it's just that, well, it's all Douglas's fault, I had to send Douglas away with Elle. He is just too much like David."'

Polly shook her head and said I wasn't

Elle bought her hands up to her ears.

'For mash get smash!' she shouted.

Then Stewart smashed all the plates of our meal, rather than him having to do the washing-up, as Polly had asked him nicely to do. I comforted her. She was, after all, only trying to do her best like me.

At Nazareth. Up at seven am, it was a race to the communal wash room. Brushed teeth, Charity tooth brushes, washed face, don't forget to Hell Mary. Freezing, still in my pants, I walked back to my bed. Get dressed, don't be sloppy, made bed. I stood to attention and waited inspection.

'Very good, young Master Porter'

The bell for breakfast rang.

Boys found their seats first, I had to be careful to choose a spare chair. The crimped-haired boy, it had been decreed, had to sit on his own. Not Elle, though. She wasn't seen as a revolutionary. Girls in next, then we queued at the food-counter. Cornflakes (too late for milk), bacon, scrambled-eggs, a very small sausage, two toasts, one dark, one light. No choice. The boy said the light toast was called fried bread. We took what was offered, thankful for what had been provided. The scrambled-eggs and sausage were good, the light toast? Well, yuk!

'No,' said the crimped haired boy. That's the breakfast from yesterday.'

'Eat ... Yuk ... Eat it,' I told myself.

Elle played with the dry cornflakes, until they were taken away. Dry toast was all that was left in front of her. Before it too could be swiped, she ripped the crusts off, sticking them into her pinny pocket for later. I was too far away to stop her.

'No, Elle, don't do it!' I shouted, knowing exactly what was going to happen next.

Elle's crusts were quickly found at inspection.

'Hands out.'

'Owww!'

Whacked over the knuckles with a wooden spoon.

She didn't cry though.

'Fucker!'

Elle!

'What did you say?'

The robed man was even more frightening to behold than the Reverend Kibble, with his ruffled hair and purple sash.

'You have to escape,' said Shed Boy.

Again, and again. I had to switch off. I couldn't stand his noise. It was worse than a when he screamed from the pavement.

On the long crocodile-walk to my new school, led by Carmen, the fried-bread I'd had earlier, started to repeat on me. I bent over.

'Master Porter?'

But Carmen was too late. I had already puked it out onto the pavement, as disgusting and bloody as the former contents of someone's burst appendix.

'Can't you do something?' asked Shed Boy.

The fat woman was laughing at all the mess I had made. 'Well, I suppose that's what the council is for.'

After school, she showed us the bare playground, stretched out like a tarmac wilderness for skateboards.

'Take out your shoe laces and your belts. We don't want any of you newen's escaping, now, do we?'

How could we play French Cricket like that?

It was then that I started to shake again, as I saw before me rising from the tarmac three weird entities, but were they Grandfather's, or Dad's?

It was the T first, I was sure. Dressed in purple, looking just like when I had first seen him in Tickencote, then the Dough, smiling and fading in and out and behind but growing ever larger, a, great judge, pulling me towards him, to punish me further, unless I was going to send Dad to him and the light.

How?

Because there were some good bits to this place too. Elle's new friend told us, 'We will all be going on a holiday soon, to Southend, with that T and Dough of yours too if you like. There will be spending money!'

Elle and I would be able to use all the pocket-money Dad gave for safe-keeping each week that we never saw.

Dad left us money?

Mum was much larger than normal when we got back home. Everything was supposed to be alright again. There was no ceremony. Mummy was sucking all the drama out of life.

As much as we knew we were expected to suffer as children and come unto her, it was not likely. Our attention turned instead to the what was in Dad's WH Smith bag.

In recognition of my help and sacrifice, Dad produced a red battery-operated helicopter that would fly around in circles on a piece of string.

It was the first time Dad came anywhere near to saying sorry. I took a leaf out of Stewart's book, and decided he and Mum should go fuck themselves, for being such awful parents.

They did, for a while, noisily, every third Thursday in the month after Dad's bath.

'Oh, oh, oh!'

I would then go to my bedroom to strangle my Action-Man with the cord of my red-plastic helicopter when they did, just like Auntie Eileen had done with a holy light cord, after Dad's father had died too.

I didn't need a helicopter, I needed a spaceship, that was the only way to save him, I wrote in my Discover's Workbook.

Miss Dobson seemed pleased to see me back. She welcomed me into class with her proper believer in the coming of Thelma smile and was far less severe in her new pink polka-dot dress.

Maybe that was why she then took me to see the rugged-fingered caretaker again.

He was sitting in his own shed, trying to rid himself of his dandruff. I wanted to clear it away.

'You know, it's not his fault you children don't trust him,' said Mrs. Dobson, as she read my latest attempt at homework about the prophecy. 'Or that your mother hasn't space anymore to care. It's not fair to expect it from her. It's not fair to expect from any of them'

Miss Dobson nodded her head, not surprised at this at all. 'By the way,' she said, 'I got a report from your teacher at the other school, near Nazareth House. She thought you were the saddest boy she had ever met. Are you really so sad, Douglas?'

It wasn't that something happened to cause it, during that summer holiday between schools, like a great revelation of the light. Or if it did, I somehow always seemed to forget, get lost in the search.

Only, in the mouldy-green shed could I withdraw to try and understand, construct ways to bring it all about. It wasn't good enough to be just accused of being a divvy-spaz, I needed to become one, to invite and become worthy of the bullying, yet still have time to do the washing up, their washing before my own. I would do as they all wanted, and sometimes when they didn't know themselves.

For isn't that what they needed, deserved, so that I could be recognized as the great Captain Lollop, swinging into every discord to take responsibility from them, the best superstar, the best martyr, do for them and better, for everyone's sake and then withdraw, forget, or shut it away.

Great chunks of selflessness shut away in the safety of my self-claimed withdrawal to help my father, into the light of his very becoming, in Babel, as was written.

Steve Porter

DAVID

'Our Father, which art in heaven,' Michael read out with the rest of them, 'hallowed be thy name; thy kingdom come; thy will be done ...'

But what was this will to be done and how would it impact on Michael's journey with me?

'That which is acceptable and perfect and good.'

Pastor Mead, the new reader and Michael in the bible study that Michael had started to attend, just before communion, confirmed it, like it was some sort of pact.

It was also Michael's adopted new way of understanding his getting Stewart baptized, when he really shouldn't have.

'Have you never heard of the Tower of Babel?' the reader asked of Michael.

'Uhm, well, yes.'

'Come, come, we must not bully him,' the pastor said to the reader. 'As we all know, some of the voices are to be ignored, and some are accepted. We each get to choose.'

It was right and it was good.

As the pastor and reader left to change into their robes, Michael noticed the bible lying on the empty seat next to him, a page extended from the middle, and with text underlined.

'...do not be conformed to this world...' it read, '....be transformed by the renewal of your mind in mine.'

Did it really matter where it had come from?

I was glad Michael hadn't worked it out.

It was time for communion.

Michael picked up his bible, made his way to his pew, joined in with the service.

Hymn, Prayers, Collect, Readings, Sermon, Creed.

It was a younger sound, Michael heard, or it felt like it, as he made his way up front to receive the sacrament. In harmonic dissonance, like an echo from somewhere far away.

'He doesn't even recognize its importance.'

'Not here,' said Michael. Not now.'

'From Mona, you say. Oh, sorry, Great "M", your wonderful...'

Interference, then. Maybe Thelemic static, or a Skylark flying into the clouds.

Was it male or female, this new message, Michael wondered? Child, adult, or a chorus, like a choir of angels, or perhaps just one?

The importance of this as some sort of alternative way was all that mattered.

It was as though this angel was calling him into a new light, willing him to play, and me, because, as Michael's twin brother and adventurer supreme, I wasn't going to be left out in the cold.

'Thy will be done.'

'But not with Delius?' pleaded Michael.

Hannah was holding his hand as Pastor Mead placed a wafer in his mouth

Which was the one true faith, with Hannah surely, and so the Delius sirens were to be ignored. It was to be by this way and by this will.

'Exactly, Michael.'

And all the women in Michael's life were there before him then in his mind, Hannah, Patricia Grimshaw, his mother up front, of course, with her dark eyes.

'There is no need to be so scared, Michael,' they said, but the Angel to his left took over with the great battle of Babel.

'Will the walls come tumbling down?'

In Babel, there were many walls, many voices, but only one will, for each to choose. But not if Hannah was there, preventing Michael from all that Babel had to offer, against the teachings of great 'M's' modern gospel of how the world is not always supposed to go by the way of *Onward Christian Soldiers,* that there is always too, don't you know, the round and round.

On the way back from the service on his bicycle, I had Michael consider again his findings in that bible. All the 'your mind in mine', or from his point of view the other way around.

Why was he going against our pact? Why would he refuse our journey, in favour of his own, despite all that they were doing to him, had done, all the women, or girls, that he had never found the courage to trust?

Steve Porter

POLLY

I n Vicar Morgan's garden by the podium on the stage, the cameras were ready, the lights were positioned and glaring. Stewart beamed at Vicar Morgan's lifting of the plastic-silver first-place trophy from the table, and Douglas, about to be lifted onto the second-place step, looked so much prouder than I had ever seen him.

'No, it cannot be!'

Even the Magaluf, a voice that had recently decided to take me over every now and then, was surprised. It was the only time Douglas had ever got near to winning everything.

I was very happy for him.

'Oh, and you don't have to worry about Miss Byatt,' said the Magaluf. 'She will now be dressed up in sequins and raised to the top of the Christmas tree, or maybe further, maybe even as far as the Skylark space ship to get your Daddy to the light.'

Mrs Byatt had been our French teacher. She was a Christian who apparently, according to Mr Singleton at last Friday's assembly, fell out of a plane on fire on her return from Spain.

'It wasn't Concorde, was it,' asked Daddy?

But what was the Magaluf on about? What was a Skylark space ship? What light? And why did he think Daddy would want to get to it?

'Possibly,' the Magaluf had it, 'because Miss Byatt's effect on you when she was alive made you want to become your very own little Christian light, just like her.'

91

She had earned this right, apparently, because she was a Christian and had been to Lourdes and, on her descent, she had met with the Magaluf, and they had had a lovely conversation, apparently, about the benefits of the light above the Christmas tree, which they determined, could be my destiny too, if I could just bring myself to believe that miracles were possible if I chose the right religion and space ship.

What right space ship?

Douglas was trying to tell me something, then.

'Don't...'

But he was inhibited by the roll of carpet surrounding him and obscuring his vision from the light.

And Mummy, with her attention temporarily taken up with her tray of what-nots on the seat beside me by the teapot, knocked my Skylark sponge and its attached balloon to the hard podium floor.

'Pelmanism,' she said. 'It's messy child-centred play between strange parables and plenty of tea.'

The Skylark's balloon popped, preventing me from reaching the light, as was supposed to happen, I reasoned.

This was just as well because there was a better time, and as I was about to find out, I was far from ready.

Vicar Morgan approached Stewart, the true first-prize winner of St Richard's holiday club fancy dress competition. He held out his hands, ready to administer one of his blessings.

Douglas started to jump up and down and was about to topple into Stewart, threatening to ruin Stewart's prize-winning costume of a bright red tube of angelic toothpaste, with fluorigard, too.

It was the only proven decay fighter in the world, apparently.

'Fucker.'

I looked to Daddy for help, but he was too busy talking to himself again.

'I really wish I understood girls.'

'Polly, will you get out of the way," said Mummy. 'You are not supposed to be in the shot. This is your brother's best-ever moment. Can't you see the greatness he has earned by winning the plastic silver first-place cup?'

Vicar Morgan gave Stewart the prize, as Mummy looked at Douglas and me with the scorn of a mad woman possessed.

But this didn't last long because Vicar Morgan started leading us all in prayer over that poor Miss Byatt.

'May God give to" he looked at his note cards, nodded, 'Miss Byatt, the French teacher with the Skylark balloon ship, and all whom she loves, his comfort and peace, his light and his joy, in this world and the next, and the blessing of the eternal light.'

Mummy stomped over and cuffed me about my ears, obviously thinking I'd been the one to swear.

'Owww!'

This despite my new desire to find a Christian light with Mrs Byatt again.

'And don't you start again,' said Mummy, 'with all your ideas about bowing and scraping to the Immaculate and such.'

Because Stewart never did, and as Mummy wanted us all to know, she didn't see the need for anyone to bow to anyone.

The light dimmed behind a cloud.

But Miss Byatt had given me a *Miraculeuse* – Sound it out, Polly – Sindy Madonna doll from the gift shop in Lourdes, and as I'd tried to tell Mummy earlier, it had been blessed. 'Like a holy relic,' Miss Byatt had told me.

'Because I sense you of all my truly wonderful pupils will be able to understand.'

'Would I,' I asked? 'Why?

The sky darkened.

So I stepped aside, as Mummy wanted and picked up my Skylark sponge and popped balloon.

'May the Lord Bless you all and keep you and...'

There was a tremendous thunderclap in protest, probably because I was distracted from the Magaluf earlier.

In all the confusion, a figure started to creep out from behind one of the heavier clouds.

His clothes were far from sparkly and gay or with wings, and he was washing Daddy's feet in our just-bought washing machine. A twin-tub.'

'It's him,' said Douglas. 'It's Uncle David. You'd better watch out, Polly!'

Then the rain started. At first, it was just some light spitting.

'Polly,' said Mummy. 'Will you stop gawping like that and help Elle put her clothes back on.'

She hastened me off the stage, all of us, as the Magaluf reminded me of the purpose of the Skylark sponge ship, with a head on each end, Daddy and the Magaluf, four port hole windows, one for each of us children.

But what about the cat?

'There were no cats in the 'Bible', she said. Not even cats called, Tingle Two, sent to keep Michael from me.'

A balloon was also supposed to be attached to the top of the ship as its primary means of ascent, as it travelled to the light.

Well, that's what the Magaluf wanted me to see and believe.

'Look, you're going to have so much fun flying about with your Daddy in that,' she said.

But as the clouds thickened and the rain increased, I concentrated on securing the poppers of Elle's clothes, as Mummy had ordered.

On the way home, we had to march crocodile file to the rhythm of *Onward Christian Soldiers.*

'A good, true and very Catholic hymn,' agreed the Magaluf.

'Come now, children,' Mummy was in her voice. 'I want no sloping off or slouching, and I'm not going to be embarrassed like the last time you went to school, Polly, and started dancing in the middle of the pavement like you were some sort of God-awful pagan.'

I said nothing.

Even though dance was all I had to find and express my true self, and some had even compared me to the Lady of the Dance, atop the Christmas tree, or Douglas had, I knew, I hadn't a chance to convince Mummy of my skills.

'What is this Lady of the Dance, of which you speak,' asked Mummy, which was something.

But by then, the rain, as fast, loud, and fearful as Mrs Byatt's descent to Spain, was enough for us all to concentrate on, leaving no space in our heads to answer. When we did finally arrive home, Tingle Two, maybe because she was so unloved, died.

'Good to be rid,' said Mummy. 'Mangy, bloody, flea-infested moggy thing!'

Daddy had called the vet earlier, apparently and when he'd arrived, Tingle Two had tried to get up from her basket but had failed, like Douglas with his Pelmanism trials, so the vet had to hold her and stick her with a massive needle.

'Will she go to the light of Lourdes with Miss Byatt,' I asked, imagining her smiling down at me, as Douglas picked his nose.

'Stop that. You'll hurt yourself!'

But I had never seen Daddy cry before. None of us children had. I wanted to comfort him. I wanted to comfort them all. Well, apart from Mummy, who really didn't deserve it, with her lack of respect or knowledge for my skills at dance.

'Daddy,' I said. 'Don't cry so much! Do you want me to wash your feet?' It seemed appropriate.

But Daddy seemed so much more interested in writing it all down in his diary because, unlike it was with his love of the Lord, he never thought he deserved to cry for himself or have his feet ritually submerged and his stumpy toes simultaneously washed.

That *was* in the bible. I had read it.

So there we all were, except Elle, behind the telly box in the front room. Tingle Two, the dead cat, in the wicker chair, Stewart and Douglas, now free of their costumes and trying to work out why it hurt when they pulled snot globs out of each other's hair.

And as Noah and Nelly jumped about on the television, in their own dance, or that's how it seemed, Daddy was crying in the reflection, in his black-leather swivel-chair of their two-headed Skylark space ship.

'Oh, that was what my sponge was all about?'

Mummy flopped on the black leather swivel chair, pasty-faced and almost monosyllabic in her death-like depression, like Eeyore from Winnie the Pooh on a very bad day.

'It's not my fault,' she said. 'It's not my fault I don't fit in here, anymore.'

But none of that mattered much at all because what I heard from the Magaluf then, about Daddy's religion being our only way and salvation, was not quite right.

Douglas agreed.

'Got himself struck up on a cross, that Jesus,' he said. 'Bled too – an abdomen wound. And would he miracle himself down? Oh, no. Even when his own Mis Byatt given, *Miraculeuse* Sindy-Doll, Mary, was crying for him with her painted purple hair at how everyone was being treated. Someone should have put him in a space ship with a balloon up top instead!'

But why did the Magaluf want to take my Daddy away from us in a Skylark ship?

I had him then. Douglas didn't know.

Which was just as well because when Elle came bouncing in.

'Polly, it's Bay City Rollers on radio! We do dance now?'

And it might have been what Miss Byatt wanted.

'Arms up, Elle,' I said. 'That's right, well done. Two, three...'

'Is good, you count like, Polly. Show me?'

Poor Elle. How she had her troubles.

'Yeah, and we sang Shang-a-lang. And we ran with the gang...'

'What's a gang, Polly?'

'A gang, Elle,' I said, 'is like a lot of people, under the watchful eye of Miss Byatt from up in the Lourdes clouds, smiling at us from the light with all the angels.'

'Oh!'

'And the Skylark,' said the Magaluf, suggesting he had an interest in the antics of Mrs Byatt and the angels.

'But Mr Magaluf,' I said, 'your ship with a balloon to take us all into the light is also not in the good book!'

'I know,' he said. 'And maybe, Polly, that's what your father doesn't understand and why he needs your help.'

I didn't like his tone.

Yes, I wanted to help my Daddy, but I didn't know what it was that he didn't understand.

It was three days later when Mummy got taken off to hospital again. The ambulance men were very kind and quiet about it.

'Just as all the grey-suited angels should be,' the Magaluf tried to convince me.

'Mmmm, eee, ayyy, ahhh, ohhh, for the wings, for the wings, of a dove!'

The grey-suited angels rescued Mummy from her singing of this and a particularly tuneless rendition of *Amazing Grace* up the cobwebbed stairwell, then gently escorting her out of the front door of number twenty-six.

So I was in charge now, the eldest female in the house, as it should be. It was my job and a chance to look after Daddy and the rest, my way, and that, I said to the Magaluf, 'is exactly what I am going to do.'

Daddy looked depressed again.

'It won't be easy, child,' said the Magaluf, 'with that Daddy of yours and his escapes. I mean, he is not really, very much, is he? You should think again about the ship and get some help. Wouldn't you agree?'

I wasn't sure, but what I was sure of was that soon, it would be my job to wash my Daddy's stumpy-toed feet because that would make things alright again.

I had prepared for this with Elle every Sunday after Church for three weeks. I had the washing-up bowl ready, with the expensive Fairy liquid and everything.

But Daddy, even though the washing of his feet was in the Bible, had other things to do. He was looking at a pocket map of the London Underground, trying to get Stewart's attention.

'Uhm, uhm, Stewart, what colour is that dark line here?'

Daddy was a colour-blind, apparently.

And Stewart was very helpful about this.

'It's Blue,' he said. 'Blue is the colour. Football is the game.'

'Yes, I see.' Said Daddy. 'Well, thank you.'

'Yeah, and we're all together, and winning is our aim.'

'Yes, Stewart. And that will be enough.'

'Fuck off, then! You never understand!'

Indeed, Stewart was very badly behaved!

The Magaluf didn't think much of this, either.

He suggested that Stewart shouldn't get a place on the Skylark with the balloon.

It was Miss. Byatt, still smiling, as she played with Tingle Three, who was chasing her crucifix around as fast as Daddy's bicycle wheels when taking us to our school.

'Daddy,' I said, trying to regain his attention from his pocket map of the London Underground tube train system. 'Now, about your feet. Bathing them in this bowl will help you spread all the love of the Lord to all of us and keep you here.'

He looked up at me.

'Polly,' he said, 'you are not Mary Magdalene.'

Magaluf, I wanted to return, but thought better of it.

Daddy was right, it was true, I was a child but so was Stewart and a very rude one at that.

He knocked over the washing-up bowl, wasting all the fairy liquid I had used to prepare my Skylark sponge.

'Bastard!'

'You can't get to space and shit in that.'

Quite a lot of the time, I really didn't know what to do about Stewart's naughty.

The next day was better.

'A surprise', Daddy said. 'On a trip, we shall go on the overground tube. So you must all behave yourselves well.'

Eight little legs and two daddy-long ones were marching in perfect unison.

'Onward Christian Soldiers,' we sang, 'marching as to ... But then, 'Douglas, stop that, this instant. If you must know, we are going to find an elephant that lives in a magic fairy castle!'

Douglas was tripping up from his arch supports constantly, trying to escape Stewart's kicking.

Indeed, the tube train, as we called it, was very welcome after the four-mile walk to Hounslow Tube Station to save money on the bus fare.

'We take the blue line,' said Douglas, 'all the way to Leicester Square before we change to the proper overground trains.'

Douglas didn't have that much confidence in tube journeys or miracles since he learned from Daddy's diary about 'him not being a perfect hero, whilst Elle..,

'Are we there yet? Toilet! Now! Need it!'

Luckily, I'd remembered to bring her bucket for such an occasion. The other passengers didn't look too pleased, which wasn't very Christian of them. Didn't they know that someone had to ensure Elle had dry knickers.

It was a long journey, with the train stopping at every milk bottle, or so it seemed. And preparation had been everything.

'Remember your Discoverer's Workbook,' said my *Miraculeuse* Sindy-doll in the distant voice of Miss Byatt.

Because what was in my workbook differed somewhat from what was in Douglas's.

In year twelve, I read in this that the Magaluf wasn't in Nazareth for much of his childhood. He was in Jerusalem, having been abandoned there by his God-awful parents. And he had tried to argue himself out of the rather difficult situation in which he had found himself, like me.

The other passengers looked to Daddy when I emptied the whole bucket of wee on the train tracks at Hammersmith.

'It's not Daddy's fault,' I said back to them. 'I am in charge here, and I am trying!'

When we got to our destination, there was another, new problem. Well, two.

The elephant I'd promised them all wasn't real, and there wasn't any castle either.

But miracle of miracles, a Jesus-like man in a potpourri-patterned, open-necked shirt with a beard and collar almost the size of elephant ears turned up.

After my greeting – 'Pleased to meet you' – and a quickly gobbled plate of bourbons, Jesus Man told us about the next long journey ahead. 'It's going to be alright, though,' he said. 'For your trouble, I am going to give you each a lumpy Swiss roll.'

'Well-cushty!' said Stewart.

Douglas and Elle picked at their scabs, whilst Daddy waved us goodbye.

Why? Where was he going? I hoped he hadn't taken my two-headed Skylark sponge ship with him.

We had our swiss-rolls to consider, and soon after were shepherded into a blue frog-eyed transit van, with its lights blinking like a disco.

'Dance, then wherever you may be,' sang the Jesus Man, who was also our pilot, driver.

I joined in loudly. I had to. I was the new Lady of the Dance.

'Shut up!' said Stewart.

'You shut up!'

There were other songs, too.

This was all very good and pleased the Magaluf immensely, enough to reveal in *Miraculeuse*, our destination by the disco lights of the frog-eyed transit. And behold, the road signs were showing we were well on our way on the M3 all the way to fucking Woking

Stewart had observed in his eldest and bestness that the journey was a 'waste of time', as 'frog-van' could have picked us up on the way, in the first place.

Jesus Man's bunting-shaped collar obstructed my view when he leant forward to clip Stewart about the ear for his wanton cheek. For, as it was learnt in Jerusalem, it was in the way of things in nineteen seventy-four. Jesus Men had every right to clip naughty boys, around the ears as was good and very proper.

Ockenden Adventure was a holiday home, yes, but it was a holiday home with a difference. A place for the maladjusted and really, really awful, bad!

It was all Stewart's fault, of course.

'Christian?' I asked the new bearded man, hopefully, who was sitting under a photo of the Beatles on the suede settee.

'Of course, my child.'

The bearded man was from one of those new Peanut-Butter Ministries, the Magaluf said, as Stewart screwed up his nose and then spat out a most lumpy piece of swiss-roll.

Peanut Butter man wanted to know if anyone had any questions. 'Anything really, anything at all?'

Stewart recovered quickly, 'You know Chelsea?' he asked.

'What, Peter Bonetti and Osgood,' said Peanut Butter Man bearded one, 'the best players in the western hemisphere? Of course, I bloody know them!'

I leaned forward and tapped Peanut Butter Man on the edge of his knee.

'So if Jesus is the son of God and not Joseph,' I interrupted him, covering my knees with the Indian wrap-around skirt that Mummy had given me after cutting off the hem with her pinking scissors, 'Could it be that I might be the daughter of an archangel, like Douglas told me, and will be sent to go find both the light and the coming of the Thelma?'

Douglas sort of nodded his approval at this, but he didn't seem very sure.

Stewart and Elle might have been thinking about it, too, if they were prepared to be bought into the light, so to speak, and the gates, but they were soon occupied with an earnest search of the too-high food cupboards, just like at home.

'Where's the Peanut Butter?'

My Sindy Doll started to glow then. Or that's what I thought gave me all my powers of the light of Jerusalem.

Douglas had said it was written, somewhere.

I started an almighty discussion, in which I had to explain how it wasn't any wonder, with me being the daughter of an archangel, that life would always be very hard and I would indeed, have to suffer?

Stewart found an ominous-looking elasticated slingshot and started twanging the elastic faster and faster, almost to the same rhythm as the Wolf theme from *Peter and the Wolf* by Daddy's *That Prokofiev*.

A piece of piecrust flew past my left cheek, missing it by, I didn't know how much, given Mr Singleton's much earlier confusing lesson on the difference between the new metric and imperial measurements when it comes to Skylark space ships.

Peanut-butter Man stopped me right there, with the only measurement that meant anything to anyone.

'Do you believe in Jesus Christ?' he asked.

I knew what I had to say, but would I say it and then with the grace of the Magaluf filling up my faith pot.

'Oh, yes, I believe,' I said as Stewart took off with his slingshot. 'He's a real, rare one,' I said, and that's the God only knows truth. But the question is, do you, with all your football worshiping ways?

Elle held my hand as Peanut Butter Man looked back at me with his mouth open.

'Because,' I continued, 'if you do, then you are ready for our Father's kingdom. But what of the Magaluf? Should I trust him?'

Neither Peanut Butter Man or Stewart said anything.

'Is the Magaluf not the true reason behind Mummy's shouting and mad?' I continued as Douglas snorted out his own big one. 'What is his true role in this? Tell me!'

Douglas picked up the bogey, tasted it with his tongue and then started spitting in what seemed like absolute disgust.

Further exploration by Peanut Butter Man as to what I meant by the archangel, Mummy's madness, and the importance of the Magaluf left him looking very tired.

'Can I touch your beard?' asked Elle.

'I'll say this for you, Polly,' answered Peanut Butter Man, as Elle started her stroke, 'you are quite a something to be reckoned with.'

But I thought this was supposed to be a place for the really bad, wasn't it?

And when Elle said. 'Me not know, what Lady da Dance is,' and Peanut Butter Man took her by the hand, with comfort, and tried to explain.

'Do you know of Shiva?'

'No!' said Elle.

I argued with him.

'That's Indeean.'

'Yes, but it's also a hymn, like Jerusalem'

Peanut Butter Man stepped back then, looked at me and asked me how I could know so much about the ways of the Lord, or the Magaluf, at eight years of age, when it took Jesus himself until he was twelve, and he was at a temple and maybe was even an Indian!'

'Perhaps it's a *Miraculeuse*?' I said.

A year later, with Miss Byatt still smiling down from the clouds at me, Tingle Three scratching at some newly found fleas back at number twenty-six, the stage was set for my debut at Feltham Village Hall, with flickering fairy lights.

There wasn't any fanfare to speak of. But there was an introduction of Tchaikovsky's famous Sugarplum piece, from the scratchy sound of what, according to Daddy, who was then twiddling his nose in the cheap seats, with Vicar Morgan and the Right Reverend Kibble, had to be a Fidelity Mono HF45, turntable, with anachronistic valves', or something with as much attention paid to the quality of sound.

The curtains opened. Vicar Morgan beamed at the delighted whispers of excitement from all the little ones as they hoovered up all the mincemeat crumbs left behind from the earlier, tea time, dress rehearsal.

The clever Case from the left theatre wing seemed to look at me with such hate for having taken over her role, having injured her foot the day before.

'Please, Miranda, show me how I can do it well, like you.'

'You will do so well,' said the Magaluf. 'You will win them all over and earn your and your Daddy's place in the space ship.'

Then the whole of Barbara Billings Dance School skipped onto the stage, a feast of taffeta and lace, with stars stuck on to their costumes with Sellotape, flour, and lumpy paste glue.

I was in the middle, sparkling from top to toe as a protection from all the evil I had learnt to feel from Mummy about how bad I really was.

'A lollipop dunked in glitter', I heard one of the other dancers describe me. And I thought Miranda was supposed to be my best friend.

But the Magaluf was with me, I could tell. I could feel it, which was just as well with the Reverend Kibble's hand up, ready, to start the performance with its drop.

Where were Douglas and Stewart? Oh, yes, in the cheap seats at the back of the village hall.

The Reverend's hand fell.

'Now!'

First, the littl'uns went to their places, followed by the rest of us. Tissue confetti fluttered down, thrown by the ones that could not be trusted to be without nappies, or buckets on tube trains, of which Elle was most definitely the needy.

The illustrious so-lucky-to-have-as a dance-teacher, Barbara Billings then glissaded over to the allocated spot marked out in red chalk in the middle of the stage carpet.

She smiled, bowed her head. All that could be heard was a leaking tap from the hallway water closet, like the trickle of water from a just-dunked body at the first baptism in the Bible.

It was a blessing indeed and with the strong possibility that might even make Daddy really proud of me.

The scratch from the Fidelity HF45 moved from crackle to the recorded soft bells of the celesta of Tchaikovsky's opening.

Barbara Billings looked at me and beckoned her star.

As gracefully as possible, I stork-pointed my way to the middle of the stage. Upon my arrival, alone and scared, I looked to the audience for Daddy's reaction. Nothing. He was too far away to see.

Douglas waved, I could see, but then Mummy slapped him.

It started with a piece of choreography that Barbara Billings had borrowed from the Tiny-Tots dance manual.

In perfect harmony with the music, I performed, with the audience showing their obvious heartfelt appreciation.

'Oh, will you look at that?'

'Ahh!'

Plié, Straight, Pause. Passé, Down, Passé, Down, No pause, Point, Point, Point.

It was a near perfect performance. I had good reason to believe I could become an angelic host and maybe, even, make a proclamation.

Again. Plié, Straight, Pause. Passé, Down, Passé, Down, No pause, Point, Pointy point. Point.

Indeed, Barbara Billings looked like Mrs Byatt when she gave me my miracle Sindy Doll.

By the beginning of the third section, I saw Auntie Belinda dig Mummy in the side.

'Will you look at that, Hannah. That's your daughter, that is. Even though it should have been mine, I have to say that she is like a proper, darling little angel.'

But what kind of angel?

I saw Mummy cough and look around the audience, perhaps waiting for the adulation I would bring her, letting everyone see her not so ashamed of me, bucked-tooth smile.

'Ere, that ain't Mrs Porter is it, the pasty-faced teacher wot put on that Peter Pan up at Oriel? Well, we are blessed. I thought she'd be up at Buck House by now, busy sequinning the corgis in preparation for Billy Graham's next production!'

Passé, Down. Point, Point, Point. Now arabesque to the right. Back to first. Arabesque to the left.

Elle waved, and Mummy acknowledged this with a faint movement of her fingers. She didn't wave at me because I realised that even though it was just a trifle of a show compared to her latest and most talented production of *The Adventures of Peter Pan*, she didn't want to distract her first-born daughter, the brilliant star of the show, and affect my concentration.

Back to first. Arabesque to the right. Back again to first.

It was all perfectly timed but also short-lived because, as Mummy would make sure everyone realised later, children needed very little support after they had passed the age of seven, as unloved husbands required none.

At least that was Mummy's take on *Froebel*, who she'd once said had been in charge of her college training at Roehampton.

Elle was dribbling into her tights, but the Magaluf, in a warm voice that was like Daddy's, when about to sneeze, said, 'You are really earning your place on the Skylark, and you are my daughter, whom I love. With you, I am well pleased, but you will have to fight, Polly, and you will have to suffer.'

Demi-pointe, Turn, Arms in fifth.

I was the princess of my moment then. Not a thing or person could take any of it away from me.

'Very good. Higher, Polly. Very good.'

I began to smile as I repeated the moves to myself over and over, encouraged by the higher power of the Magaluf's assuring voice, straight out of the Bible: '...led by the Spirit into the wilderness, to be tempted by...'

But all the lights went out, and the music from the record player slowed.

'That Mr Heath and his blessed power cuts,' I could hear Barbara Billings curse.

I held position just like I'd been trained for this situation as the backup generator kicked in, and I waited for Mrs Boulting to make her way over to the pianoforte, as she called it.

Everyone turned together to look.

Mrs Boulting stared out her invitation for silence, and it worked. She gave a swift nod to Barbara Billings.

But Miss Byatt wasn't there anymore, nor Tingle Three. They had been taken out by the power cut.

Mummy shook her head. I secretly hoped that she wanted to cry for her little girl. If Mummy could acknowledge me as a worthwhile daughter who would do right by her, just once, then I would have realised what being a woman, wife, and mother in the future is all about.

Elle tried to copy me as I pointed my right leg out to the side, but she was also greatly affected by her oversized nappies and needed to fiddle with them, it seemed.

Brush your leg. Then, a quick hop onto the right. Up. Brush your leg. Up. Repeated. Twice.

Mrs Boulting revealed herself to be quite the 'tinkler' when she was allowed to get into her Tchaikovsky.

The whole tone of the performance changed.

'After fasting forty days and forty nights,' continued the Magaluf from his own bible study, I imagined, or what he'd interpreted from mine, because he really didn't understand the Bible as much as me, or did he?

'The tempter came to him and said, "If you are the blessed daughter of the almighty, tell these stones to become bread.'

There was no bread.

Instead, Elle picked up a large piece of mincemeat pastry from the floor and started chomping with so much enthusiasm the sweet mince squeezed out and landed all over her carefully prepared crepe-paper tights.

'Oh.'

And then.

'Mu-u-ummy!'

Mrs Boulting plonked up the volume of her grievous playing.

Arrière back, Point forward, Point. Pointy point. Point.

'Mu-u-ummy, it's all sticky!'

That brought the whole village hall down with a massive round of applause.

'Ere, look at her go.'

Auntie Belinda's gait, following Mummy, was causing all kinds of interesting strides as she stomped over to the front of the stage.

As the applause died down, and to the apparent relief of the embarrassed Barbara Billings, Mummy picked Elle up and silenced her cries, allowing the show to continue.

'Thank you, my dears! Thank you so much for your understanding!'

Mrs Boulting nodded to Mummy, who managed to force from the empty space where her shrivelled-prune heart was to be a response to Mrs Boulting.

'Thank you!'

It was then, as though I was launched to the realization of Daddy's dreams by a higher existence that wasn't anymore there, in a far-flung winged jete to beyond the Babel clouds and from there, to the light from whence Thelma would come, according to Douglas's Discoverer's Workbook, from the Temple of Jerusalem, or fiery wake, where, through the window, I could see Daddy marking down in his diary, how I had caused him so much happiness that day.

But who was this Thelma?

Douglas, I remembered once had tried to tell me, but I didn't believe it. And in truth, I could see that Daddy wasn't anywhere near the light. He wasn't even in the village hall.

It was probably work that took him. It was always his work or Mummy's need for bubble bath because Mummy was so very selfish, like that, or so Daddy always said.

Barbara Billings had the whole troupe bounce onto the stage to take a bow. I was first.

Records. No, Daddy wouldn't have left me for a trip to Richmond Records to buy something other than Tchaikovsky or Delius, would he?

'To save him,' said the Magaluf. 'To save your Daddy and you all from his selfishness, Polly, you have to get him on that two-headed sponge Skylark ship of yours!'

'No,' I said. Because I couldn't believe it. 'My daddy's not selfish, he is just misunderstood.'

On our way home, I skipped down the avenue of trees with Mummy, halfway to Castle Road, on our way to number twenty-six. It wasn't right or fair that Mummy should say nothing about how well I had done, so I took a leaf out of Stewart's book.

'Did I do well, Mummy?' I asked.

'Stop right there!'

I stopped and looked Mummy up and down with the respect she always demanded.

'You were acceptable, Polly,' she said. 'Quite acceptable, I will say that for you. Thank you for asking. Now, that is all.'

Acceptable to who? And again, who was this Thelma that Douglas was always reading and telling me about from his Discoverer's Workbook?

With Mummy and Miss Byatt gone, there was time for play and imagination. There was time for the house chores and the shopping and taking over from Mummy, like the Magaluf wanted, to facilitate the environment in which Daddy might learn to become a real man and be respectable in the light.

'Daddy, you haven't washed your socks for two weeks!'

I had counted.

'How am I to wash your feet and stumpy toes like the Magaluf wants when you haven't even washed your socks?'

'Leave me alone, child?'

And if Stewart would stop going on about his Chelsea and help with the washing-up, and Douglas could find his arch-supports to help with his lolloping gait, so he could help carry the big boxes of corn-flakes home from the weekly shop at Sainsbury's, due that day. Daddy might just see that he could place his faith in me entirely.

The whole family sat in the sitting room, waiting for Brucie.

I had to explain to the Magaluf why I had cut my Sindy-doll's hair off in a group session at that St Bernard's Hospital of the Mentals place.

'It was stiff plastic,' I told him. 'Stringy hair, like my Sindy Doll, not to be trusted. Purchased from the family accounts, and without consulting me, who, ever since I started shopping, was now supposed to be in charge of the family, and the family allowance too.'

Douglas understood. It was my way of not being a nuisance and talking. That was how we bought ourselves up.

'Lovely to see you, to see you...,' came Brucie's introduction.

'Lovely,' we chorused.

'Thank-you. Thank you,' said Brucie. 'Well, shall we meet our contestants? Come on now, stand over here, nice and close. So you are Hannah, and you like to make costumes with sequins, I see.'

Mum was on the telly!

'Well, the world's big enough for all of us. And it says here that you like to sing from the top of the stairs. Do you play dressing up with the children when you do that?'

Dad was nose-deep into his books, not deserving any help.

'Yes, I see. And this is your daughter, Polly, with a rather extraordinary skirt. And you like the Bay-City Rollers, Polly, or so I hear.'

I smiled.

Stewart, Douglas and Elle sat cross-legged on the floor, taking it all in.

'Well then, game number one! We have one to test any relationship between a mother and daughter. Over here. Now, Polly, have you got any idea what this is?'

On the telly, I picked up the shiny item, looked it up and down, and then turned it over. I beckoned Brucie over and whispered in his ear. At least someone was prepared to listen.

'A large cheese grater without the holes,' I said. Proud as any post-twin-tub matriarch.

Brucie looked to Mum.

'I'd have thought, as a teacher,' he said, 'you would have educated your daughter better!'

How I loved my Brucie!

'It's a washboard,' said Mum.

'Indeed, it is, said Brucie.' And this?'

He picked up a large copper pot and a stick with five prongs long enough to support sails on a ship. He looked earnestly to the audience.

'Anyone?

Elle was so excited. 'It's Jake's leg,' she said. 'Wiv its extra peg and everyfing.'

Stewart laughed as Mum, on the telly, explained all about washing dollies and how some of our grandparents' generation used to do the washing before twin tubs and the new modernism bought about by Sputnik.

Brucie patted me on the head as he brought out an expert washer in the form of Mrs Grigg, the Child Psychologist; I wondered how she protected her painted nails when she had to use her twin-tub.

'Shall we start?' Brucie asked.

The mum on the telly with me strode over.

'You don't do it like that,' she said, taking the dolly and rubbing the handle in her hands.

'Polly, poppet,' Mum said in a false, kind voice, 'bring me some soap flakes, dear.'

I poked out my chin at being ordered about like this by someone, who, as the Magaluf reminded me, 'doesn't care a Skylark flying-fuck about you!'

'No!' I refused.

I could see the anger flashing across Mum's cheeks.

'What do you mean, no? It is your duty, as my daughter!'

Brucie pulled a funny face, then. It was hard to work out whose side he was on.

Instead, I acted out separating the woollens, cotton, and colours, precisely placing the imaginary garments in neat separate piles.

Brucie smiled at me like he was in love.

Someone had to be.

'Didn't she do acceptably?'

Mum, in response, showed her bad face.

'Then a programme for all colours?' she asked, offering a new solution to the problem of raising a young family.

'Never mind, Hannah,' said Brucie.

He looked to the audience. To me.

Stewart then tried to teach Elle a new game he called 'Let's break Polly's unflyable ship and punch the new cat'. I should have been there to stop him, but I was with Brucie, and Stewart was older and bigger than me!

'Now, game number two,' said Brucie. 'The idea is to fill the trolley with as much value as possible, with the winner being the one with the largest amount and the most expensive items, as authenticated by the banker chap in a tight tie and holding a plastic wallet.'

'Ooh,' the sound was supposed to come from the audience, but I didn't think it did.

'Or at least he likes to think he does', continued Brucie. 'Ladies and Gentlemen, boys and girls, please welcome, Mr Michael Harry Porter.'

Dad was on the telly then, too. He had an extensive black diary and a checked jacket with oversized nineteen-fifties lapels.

I was astonished.

Dad?

'He deserves just as much as you to find happiness in the light in the ship,' the Magaluf told me. 'And it's your job, Polly, to find him a place on the ship so he can find his light and gate, with your mummy not being capable of doing so.'

I really wanted Brucie to fire his gun.

Bang!

I ran around the aisles, throwing sweets and packets of Angel Delight into the trolley.

Mummy walked over to the cleaning section, picked up four vacuum cleaners, strolled back to Daddy, who added up the accumulated value in a big black book.

'Four pounds more to Hannah,' said Dad.

My chin jutted out like the end of the bag on one of Mummy's vacuum cleaners. I realised I had been beaten and very soundly too. I sulked back to the others.

'Didn't she do acceptably?' said Brucie.

Then, to rapturous applause, in strode my grandmother from Gillingham, in her second-hand charity wool coat, just like Mary Poppins, with her famous umbrella.

'Are we going to fly now?' I asked.

'Are we going to fly?' Brucie laughed. 'What on your silly balloon ship? No, Polly, this game is about acceptable child-rearing. You have to play with your children. Mary Poppins will judge your skills and let you know how well you do.'

'But I don't have a balloon ship or any children,' I said! 'I am not like her. I am not and will not be my mother.'

Brucie looked to the audience. 'I honestly don't know with

this one. If, like her mother says, she is just too evil, like her brother Douglas is described alSo or she is simply too stupid for her own good?'

On the telly, Mum quickly answered: 'Oh, she's evil all right,' she said. 'Flying, indeed. It's against God; it is. As bad as Judas she is and those at Oriel that have betrayed me and refuse to allow me the chance to put on Chitty, Chitty Bang Bang.'

Some television prop hands entered, kicked out fake grass rolls and attached them to the table.

On my team was a pale-looking boy with a slightly red, bloated stomach, myself, of course, and a Sindy doll with chopped hair. On Mum on the telly's team were Douglas, Stewart and Elle.

Grandmother Poppins, according to the Magaluf, was studying the play closely.

'That's a six, that is,' said Stewart. 'Course it fucking is. Went into the laurel bushes, it did.'

Mum replied, 'Stewart, dearest. What will the neighbours think if they heard such language?'

As Brucie watched over her shoulder, Mrs Grigg was busy writing everything down.

'Oh, yes. I see. I can see where you are going with that.' Brucie placed his hand over his mouth.

'And you are a child psychologist, you say?'

The audience let out a cheer as I was revealed, by the Magaluf, to be the much better Mummy for this round.

Then, an even bigger cheer sounded as it was shared with the audience that I had, in fact, won the whole game.

Mum on the telly was sent off back to the hospital, her buck teeth pointing.

'Well, Polly,' said Brucie. 'Are you now ready for the conveyor belt?'

I nodded with enthusiasm and sat behind the screen as it slowly opened.

'A bottle of bubble bath. A pair of pinking scissors. A curl of butter. A piece of bunting. An old roll of carpet. A skateboard. Some peanut-butter. Angel Delight. A cheese grater without holes. An Indian wrap-around skirt. A rather rude picture of

Dad's. A football. A sponge Skylark spaceship. One of Douglas's socks, the family allowance and Dad's diary.'

A buzzer sounded.

'Come over here, my dear, Polly, and keep thinking, keep thinking. Yes, that's right. Now, let's see what you can remember?' Brucie asked.

I said nothing.

'You can begin,' he said.

'Nothing here to convince me to follow your light,' I said. 'I don't trust you anymore!'

Brucie looked to the audience again and back at me. 'What about the family allowance? Every mother needs a family allowance, enough to afford tights from Debenham's!'

'Your game,' I returned. 'I don't want to be anyone's Mum. I just want to be me!'

Then Brucie pulled out a box behind his back and tried to hand me a new Sindy doll.

'I don't want it,' I said. 'It's from Mum, isn't it? I know!'

Mrs Grigg picked up her pen and started to write it all down.

The title music played, and we were all unceremoniously dumped by the telly back into the living room. I went upstairs thinking that I didn't do very acceptably at all; in fact, I was atrocious and probably evil, just like Mum had said.

Douglas disagreed.

I was twelve when I realized I wasn't allowed into the boys' bedroom. Stewart always wanted to be quick under the eiderdown with his new girlfriend, Melissa.

But wasn't I supposed to be the mum and in charge? Wasn't it up to me to exert some control to prevent her from returning?

'No, you show first,' I heard.

The Magaluf was most insistent.

Melissa giggled, and then Stewart's head rose from underneath the eiderdown. Then he popped his fist, and I was slapped across the face.

'Slag! You fucking tart!' Stewart snarled.

I remember talking to Vicar Morgan once about Dad and how bullied he was in the temple in Jerusalem.

But Dad wasn't anywhere near the temple at Jerusalem. He was downstairs, depressed again or with another of his colds, probably listening to it all over his Delius.

Poor Archangel, I thought, if it was me, actually, doing the thinking. By then, there were times when I just couldn't tell.

Help me, Douglas?

But Douglas couldn't because Stewart was the eldest and always the best.

'I said, get out! You fucking cow!'

I got out, but it wasn't very fair. I had every right to play and take control.

So I took Elle into the bedroom with me and boldly made the announcement.

'Dad says that we must all be very quiet so he can listen to his music. And Elle wants to play.'

Stewart had other things on his mind, like his trying to speak in tongues.

Melissa, his new girlfriend, was staring at Elle and me from the other side of the bedroom.

'Ooh, are you playing shops?'

Elle offered Melissa a diary. 'two new pennies, pease.'

Melissa laughed and handed over some play money.

Stewart's friend, Simon Sullivan, laughed. 'Two new pennies? Someone, please give that girl some help.'

Stewart stared, his finger wagging a warning at him.

It worked, but Stewart got distracted again by Melissa's attention towards him, which I thought that was my way to get in without being slapped again. I was grateful to Melissa. She had never been so helpful.

With the coast clear, I bought some sachets of Angel Delight powder in my now chopped-haired Sindy doll, which had been raided from the kitchen cabinet only two days before.

Like gold dust was Angel Delight powder, at least it to me.

Enough to power a ship to find the light and maybe the coming of Thelma.

Douglas had told us all about Thelma from his printing that he would give out occasionally.

But Alistair was there too, in the bedroom, having already

learnt to shave from stealing Dad's razor and if I was kind to him and didn't tell, then he might like me too.

The Magaluf started laughing at me and the idea. It was such a ridiculous proposition.

It was then that Dad entered, which was good because by then, I had become a little more concerned and confused about the type of kissing that was actually going on.

Dad's creased trousers, which I had not been able to get off him to wash, stank up the room for the life of Miss Byatt. His nineteen-fifties tie was crammed up into a perfect triangle knot.

'Give me back my diary,' he said, holding out a gnarled hand, 'and I'll have you turn your music down, or all your friends will have to leave.'

But he didn't have any authority anymore.

'No, Stewart, don't,' said Douglas.

Then, the Magaluf piped up, trying to drown out everything else with his own false interpretation of the bible.

'And making a whip of cords, she would drive them all, with the sheep and oxen, out of the temple, and she poured out the money changers' coins and overturned their tables. And she told those who sold the pigeons or doves, "You shall not make this a ship of trade",' lest your mother return from your failure.'

When Stewart came over to hit me again, it didn't matter whether he succeeded or not because as I could see his fist approaching, I knew I would feel nothing, as I would simply not feel it. I wouldn't allow myself too. If Douglas could switch off his hearing aid, why couldn't I also?

'Because you want to help your father,' said the Magaluf. 'You need to help your father into the light to get to the gate.'

At the grand reckoning in the living room, I knew I needed something to defend myself against the shame.

Dad had no money again. Dad always had no money, but this time, he really didn't have any because it had been stolen, he'd said, and he might have to get Mummy back to raid her pension again. He'd also said he had gone through everyone's pockets and couldn't find it, but he wanted to know who was responsible.

Elle asked him, 'Who took the money?'

'Not me,' said Stewart, and not Douglas, either.

He looked at me, all sorry and about to admit it for me, but I shook my head. I squeezed Elle's hand in support or defiance; I wasn't really sure.

Dad's overgrown eyebrows were very scary.

'You know what happens if you lie.'

Dad looked at us all.

'Remember when PC Biggs came around last time and said you could all end up in court.'

Stewart turned to me as Douglas tried to hold him off.

I screamed as Stewart grabbed me, but not like I'd ever been grabbed before.

This time, his hand pointed and plunged down my top and into my bra. I could feel my anger grow with my screams.

Stewart pulled out the missing five-pound note, marched over to Dad and presented it to him.

'See,' he said, 'I told you!'

Dad looked at the floor.

'But isn't your daddy supposed to protect you,' asked the Magaluf, laughing again?

It was like I was the Mummy I was destined to be and just as bloody about the knickers, too.

'Send him to me in your Skylark,' said the Magaluf. 'I'll know what to do with him.'

That Dad hadn't bought me any sanitary towels, not knowing that I might need them was the only reason I had stolen the five-pound note in the first place.

He didn't seem to care.

'What is tarry towels about?' asked Elle.

At tea later, Dad, depressed again, chased cherry tomatoes around a Melton Mowbray on his plate with a fork while Elle spooned copious amounts of salad cream into her mouth.

'I know one of you will betray me,' said Dad. But none of the others were religious or had ever heard about the betrayal of the Magaluf!

I looked up.

Elle held Dad's hand.

Douglas was in the corner, hiding.

It wasn't one of Stewart's friends who would betray me, not that they could anyway, or Stewart because there wasn't enough of a relationship between us for him to betray.

'I'm fed up of all this, of all of you,' said Douglas, in a way that felt like a departure.

Of what? Who?

It wasn't as though I had much left inside that hadn't already departed. What was happening here, and why was it all happening so fast?

'Are you alright, Douglas?' I asked.

Dad looked at Elle, shook his head, and then got up to leave the table, with me and the others following close behind.

Later, Douglas came down from his room with a plastic bag of clothes. He stared at Dad.

'Alright, then,' said Dad. 'Take a plate and one set of cutlery if you must leave,' said Dad, 'if it is all my fault, as you say.

It wasn't, but I was on the sewing machine, and anyway, I knew Douglas wouldn't listen.

There was a hard rap on the door. Elle went.

'Pleased to meet you,' said a young woman at the door, I heard. 'Would you be Polly or Elle?'

I recognised the voice of Ginny, Stewart's friend. She wasn't a 'debutante tart'. She had her own Ford Capri, and at seventeen, she was the envy of all.

Douglas, or so it was described afterwards, grabbed his plastic bag full of clothes, plates and cutlery, pushed past everyone and slammed the front door behind him.

Dad came out of the music room.

'Where's Douglas gone?' asked Elle. She looked up to him.

Dad shuffled his feet in his slippers. He looked back at Elle. 'You mean Douglas? He's left home.'

'What do you mean, left home?' I asked.

'Left home,' Dad said. 'He thinks I betrayed him by never being there for him or any of you.'

I was mortified.

'Isn't it me, the eldest,' asked Stewart, 'that's supposed to do things first?'

The Magaluf asked me the same.

'Where did you take him?' Stewart demanded of Ginny when she returned.

'Hounslow,' she answered.

'Where in Hounslow?'

'A pub.'

'He's too young.' Stewart's tone was becoming more and more accusatory.

'I took him to a room above a pub.'

'Which one?'

Stewart wanted to know everything. So did I, but with Stewart, getting all het up, I couldn't ask. What was this place like? Did he have a telly? Was it because he was bullied? Could he have visitors?

'He looked so sad when I left,' said Ginny, 'like he couldn't understand why his dad would let him go and I didn't either. I didn't know he was leaving home,' she snivelled. 'I just did him a favour, is all. He wanted to go, so I took him.'

Stewart was immediately searching the Yellow Pages telephone directory.

'Dad, can I have the key to the phone lock?'

I called through the music room door, but Dad wouldn't answer, not even when I banged loudly on the door. 'Dad, how could even think of letting him leave home?'

It didn't take long before Stewart found the pub's number and tapped out the number on the phone, bypassing the phone lock: ten taps for zero, one tap for one and when it didn't work, doing it all over again.

'Hello, yes, Douglas. He's a bit of a spaz. Moved in about half an hour ago.'

'After the Jewish leaders had arrested and wanted to condemn Polly to death, by hanging her from a holy light cord, for not being able to save Douglas,' the Magaluf continued, 'they took her to the Mansfield Roman governor to have her tried.'

'He's my brother!'

But when Douglas came back for his Discoverer's workbook, he had said nothing to me. He never even acknowledged me.

I didn't want to show I was upset with him. I just wanted to talk. It was time for him to speak to me about his troubles and all this Evolutionary Above Human existence stuff he had gotten himself into from his own writings he had started.

The Magaluf was upset when he spoke, unable to question and ridicule me to the quiet audience of all the unbelievers.

'It's like Babel,' he said. No one cares or understands. So I'm leaving home with Stewart. He knows what's best. He knows how to escape. He is the first-born, eldest and the best.'

I was fourteen, sat in the bath, and in my mind, like before, in the expansive field of St Bernard's Hospital for the Mentals.

Because my immediate family was no good, I borrowed from Mum's way of seeing the big bad world.

I searched the bathroom cabinet: Mogadon, Valium, Paracetamol. I had found the first two but not the last. Mum had probably finished them all off in her most recent attempt.

'Shall we do dance 'gain?'

I wasn't exactly in the mood. 'Search the house,' I snapped back at Elle.

She did, with me.

They weren't in the bin, and there wasn't any under the sofa.

'Found...'

'No, Elle. That's just an old WH Smith bag.'

Were they outside Dad's cabinet, where I always found everything? No. Behind the clock? No. Tucked behind the Skylark, then? No, again. Together, we rummaged every crevice as all the accusations I could muster against myself started up, growing in volume, all the time.

'Slut.'

'Thief.'

'Look in the cupboard under the stairs,' I screamed at Elle.

She emptied each shoe whilst I raided the cutlery drawer.

'Thinks she's their Mum, she does.'

'Help me, Douglas!'

'Ooh, are you playing shops?'

'Plié, straight. Pause. Passe, down.'

'You evil child.'

'It's just not acceptable, Polly!'

'Don't do it, Stewart.'

'Found them!'

Elle poured out the pills from the little plastic bag. At least sixty of them must have been stuffed into a bag at the toe end of one of Mummy's old Wellington boots.

I had them now. It was my time. And in having them, I could achieve the rewards of my failure, to do precisely as Mum had done, as was expected.

'What do I get,' asked Elle? 'What do I get for finding them so good?'

'Arabesque and up, to fifth.'

I stood next to Dad's gaberdine mac.

'You get to run and hide now, Elle,' I said, 'while I count to one hundred and whether you are ready or not, I will come!'

Elle scarpered off into the sitting room.

'One,' I shouted. 'Two, Three.'

I didn't shout loud, because I knew Elle wouldn't have gone far. She was probably watching from the edge of the door.

'Brush my leg. Up. Brush my leg.'

Soon, it would all be over.

'Twenty-seven, twenty-nine.'

I didn't have any water, but I neither had a dry mouth, like Mum had told us she had, after she took her concoction of pills.

I wasn't despairing, though. I wouldn't need electro-convulsive therapy. Because I wasn't anywhere near good enough. And I didn't do it anymore for the Magaluf. I did it because, all in all, I knew, it was precisely what I deserved for being so evil.

So it wasn't the same. It could never be the same. Mum was a completely different person.

'Forty-four, forty-five, forty-six.'

If I took more than the sixty Mum had taken, would it make me a better mother? More committed to the ultimate sacrifice?

The accusations were clearer, timed to coincide with each swallow of the pills.

'You always were evil, trying to take Michael away like that!'

'So you think it's you that wears the culottes around this place, then?

The Magaluf was in fine fettle.

'You are not her. Polly. You are...'

There was a complete absence of any hope like the pills were willing me, all on their own.

If I swallowed five at a time, it was easier.

'Stop it, Polly. Stop it, or I'll tell ...' Elle seemed very upset.

'With the jukebox playin' and everybody sayin', that music like ours couldn't die.'

Who would Elle tell, exactly? Mum?

And wouldn't she finally have a good enough reason to be proud of her daughter?

Or Dad, perhaps. But it had become evident that he only cared about his records.

'Do you think I am a bottomless pit?'

As I finished the last of the pills, I remembered the Holiday Club at St Richard's Church, and all the thoughts about how Miss Byatt was beyond the Babel clouds, by the light.

The ambulance was so very different from the one that took Mum away. It had a red stripe of failure running down the side, the same colour as the two coned horns protruding from the top. The siren was on. The same ambulance man who had come to get Mum insisted I didn't lie down.

'Who am I?' I asked.

The man had soft eyes.

'You are you, dear. You are Polly Porter, or so your sister Elle says.'

'And am I of this world? Am I here now?'

The man squeezed my hand, as soft as I imagined Jesus to be, or maybe Archangel Michael, on a good day. Had I had it so wrong for so long?

'Yes, child. You are of this world, and you are here with me. Can't you feel my hand?'

I looked down.

'It is a warm hand,' I said. 'I am not beyond the Babel clouds like Douglas says?'

'You can be wherever you want to be, child. You just have to believe, and it will be.'

They gave me some medicine to numb my throat. It was like

going to the dentist. They slipped a tube into my throat, trickled some water down the tube and switched on a suck machine.

I wanted to be at the end. I had had enough of it all, but it went on—the pain, tears, and failure at not even being able to achieve my own end!

For my failure, Mum, came back again in my life, by attending the appointment with the child psychologist. Not Mrs Grigg. I was to have one all for myself.

'Hello, Polly, my name is...'

She sat in one of the circle chairs, like in family therapy back at St Bernard's. Flouncy clothes.

'Yeah, yeah.' I faced away from her, studying the walls.

The psychologist started again: 'I know you don't want to be here, but you've come into this hospital having taken an overdose of pills, and it is my job to find out why.'

'Dunno!'

It was all I could say.

Mum sat beside the psychologist, like a witch with ruffled hair. She leant forward in the biggest lie of concern that I had ever witnessed.

'Polly,' she said. 'You have to understand, we are all very concerned. Did your father, I mean, do you feel safe at home?'

'It's not true,' I said. 'Dad never took me like that into the bath with his noddy!'

Silence. It carried on for ages.

'It's alright,' said Mum. 'I suppose I shall just have to take her if I must.'

The psychologist nodded.

I said nothing, stood up, walked towards the door, opened it, and in a moment of certainty, legged it faster than the Bay City Rollers, singing doo-op-do-dooby-doo-eh.

'Serves you right, Polly,' said the Magaluf. 'It's all your fault for not helping wash your dad's stumpies or even attempting to help him into the light.'

The whistle of the wind was the only sound in the park. I concentrated only on what I had to do. I let myself float off to my own world, where I was the only person. I didn't even let the Magaluf in.

The white sky above overwhelmed me. There were no people, family, or other determination except to leg it.

I felt the wet, grassy ground beneath my feet as I ran up a slope. It was very slippery, and hard to keep a grip. As I made my way up, my thighs hurt. I wanted to stop, but I couldn't. I pushed myself through the pain.

At the top of the hill, I ran across a narrow gravel lane. My legs kept going, and my arms moved back and forth. With every stride, it took more effort. My shoulders weakened, like they were going to collapse on my body.

I needed a drink, but I had nothing. I licked the sweat from the side of my mouth.

Over a ditch, across the road and down Queen's Avenue. A sudden rush of anxiety darted up through my body, but I was disoriented from what had just happened with that psychologist and with Mum.

I slowed as I turned into Sunbury Way, knocked on the door, and Dad opened it. He looked so helpless.

'I can't let you in, Polly.' he said. He shook and stammered, which was a first.

'But I live here,' I pleaded.

This was my dad. My own dad, who had once given me so much hope.

'I had a call from Social Services,' he said. 'Whilst you are under your mother's care, I cannot let you in.'

'Where shall I go?' I asked.

'I think you had best go back to your mother.'

Ever so slowly, he closed the door on me.

'Crucify him,' I heard the crowd in my head shout. 'Crucify the false one. Let thy true redeemer live.'

'No,' said the Magaluf, 'just bring him to me.'

I had no choice then but to let all the badness I felt place upon this a crown of thorns as I marched, and they harried me to the place called Golgotha, by the light of Babel.

I felt my body rise up outside the front door of number twenty-six. Glinting in the sun, as though on a carpet made of sequins, Miss Byatt appeared with her arms open as though offering a new life in the afterlife.

'Don't go Skylark, Polly, please, said Elle. 'Not like Mummy went. Need you, me. Need you teach me how to be me, like you, the Lady of the Dance.'

A month later, in which I had to fight, not so much for my escape from the clutches of Mum, as for the right to exist.

'Yes, I suppose it would be best to go to your room and think over what you have caused here,' Mum said. 'You had best get off to that bathroom to wash out all your evil!'

When I next saw the cheese cloth shirted psychologist at the clinic, I told her everything.

'My evil?' I said to her. 'Do you not see? Can you not see how she has no heart and certainly no resources to look after anyone. Everything is always someone else's fault, never hers. She is a really bad one and completely mad.'

But who listens to a child? Especially a child who likes to chop the hair off Sindy Dolls.

It was only after they discovered self-inflicted welt marks about my body and a washing dolly, inscribed with the words 'The Magaluf's beating stick', in the bath that they listened. The child psychologist had to agree.

The living arrangements with Mum were to be abandoned. She and I were too similar in our ways and how we saw things.

Whatever!

The child psychologist had no choice, said the small, swarthy doctor, sitting behind a table with a copy of the Babel picture behind him, but to commit me instead to my dad's care.

When I returned home, it was with all the self-questioning that drives all young women when trying to find their place in the world. What was this God that could allow us to be so treated? But more importantly, who was I?

In a moment of absolute clarity, I raced to St Richard's Church to drown it all out.

I charged into the vestry, dragged back the velvet curtains, and pulled on the ropes attached to the bells.

The first one, I pulled. Then another, until all were bouncing in unison and the peal from the low church bells joined together in an ever-growing sound, banishing the Magaluf voice that had afflicted me my entire life.

'Go away! Go away!' I screamed as the Magaluf revealed himself, bent over in his nineteen-forties clothes and very unkempt hair.

But, 'Look at me, Polly,' he said. 'Trying to drown out the need, you know, still won't bring the clarity you seek. Nor will this ridiculous religious story that you have for so long clung to.

As I have told you, if you want to shut me up, you only have to get your father into the Skylark, and I'll help.'

I didn't want any help.

All I wanted was to be left alone.

It was like a miracle when Tingle Three arrived at my side in the vestry, mooching about my legs, with fleas or not, I didn't care anymore.

But then I heard the music and saw Tingle Three prance as though inviting me home again.

I followed, and the music coming out of the window of the vicarage in the car park area of St Richard's Church was liberating. It seemed to give a spring to my step and to Tingle Three, too.

We bounced and danced, in time with the music and then with me consciously determining the journey with a skip down the Nallhead Road, with the same words ringing out defiantly against anything that might befall us when we got home.

'Onward Christian Soldiers,' I sang, to frighten off and abandon the Magaluf forever.

With each step forward it was a war that I was going to win, and with the broken figure of a fairy in a ditch at the side of the road that might have topped a Christmas tree to show the way to the light, I knew I was winning.

Until all that could be heard was my voice, and I saw Dad waiting outside the house by the pampas grass for the both of us, holding out a curly-wurly.

'You're home, Polly. Good. Quick now, Brucie is waiting for you on the telly.'

It was a new start.

As I entered, Elle jumped up from her changing channels on the telly.

'For mash, get smash! Ha ha. Hee hee.'

She hugged me, grabbed my hand, and dragged me into the living room.

'You back?'

'Yes, Elle. And no-one will take me away from you again.'

'Is good, Polly. Missed you so bad.'

Douglas came in from the kitchen then holding my old sponge skylark.

'I'm sorry,' he said.

Brucie started over as Dad made us all a pork pie salad.

And I knew Douglas and I would retrieve that which had allowed us to grow up so far, despite all that, I was different, I was not Mum, and to prove it, I decided, I would never wear Debenham's tights.

THELMA

His videocam came up on the screen, my eyes only, through my personal channel.

I would have to have words with the Intendant of security again. Nice enough, chap, Turing. And usually very good. He'd only become a little lax recently.

Credits rolled.

Him, Dave, as the Portergeist.

Michael as Michael.

Patrick Morgan as Patrick – the one with a monocle.

Jane Fonda as Tinkerbell. No, it was Novice Fonda, in practice for her future, no doubt.

All filmed in the year of the great 'M', nineteen-eighty, in the relatively new invention of Kodachrome for the colour blind. With some fairly vulgar Billy Graham Dolby boom effects too.

'Behold!'

A shady silhouette started to appear on the screen.

'I would like to say I am just too busy, Thelma,' the Portergeist opened. 'But the truth is, I am in need of you. Your skills, that is. I am just so fed up with failing. With three of them, so far, I have tried, but they keep resisting, pushing me back. What does my favourite teacher suggest I do here?'

Communicate through proper channels, perhaps?

The bells of St Richard's Church quietened, and with Polly settled, I could feel the sighs of relief from across the whole of the fiery wake.

The Portergeist gave me one of his usual, you just can't resist me looks, and I couldn't, as the view screen moved into the interior of great hall, stopping briefly at the small sign on the door of the entrance.

10 September
322nd Grand Synod of the 'M'.
In Session

It wouldn't hurt, I thought, to just take a look.

A door creaked open, and the camera zoomed in to the recently appointed Bishop of London, presiding, at the end of an oval table, her pointed hat shining back at the light generated by the camera, her purple cloak swishing as she picked up her silver gavel set decorated with all her alternative moon stars.

'W.T.F.' She stopped. 'I mean, will you stop it with all your protons, Patrick, and just let us start the Synod, as 'M' demands, long, may her socks be upon her feet!'

The others seemed to be in agreement. There was Billy Graham, who'd got so much slimmer than when I knew him. I put it down to all those Jazzercise workouts that were the talk of the fiery wake. They were a bit too energetic for me and anyway, they were hardly what was expected of an archangel. Thank the good 'M'!

Fonda was in her element, as always, swaying about in front of some awkward-looking Nuns, showing great promise, as an Apsara, perhaps, when her time comes, maybe, even as an apprentice arch.

She smiled, nervously.

All the others, that Russell chap, Moneypenny, Bakewell and Bosanquet nodded their heads in the direction of the grand lady bishop.

The subject of the symposium as shown then in the programme pages of the Synod of the 'M', opened just for the camera and in close up was supposed to be the comet, not the endless blathering's of Patrick Moore, or the latest promotional on the energetics of the ever helpful, Novice Fonda, as she liked to be called.

'The comet, this time around,' or so the lady bishop said, was to be the brightest in the starry, starry – was this a sign?

They all looked to Michael.

'Uhm, uhm, uhm.'

That the Portergeist's problem was present too, having been sent by 'Call me, Alan', apparently, the new Vicar at St Richard's, was, to me at least, a blessing. Two birds, one stone.

Michael had about him a deceptive, nervous looking smile, as he stalked in from the entrance, unsure, it seemed, if the blessed invitation had really been meant for him.

The bishop put him out of his misery.

'You are 'call me, Alan's' new treasurer, I believe, at St Richard's, are you not? For the register, you understand.'

Michael nodded.

'You may sit.'

Michael bowed and then squeezed himself as unobtrusively as possible between the silver layered, wing-backed chairs. He was directly in front of the arch-windowed, stained-glass depiction of that Babel picture – the real one.

Patrick Morgan lost no time at all, staring at Michael from his seat opposite through his all-knowing monocle, as though inspecting what the cat had dragged in this time.

'Shoo, you!'

Tingle Three mooched off into the doors of Concorde – the French version – crashed, or soon to be, in time, as an example to all of what happens when you let the imagination of science replace all that the purple-coloured faith had to offer.

'Yes, well,' continued the bishop, 'according to the prophecy, or whatever it's called, the great Ming,' the bishop checked herself, 'No, I mean, the beginning and the end, greatest bobby soxer, of all time – long, may her socks be upon her feet, was correct. We are indeed approaching the great beginning of a most dreadful end!'

A general murmuring could be heard from the hallowed hall. I thought I was going to be asked to deal with their resultant fears displayed, but it was alright. Billy Graham was there to save the day.

He stood, raised his right hand up to his chest, took in a

deep breath. With his left hand, he thumped his big book onto the rather ancient-looking alabaster table, looked around the whole, possibly for effect. Then he started, 'I have read the last page of the Bible,' he said, 'and I do believe it is all going to turn out alright.' He sat down then, in the manner he had become accustomed to, since his last meeting with the Queen. He was obviously going to get a gong, or something, sometime soon.

I was about to slip in to his presence and ask him what good it would do, with all the darkness of the Portergeist failure, sure to come, but I thought better of it. This, I remembered, wasn't exactly why the Portergeist had called for my help. What good would it do anyway?

There was some obsequious nodding in the hallowed hall, but not from the bishop, who instead acted into the responsibility with which she had been bestowed with due conviction and a Lady Gadiva-like swish of her great purple cloak. 'What on earth, as it is in heaven, are we all going to do?'

They all looked to the camera – to me!

The good bishop's question was worthy of an answer, I thought, wondering what kind of solution I was going to come up with. Because this was where this was all going, I was sure. But what manner of solution was I going to bring about for them all? This was the question. The pressure was most definitely on.

Patrick slammed his monocle on the alabaster table. The attention of the room was drawn into an expectant silence, for a bit. Maybe two bits. I had no means of knowing how long a bit in this place was supposed to last. It was never explained in the great book of purple.

'Would not this august assembly agree,' demanded Patrick, 'that there has come to this hallowed hall a great fallacy as communicated by the devil's photons, in the fiery wake behind the comet, of a view that questions whether television, or radio, is still up to the job of trustworthy communication?'

Joan Bakewell, from the side of the bishop, looked at Reginald Bosanquet at her side, who looked back at her with such commanding presence.

'Oh, stop it,' said Joan, her eyelashes fluttering, or was it a holy fly annoying her 'Why do you have to be such a one?'

Moneypenny, from the opposite side, probably under orders from the great 'M' to take the minutes, took her jealous gaze away from Novice Fonda a while, pushed up her curls seductively, as the fly changed direction in a very energetic sortie that was met with a skilful swat from which the fly was swatted and duly despatched to the other place.

So it seemed that not all of 'M's creatures were in fact equal in the 322nd Grand Synod of the 'M', as the socks upon her feet demanded. I would report it later.

It was time then for the others to display their recently appropriated 'shock and awe' at the rantings of the eccentric Moore, ne'er do well.

He was tapping his monocle on the alabaster table in front of him.

'It's all in the comet, I tell you.'

The bishop looked at the Patrick with a glaring despair.

'You have a relevant point to make?' she asked.

Patrick sat back.

'Well,' he answered, still staring at Michael, 'I once had occasion to be in contact with 'M's will, and she told me, exactly, as was prophesized, that she had already heard once of the plight here before us in this very hallowed hall.'

Had I?

But Patrick was too busy comparing the Milky Way to a fried egg to answer. I wonder what he would have made of the fiery wake, had *he* ever discovered it?

'Indeed, through my monocle,' he continued, 'a veritable third eye, you should try it. Well, I did commune with the Thelma behind her viewscreen, and she already knew of the troubles of David, and his Portergeist activities. In fact, she had seen how I had tried so hard but failed to bring Michael into the light of the fiery wake. She said she might try to attend, "if she could find the time", which, as David then pointed out to her, to score a few points for all his hard learning, since the pavement days, would be infinite.'

Patrick burbled then from behind his deadpan expression, like a suffocated chuckle that was about to explode from the engine of a hurricane. His monocle had been specially adapted for this and the task of inter-realm communication by the boffins at the BBC, back before the discovery of Pluto.

Moneypenny was shifting in her seat. She raised her hand. 'For the sake of the minutes,' she asked, 'did you say that the will of 'M', Thelma, is here with us?'

No one answered. All eyes were stealing into Michael's rather startled disposition.

'Uhm, well,' said Michael. 'I think, but...'

The bishop responded with a shaking of her head and a very impressive tut. She looked at Michael, who was all eyes open.

'So it seems, Mr. Porter,' she continued, kindly, 'that you might have something to elucidate on the order of business here, today at this Synod.'

A starry gavel then bounced off its block and the stars seemed to shake the Tinkerbell of earlier into an Electro-Convulsive-Therapy treatment inspired shock.

Michael flicked back his quiff, as any 'still to be called', or believed to be, would do, when aware that the pure will of 'M' was awaiting him, and that Patrick did seem a bit familiar.

Michael started, using the silver tongue of calculus and quadratic equations on the benefits and the truths of the energy contained within photons. He was trying to explain all he'd learnt from between the lines of Douglas's elusive Thelemic prophecy, as he called it.

All the assembled looked, from their expressions, as though their souls were in great pain, especially Bertrand Russell, as they scratched their heads.

Apart from Patrick, that was.

'Erm. Michael. Is that the Paganini theory you are using there?' he asked.

Michael looked back, as though terrified of his heresy in participating in what would certainly be a banned custom for 'called' Synodiums.

'Because I once knew a man who used Paganini Trigonometry,' pronounced Patrick. 'You will remember him, well, Michael. He was your father!'

A halo appeared above Michael's quiff, as he experienced what looked like his first 'light of the silvery moon' moment.

He looked back at Patrick.

'It was you that came to the house, trying to learn from Father,' he said. 'But Father wouldn't let you on his Radio show because you didn't understand the vital importance of comets, or the future of television, for that matter!'

Patrick's monocle dropped, his head too, and from this position he addressed Michael's challenge.

'Yes,' he said, 'and that was the most important lesson I ever learnt from your father. It is what led me to study, find my third eye, so to speak, and through this, the archangel Thelma too. Oh, at first, I didn't believe in her, of course, not very science, as you will understand, no doubt, but when she introduced me to the movement, Michael. When she introduced me to Thery T and that Dough from Auntie Brenda's blackberry pie, possibly, who told me to find my own voice on the telly. Well, what was an astronomer of fried eggs to do?'

'You mean, all of that was not just in Douglas's mind, or Discoverer's workbook?' asked Michael.

'Have you not heard of the *Night Sky*, Michael, or its fiery wake?' Patrick was shaking his head. 'Your father will be turning in his grave!'

Something beeped from under the alabaster table and a blue light appeared to shine out momentarily from the bishop's lap.

Bertrand Russell's hand shot up.

'Has it got something to do with video being more reliable as a form of communication?' he asked.

Beethoven then chose this moment to announce the opening notes of his fifth symphony.

Patrick laughed, waving away the thought. 'No, though the Tholians on that *Star Trek* that some of you sometimes watch,' he said, 'might think otherwise. No, the fiery wake is of the comet, to which the spaceship conceived by Douglas in the mouldy-green shed is to be constructed.' Then he trained his eyes back at Michael. 'To take you into the light, completely.'

Dante patted Beethoven on the back and led him off into the moonlight.

'In the Skylark?' asked Ms. Bakewell.

It wasn't clear enough whether Michael should answer, or believe in this, or not. Such strange things had never happened to him. At least, not since James Bond had shown him how to turn into a thoroughly modern man.

'It's called life, Michael,' said Moneypenny, with a smirk. 'You should try it more often.'

Michael bowed his head in complete supplication.

'Order, order,' shouted the bishop, with an accompanying heavy bang of her gavel. 'I shall not have any making up of new stories,' she banged again, 'when the old one, despite what Billy says, is under such dire threat!'

Billy Graham stared at me, as Novice Fonda strode over to the bishop, picked up the gavel and then handed it back to her.

'Do that again,' she said, 'only this time put some rhythm into it.'

The bishop did and Novice Fonda started to move her hips from left to right, slowly. Billy Graham got up to join her.

'Passe down, Plie up. Ooh, this is really good! I feel just like that Rudolph Nureyev from the other place.'

They were joined by a surprisingly nubile Joan Bakewell, in the much-pumped arms of Reginald Bosanquet.

'Oh, I say, this is so much better than Jazzercize.'

Bertrand Russell got out from his chair to join Novice Fonda in her brand of exercises and performed some gyrations in front of all the nuns who were also joining in to a funked-up, for the occasion, performance of 'How great thou art'.

Moneypenny skipped down to the space between the alabaster table and the entrance door and started to flounce about, like she was one of those too awful Bay City Rollers.

Patrick picked up a pencil, and started to use it like a conductor's baton, great swathes of protons, illuminated by their own phosphorescent halos, started swirling, pulling, pushing, with beautiful mathematical precision, against the polyester sails from Brentford Nylons – the money savers, had to be – that were flitting about the hall.

Then, as if from nowhere, a man in a Homburg hat, to the music of the *Devil's Gallop*, like the Portergeist had tried to introduce me to once, burst through the doors to the hall, with his arms flailing, and great stomp, quickly changing to an arabesque over to the right, then back to first and finished off with a lovely pirouette.

'It's coming,' the man was shouting. 'The prophecy and it's going to involve a space ship, strips of copper stolen from the rooftop of St Richard's Church to be turned into great 12-mile-long wires, the opening of the tall gates, when we get there, to show us how to get lost in space digitally, according to...'

The bishop seemed too involved in Novice Fonda's workout to care, as were all the assembled. Except for Patrick, that was, who frankly, always was going to let the side down when dancing came into it. His monocle could never stay in place. He went all thumbs in waistcoat, just like Winston Churchill. Bending his knees in time, too. One of the Nuns was heard whispering to another.

'He's very cute, don't you think, Madge?'

'Look, I told you', said the man, 'it's not the prophecy that matters here, it's the coming, *Her* coming, because she is to be sent by the Portergeist, to take over from all his failures with the others and make it alright again, show us how, as well as why, precisely, Michael must get himself quickly into the light of the fiery wake.'

Billy Graham boomed again. 'Behold, I say behold, all ye of the bobby socks faith, Yea, verily.'

The bishop adjusted her robes, opened her arms.

Michael stopped his side-to-side steps immediately, lowered himself to prostrate himself before the bishop. He looked quite overcome with it all.

'It is too much,' he said, looking up from the floor, 'it is all far too much for me, your Grace.'

The bishop took pity and laid her hands upon him.

Bless!

'But must I go into the light,' continued Michael, 'through the tall gates, and be with David again? I do not want to. For years, I have avoided such a path as going back to him.'

The bishop took some pity on Michael and extended him her best blessing hand. 'Calm, blessed child of "M",' she said. 'I can see now why "call me Alan" sent you here,' she said. 'Why, he sent you to me, the only leader of the Grand Synod of the 'M', ever to have had dealings with Thery T and Auntie Brenda's Dough. They too started in the seventies, in Tickencote, and they too didn't want to get to the light to realize their own extra-terrestrial, beyond human evolutionary existence, because they, just like you, weren't yet ready to even begin to understand.'

Michael was nodding like a character popularized by a unique blend of bubble bath.

Then the ceremony of purple. I tried to stop them, persuade them out of it, as any good archangel should, but they had bought their purple shrouds, were already in the libraries researching phenobarbital, and one of them, probably Dough, for she was the brains of the fellowship, had already created her design for cheap, practicable, black and white trainers and sent them off to Nike!

Michael shook his head so much at this that I was not sure if he heard the bishop. That and all the pounding of feet from the Novice Fonda-following nuns.

'It occurs to me, Michael, that unlike the members of the movement there is no hope for us, none at all left, anywhere – and also with you.'

Michael's head still shook.

Moneypenny was writing it all down, whilst occasionally looking up for spies, and in this way, reporting that things were about to get a whole lot worse and was in need of someone else.

Reginald Bosanquet straightened up before the camera. Joan was behind the alabaster table and Reg, out in the field, was talking straight into Patrick's all-knowing third eye.

'Streaking across the starry, starry,' he said, with due, news presenter authority, 'as I hope the viewers can see with me.'

Joan, next to Michael, was playing with a fairly long wire that had something to do with his new Pentax camera.

'I have to get this right, Reg. They won't ever believe I was here. Not even by Douglas's stories, they just won't.

The bishop smiled, as Michael handed the stories over, a huge manuscript it was, longer even than *How to Be a Husband in the Modern World*.

I knew, of course from the bishop's smile, that this was the moment she had been waiting for her entire life – the chance to read out the parts of the prophecy that she now, finally, had access too.

'Pray, silence,' she pleaded.

All readied themselves with their hands joined in prayer, even Novice Fonda and completely timed with the beat of Beethoven's Third Symphony.

He smiled, as Dante fashioned a moonwalk of sorts for their entertainment.

'In a flash of light, she will come,' began the bishop, 'and her name shall be call-ed, the Thelma. She will have Great "M's" Will to bring it all to pass and then with the Michael, she will submit to the Portergeist of David, take up his failed mission, descend to the mortal realms and Yea, she will take the Michael into the light of the blessed fiery wake.'

'In the Skylark?' asked Ms Bakewell, again.

Michael started to rise then, rise right up on his stumpy toes.

'No, no, no, no. I will not have this. I will not subject myself willingly to the greatest bully of my life, ever again.'

'Are you getting all this?' asked Billy of Moneypenny. 'Are you getting it all down properly?'

'Come and find out, if you don't trust me.'

Bertrand Russell strode over, peered over Moneypenny's shoulder. With a combination of a smiley face, as could best be managed from his craggy features, and a thumbs-up, he indicated his positive, although with Bertrand, and all his tricks, you could never really tell.

Through the stained-glass depiction of Babel behind Michael, and next to this the addition of a meteor, maybe even a comet, from behind which a Brentford Nylons polyester sheet, powered space ship, might have been hiding, a flash of light, whooshed the bishop's purple cloak to fly, near, out of sight.

The doors opened.

'I said, Yoo, hoo! Hello everyone.'

My light, so brilliant, took over then and was bathing them all, particularly Michael, who was then pushed down by the lady bishop without any protest, as though this were entirely expected and deserved and it was right for him to be prostrated before me, in such obedience.

It was my most wondrous voice. The one that I had practiced over many years, with all kinds of brightness shining, wonderful and new, just like Edwina Currie and put on just for the performance.

Well, after all this and to help Michael, really, not the Portergeist David, causing all this havoc in that mouldy-green shed of his, spilling the beans to all and sundry. I should've known, really, that it was never safe to trust a child.

'Has anyone got any Kentucky Fried Chicken?'

Everyone in the hall seemed stunned. And there wasn't a bucket, egg, or chicken-leg to be seen, or at least bought to me, as any angel of the 'M' might rightly expect. They were probably all too bedazzled by my beauty and shining presence.

I switched my light off. It helped, a bit.

'Where is he, then?' I said, and some would say after that these my first words came across as a bit bossy, but how can a question be bossy, I wondered? It didn't matter. It was having the desired effect. The Nuns stopped their dancing and started to scratch around in their starched bibs, all flibbertigibbety, searching all about the great, hallowed, hall for some Kentucky Fried Chicken.

The lay-people, extras, searched their pockets, was that Kate Bush, despite knowing that miracles could only ever be found in the pages of *How to get a husband in the modern world*. Why? I didn't know.

The bishop had a Curly-Wurly. Well, what remained of one, beneath her purple robe. Novice Fonda offered up a protein pill, alongside Billy Graham's rather meagre looking sprat, fished from his deep inside his very righteous pocket.

But it was Bertrand Russell who got my attention. He approached me, like an alternative Fagin, lopping along like he'd just escaped Babel.

Oh, the depths to which a philosopher would go and he wasn't even French.

'We are sorry,' he said, 'for our sad lack of Kentucky fried.'

He was such a charmer.

'It appears that this has not been video sequenced yet, or at least no one has thought to apply the necessary photonic charge to bring about your obviously wanted desire.'

But I couldn't let him know how enamoured I was with him.

'Well, where is he then?' I asked, instead. All before me trembling, even the one with dandruff bent down before me.

The bishop stepped forward. 'Pray, tell us of whom you speak, oh, unlighted one, your Grace. Bring us into the light of your quest and we shall accommodate.'

What a ridiculous looking woman she was.

'Don't you be praying to me, you daft ha'p'orth,' I said, 'I am not the Lord, I am only the will of her, just as she likes to take her pills, you see. Now, where is that silly man with a quiff?'

From the floor in front, Michael arose.

'So there you are! So what's all this that Patrick tells me about you not wanting anything to do with your dead brother?'

Michael was shaking like when he was a child.

'I am frightened of him,' he said, then, gathering himself together, 'I am frightened of what David will do when he learns from either me, or the children, that I didn't hurry to get help and rescue him, when he fell and started dying on the pavement.'

I decided it would be a good time then to clean the insides of my teeth with my long nails, trying to look very earnest in a comforting sort of way.

'And you think David doesn't know this already?'

'Uhm, uhm!'

I grabbed Michael by the arm and started to walk with him.

'You know, I don't think you are telling me the entire truth here,' I said. 'It's not him that you fear. It's what you have done to him and the others that you cannot face up to, now isn't it? This is why you don't want to go into the fiery wake.'

I could see a bold redness in his eye.

'I have done nothing to David,' he said. 'It was he that bullied me!'

The bishop was busy trying to unstick her fingers from a Curly Wurly, given her by the Magaluf.

'Why you hid in a mouldy-green shed in your back garden,

with a switched off hearing-aid, so he didn't have to listen to any of your passive depression?'

Michael looked puzzled at first, before asserting most marvellous defence.

'David doesn't have a hearing aid, that's Douglas, my second son. What has he to do with any of this?'

Well, it's not often that archangels make mistakes.

'He looks like David,' I said. 'He has the same type of thinking, always whingeingly so. Oh, lumme, and I sent him the prophecy, all of it, after David asked and I thought I would show willing. Poor boy, stuck in his limbo like that, for so long.'

'Ahem,' said Patrick. 'You mean that I asked you to send to David to show him how it was all going to turn out in the end, and you sent it to the wrong person.'

Well, an archangel cannot lie.

'Yes,' I said. 'It seems that I sent Douglas the prophecy, in little bits, mind, maybe four, or five, and then the rest, inserted into passages within his Discoverer's workbook at St Richard's, and he, Douglas, from all the connections so far, must have been the one to spread it all about the family.

'But where is the great prophecy?' asked the bishop. Where has all the fiery wake gone, T and Dough too. What is it that we are supposed to learn about from within it and do?'

Novice Fonda, Reginald and Joan, Bertrand and even Michael, were all looking me with expectation, then, So I whipped it out the prophecy from under my left wing. Billy Graham quickly set it up as a video power-point on the bishop's fax machine and the bishop, just as she'd always wanted, in her best monotoned voice, started to read it out loud.

The Thelemic Prophecy

There once was a man. The man lived alone in number twenty-six, a three-bedroom house, by a dairy, in a village called Hanworth. The house, was near fit to bursting with his hoarding of all the papers of the man and his dead brother's life, a television, a garden with laurel leaf bushes and pampas grass.

Now, it was true that the man felt alone in number twenty-six, and deservedly So for the way he bought his children up. The isolation he would experience as a result of this and his rejection of his third born child's Skylark did not make the man feel awkward, or difficult. On the contrary, it was what allowed him, with his bicycle, set-square and calculator, to seek his destiny, which was so much better than sculpting, or bashing Maris Pipers in the RAF, or for even trying to understand the light and how it comprehended nothing, not even the architraves on the ceiling, or the shadows on his life, or mind, that these could sometimes appear to produce.

For the man also had a dead brother that was somehow always alive in his head. Bothersome, very. Mostly, even. But the man knew he probably deserved it. That was alright, though, because the man did have God to defend him, who was a good God. Of this, the man had great faith and gained much inner strength from which to negotiate his daily life.

Every day at six am the man would wake up and greet the sun, and after fixing a clothes peg, or two he would attend to his cornflakes with a tiny teaspoon.

'Why do you sink so quickly?' he would whisper to the smallest flake.

And when his children wouldn't arise, for not being there – what could the man do – he wasn't able to encourage them to play hide 'n' seek with each other, which always allowed him to get very obsessed with his calculator, fix the many holes in the former treasurer's double-entry for his church, for which he was happy for the purpose that it gave him.

After all Vicar 'Call me' had beseeched him.

And he would trip over his hoarding papers at least fifty times a day, and he also liked to speak to his best friend, Tingle Three, who never, ever, talked back.

Shame on her!

Sometimes, he would just stare out of the window, and this would allow him to calculate the trajectory of Venus in its conjunction with the moon to please anyone that might care.

Reginald Bosanquet, or Patrick Moore, the man would often forget which, had once suggested this from in front of this televisual light, and because the man thought it might counter the effects of the man's former wife, who was for certain sure, not to blame for anything, it would always be the fault of everyone else and especially the man.

She was called *That* Hannah and from her sheltered housing scheme development for the fat, she still held great court over the man,

So the man had a dead brother, a job as Church Treasurer, a cat called Tingle Three, two girls he didn't have any idea what to do with, a fat ex-wife who was supreme in her power, two sons who had abandoned him, but most comfortingly, he had God!

What more could any man expect?

Indeed, the strange writings of the prophecy, given to the man, by Douglas, his second son, straight from his printing press in the mouldy-green shed, by the laurel leaves of the man's garden, in revenge for his only getting a plate upon leaving home, were obviously the work of a false prophet, but would it be enough to answer the confusion of Babel?

The man wanted to unlock his telephone that Social Services had paid for, to find out, and to pour out his grievous heart to someone, anyone. But with the great Reverend Kibble, having been sacked, or moved on, for his views on women rising in the Church to be anything but Deacons, there was only 'Call me, Alan' to ask and he never would answer his phone.

The man sought instead from the television and other devices of mass communication to beat this confusion of Babel and peace be upon him for hoping himself worthy of his praise unto God, or even unto the great 'M', a bobby soxer, whichever would not bring about the most dreadful end feared, first!

And what was in his second son's Discovers Workbook, or printed from the mouldy-green shed was not mad. It made no money, either, which was quite a shame for the man, for he so wanted to make up for what his children stole from the Church collection plate for bonbons.

In fact, what was written was an extraordinary, justifiable, miracle, and certainly deserving, of a much-praised Hallelujah.

A beautiful bossy woman would come, it would say, declaring herself by the name of Thelma, that in Ancient Greek was often translated, as the 'will of God', not 'M', even though, unto this 'M' and her hoped for will of him, the man was enamoured and much disposed to worship.

Except Thelma wasn't really a God, she came down as the occupant of an interplanetary space ship, for most of the way past the Blue Clanger Moon, in the centre of a comet's tail, to bring unto the great synod the will of all things.

In a leather jacket, fairy costume, up down polyester skirt and long purple painted finger nails. Or at least, that's how the women at the introduction agency would later describe her, she came, not to help the man out of his loneliness, because he still had his cat and he was fine to still have his God, if he could only begin to imagine it, of just a little bit of love.

Hallelujah again!

And it was to be so.

For after this, the Thelma's coming and the mysterious loss of copper from the roof of the man's Church of St Richard's, the beautiful, bossy one was introduced and accepted into the congregation, especially after she agreed to wed the man, despite his not understanding her at all, but nevertheless he was prepared to give it a go.

Indeed, the beautiful bossy one would become known as an angel, the man's, by the congregation, as led by Vicar 'call me', after he had searched his heart about his contribution to the plight of Polly, and how he had allowed the balloon of her Skylark to get shot by an arrow and popped.

But the archangel, didn't seek to avenge the congregation, for her ostracization for being too bossy, as spread by the Hannah by her telephone.

Thelma would help the man to live the life to which he had been called, creating swathes of accounts in their Shepperton house, after he had sold number twenty-six, and he grew in confidence to feel the blessed light of a former archangel's love.by which the will of 'M' be done.

Steve Porter

STEWART

I was staring at the woman in the wake by the great tower. The only woman, as far as I could see.

She stood humble, with her leather jacket, fairy like skirt, her hands outstretched, palms up, as though about to receive something from someone important.

What was she about to receive? Why was she there? What was her significance and why was she talking to me again, when I thought I had long ago escaped all this?

Memories? Fantasies?

I didn't know.

Yes, I did, I just didn't want to go over it all again., but the image demanded it of me.

Really, Lady? I'm surprised your predecessor never told you what happened, why I had to do it.

Because deep down, we only want to help one another, don't we? We only want to be the good guy, girl, or whatever it is you are. I never could tell. I still can't.

And what was it like, Lady, giving up the life and the way that you had up there?

How to explain it?

As Dad sometimes said, Lady, when he was in his better moods, with his fingers dancing to Rimsky Korsakov, in the

145

living room, 'No man is an island, children,' and then he would attempt to lead us in this by his example.

Morally correct, of course. Wholly absorbed in the love of his God!

No, Lady?

But I thought, with his conversion in the RAF and then the with Patrick, and the Lady bishop at the Synod – Yes, I have read the prophecy – and with our support, at least, that he was going to be a Christian and alright.

Because before, Lady, when I was old enough to understand its beginning, Dad had only really ever been able to use closed body language: slump his shoulders and keep his head down because, as he often told me, 'If you genuinely want to be the power behind the family throne, Stewart, you have to appear socially unreceptive, pout a little, and you must, most definitely learn how to fiddle with your nose.

You see, Lady, Dad wanted no one to have anything to do with him. He would often say a great line about how not to be like Job in the bible, but I thought, actually, he was just scared and sulky, just like his taste in classical music.

To Mum, in particular.

'I do not deserve this, Anna.'

Because Mum, as a strung woman, always did like to suffer and shout about him and their marriage. And she always needed to put herself in uncomfortable situations.

If she did easy things, or so she said, like being a loving wife and mother, she was convinced that she was going to have a hard life. But, if she did hard things, like protest everything, maintain all her problems as the only way to live, she was sure she could graduate to the life she knew she had inherited and deserved. Happy, in the uncomfortable she would create for herself and marvellously, maybe even as a miracle, and with a lot of sequins too, in her great performance of the role she had chosen and was determined to bring about to pass on.

Because Never Never Land was a shiny place of wonder, her dream goal, especially if she could portray it as such, in her latest production at the Oriel Junior and Infant school and I, Lady, as the eldest and the best...

'You are my greatest, and we shall surely overcome together, my poppet.'

For I was to be very much a part of Mum's role. I was to be the fruit of all her efforts, her shiny diamond in the rough. I was to be her Peter Pan.

Whereas, the others, Lady?

Being a bit out there, Douglas would never be good enough to be the best, like me, or even have a part, even in music, as I tried to teach him on our clarinets, which, of course, I excelled in, with Mum's help and the loneliness of her Solveig's Song.

I hoped from this that Douglas could avoid all that silliness about his imaginary Shed Boy, play, and become my ally in defence. And I did try with Douglas, but he was just always so different. I tried so hard.

Or Polly, who would not be Mum's replacement, after she'd left, playing with her silly Skylark sponge space ship to get her and Dad away from all she felt expected of her, just as Douglas stroked her with his alternative prescription of his prophecy, as the only way.

I think, Lady, that was your predecessor's fault – David, wasn't it, or the Magaluf? – that put them up to it.

Whilst Elle – emotional, sensitive, cheerful, enthusiastic, naïve – could never quite fathom why the chicken crossed the road and other things, at least on a level that anyone other than she could understand.

'Why it not catch bus?'

And how all this and the sought-after discomfort caused Mum's inevitable departure to the local mental hospital.

'You will be good, my poppets,' her note had read, Lady.

I remember it being nervously squeezed into my hand by Dad, in hope, I could only imagine, that I would be able to convey a suitable response, it being completely beyond him to find the words, any.

'And after school, you will go to the Cygnets with Auntie Annie while you wait for your father to come and pick you up. Yes, he will pick you up, poppets, because he loves you as much as I do, or at least he says he thinks he does, though I see you all hiding away from him in the corner sometimes.'

It was this that first burst the gum bubble that I had only just learned how to blow, my first conscious imagining of it being – well, a bit wrong in the house of number twenty-six.

As the eldest and best, I needed to do something about it. I wanted to show, against the rising tension in the family due to Mum's departure, how safe, naïve, and ignorant we all could be if I were only up to the job of being able to do as expected.

I ran back into the kitchen and started taking it out on the washing up, which was my turn to do as a chore.

I smashed, and I smashed all the plates to the floor. Not because I was troubled or unhappy that Mum had gone. It was because I had not been able to succeed in preventing her latest acting out with her overdose, leaving me in charge of all the tears, Polly's cutting off her Sindy Doll's hair, and Douglas's bending of his in-step supports to be fitting of his newly adopted Captain Lollop. Elle just wet herself.

Practical, I would be, I decided, to rise to the challenge. Focused. Responsible, as the eldest and best, should always be.

No, Lady, the ship idea, the proper one, which was to be my method, was yet to come. Like the practice required of me to pull off a performance of the *Monster Mash* in in the style of a Brahms, it would surely turn out alright in the end.

'Stop all that crying,' I said. 'Polish your shoes. We don't want to look like council house kids when we march like a proper family to the Cygnet's children's home.'

For Polly and Douglas, that just made it worse.

Nevertheless, and precisely because 'No Man is an Island' or because a woman or little girl could never be in charge, I did manage, Lady, to get them to try to polish their shoes. Well, what remained of them after the way they had treated them. Not a care at all for the stains and their scuffs.

'But they're falling apart,' said Douglas. 'and anyway, you can't polish plastic.

'Yes, you can.'

Whereas with Polly?

'Mine are like they wear in the Janet and John primer books, and what's this rag of a coat she expects us to wear to school, let alone to the Cygnets? Does she expect us to be happy?'

She was right. The holes and tears were pretty grievous.

'And them charity toofbrushes.'

Elle?

And that was my fault, too, to make alright. I, as the eldest, from which all good things were to come, but all I had was the fervent belief that we should hold our heads high and grin and bear it all, for the sake of the family, us, and any chance of our survival of them.

But Polly didn't want to play that game.

Almost as soon as Mum had left, Polly pulled out her sponge from the folds of her thousand times repaired Indian wrap-around skirt.

'All aboard the Skylark,' she said, 'to be off to the light and better things,' taking away from my moral right to determine how to be and make good, or at least better than it was.

Well, I had to defend my position, Lady, but how? What was I to do?

Elle put her ladybird red Mac of holes on, as Douglas squeezed his bent in-step supports into his plastic slip-ons. Polly fought with her knitted shawl for a bit, kept two steps behind me at first, on the way to the Cygnets, then lurched forward as though she could lead with the promise of all her sponge Skylark could bring in flight. 'Follow me, follow me.'

So, you see, Lady, why I had to do it. I had to slap her across the face and hard, for trying to upstage me. I mean, how could she be Peter Pan and make things alright again? She was a girl!

It was alright, Lady. As Polly's tears protested, she at least knew then who was really in charge. She had learnt her lesson of how to achieve a better, proper reality, when without a mother to look up to, or father that was any good.

'Is Mummy not well, in 'opital, or in sky wiv Polly's sponge?'

Elle never really got what was needed to find the light. She was just like before the hospital, when Mum had been around.

'But it's against God!' she'd complained.

I tried to explain it. I tried to explain it to Polly, too, but...

'Shsh, there's Patrick, she interrupted, refusing to listen to me, take my direction, or to attend to the clothes washing that by then had become most urgent.'

'And Patrick Moore,' I had to agree, from the box television in the corner of the living room, then,' I continued to Polly, now that I had her attention, like Dad might have done if he ever had a voice that anyone would listen to, which he would, use no doubt, to explain about the technical variances of our life-changing future mission, concentrating on the science of it all and of course the maths.'

Polly didn't care. She was examining with disgust the straps of her woe-begotten sandals.

'Whilst Dad,' I continued, 'in a rare offering of peace to Mum, by way of explanation in case she didn't understand.

'It is the greatest feat of science that the world has ever known, Anna.'

Polly tried to insert the filthy strap in the buckle, Lady, pushing this in with her knuckles.

'Well, I hope the Magaluf works in mysterious ways for you, with all that.'

Her buckle broke.

Then Polly picked up her Skylark, waved it about in the air and asked me, in defiance, if I thought that with my earlier gum bubble and her stupid Skylark, we might one day be able to fly off her way?'

'Don't be daft,' I said.

Then a man in a puffy white jumper suit and helmet, instead of the costume that Mum had once made for me on her Singer, had begun to open the door to a space ship.'

Polly threw her broken sandal at me.

I wasn't hard with her, or upset. I only wanted to show her the true way, so I informed her. 'He'll need at least twelve latches and a seal for the door,' I said, repeating what Patrick had said on the television. 'Take it from one who watched your granddad build his aerials for the polyester sails and witnessed the might of Billy Graham at the Synod.'

Polly picked up her buckle again, as Dad, seemed to wake up from his malaise.

'That's Armstrong,' he said. 'Neil Armstrong, one of NASA's finest on the Apollo programme. I met him once on a trip to America where I had to explain the Concorde concept.

'You need more slack, Buzz,' from the box telly, he continued, 'and Douglas had jumped up and down,' as Polly picked out a needle and thread.

'Is that the black and white moon, Daddy?'

Polly was going for the sequins.

Still, I continued to try, Lady.

'It's to be,' I told Polly, 'a performance to better even my most outstanding performance as Peter Pan.

Polly started to sew back the buckle.

'And how Dad, at the time, had shaken his head and held my hand, preventing me from going to get measured for my silly Peter Pan hat.

'I'll go instead,' offered Douglas.

But Mum was concentrating instead on how bright I was to shine, in her performance and not the journey Polly was creating in the reflection of the light in her buckle.

'I'm going to step off the LM now.'

Polly had nearly finished.

'That's one small step for a man. One giant leap for mankind.'

But Polly, Lady, didn't seem very impressed with this, or even that she understood a word of what I had been trying to tell her, as she goaded me with the shining of her light, straight into my eye.

She took out her toy sponge Skylark from her pocket and started to wave this about like she had once before on the way to the Cygnets.

'We will go to the light,' she said, and very definitely, in my Skylark, or not at all!'

So, I had to hit her again. This time in her teeth.

We played a rather sedate game of French Cricket then. It was the best and only way to calm the situation down, until the stars would come out, and we would all go to bed with Polly in a sulk and Dad crying about his failures in life.

Douglas cried too, when he didn't get the plate that he wanted from Dad, or a sliver of Mars Bar, so he could feed his imaginary friend in the shed.

And later, Douglas wasn't interested in the Airfix model that Dad had got him with my choosing it and getting the glue to get him away from Shed Boy. For if anyone knew what Douglas needed, it was me, as the eldest. And anyway, as I already said, Lady, I really needed him as an ally.

But he wasn't interested, that was, until in a rare moment of trying to connect with his second-born, Dad tried to assist Douglas in building the Airfix model.

'That really should have been a Gloster Meteor or a fixed-winged Mosquito,' he mumbled, 'but I suppose space exploration is the future.'

Polly tried to join in and sprinkled Douglas with some Angel Delight powder she'd nicked from the kitchen, as Elle sang another song.

'Love me tender, love me true.'

It was a forty-fourth-scale Saturn V rocket, just like the one I had always suspected would fly me to the moon. So much better than that *Flash Gordon* ship that Dad used to like us to watch on the box television in the corner.

'But that's not going to get you anywhere,' said Polly, with her Skylark in hand, arcing over her head, from a move learnt from the Tiny-Tots choreography of Tchaikovsky, nearly to the cobwebs hanging from the broken light shade.

'It's and plastic and one forty-fourth of the size! You couldn't fly that, even with a miracle.'

Your predecessor, Lady – I think it was David, or so Douglas had it – came at me then, with his usual, from what he had learnt in his shed.

'Are you going to let your sister win the hour here to get your father to the light, or are you supposed to be the eldest, best and in charge?'

For without question, Polly was flying her Skylark about again, all over the living room, regardless of the consequences she should have known to expect.

'Oww!'

And Douglas, as Dad broke off each piece of plastic from the frame and laid them out symmetrically and equally distanced from the sides of the squares in the rug, through Dad's lack of guidance, had managed to glue his fingers together with Bostick and was trying to pull them apart, frustration all over his now, increasingly spaz-like expression.

He took his fingers out of his again ruffled hair, picked up the pilot seat, dunked it in a pool of glue, and thrust the figure into the cockpit of the tiny lunar module of the Saturn V with such force that it broke.

Polly's foot-stomping was also a distracting factor, I was sure, even if your predecessors wasn't, Lady.

'Yes, your brother is a little clumsy,' he said. 'Not the eldest, not the best, and so surely it's up to you to help.'

Then, another piece of the model broke.

'No, Douglas,' I said, 'patience!'

Because neither he nor Dad seemed to have any idea what this was.

By then, crying, Douglas rolled over, kicked the construction, so it looked more like a Miss Byatt plane crash than the construction of a model that could change our perspective of the world and all that we ever knew of it.

Then, in melt down, Douglas stood, stamped on the launch escape system, nearly smashing any chance of it working in the future to smithereens.

It wasn't right. Douglas behaved this way as if some poor kid had abandoned his brother on the pavement and did not know how to cope with the guilt. And Dad wasn't right either, Lady, Dad was not right at all.

He got up and walked back to his black swivel-chair, leaving Douglas to gunk up his hair with his gluey fingers and scream.

'It's just too hard. I can't be as clever as you,' he said. 'or that T from Tickencote!'

I remembered thinking, Lady, even then, that Dad had no idea how to be with his children, any children, how to play with us, how to put his wife in order, or how to be a man to be looked up to, even if he might one day, if we were lucky, actually bring home for us some Curly Wurly's.

'Don't tell. Don't say nothing about what happened,' I remembered telling Douglas in that old church.

Which was very fitting. I was the eldest and in charge. It wasn't up to Douglas. It wasn't up to anyone else but me to spill any beans about what had happened.

'Exactly,' said your predecessor, Lady, 'and he needed to be punished for that, just like you, if you don't buck up!'

So, I picked up the broken pieces of Douglas's ship and sat beside him. I was going to show him the way back to reality.

I would be the dad figure he needed if that was what he needed, or I thought I would at least like to try.

'Concentrate on building the ship,' said your predecessor, 'for your dad that he might be able to come. Not your idiot of a divvy spaz brother.'

Holding Douglas's hand, I guided him to put the Airfix kit Saturn V together again. I didn't know he could be so careful.

Douglas smiled.

Dad frowned.

On seeing this, Douglas stamped on the door assembly, nearly destroying eight of the twelve latches needed to secure it to the LM.

It was left to me, alone and with patience, Bostick glue, and determination, to put all the broken pieces of the ship back together.

I thought, Lady, that it might have been, the beginning of a new life with Douglas.

But, no. That wasn't it. That wasn't what happened back then, as I tried to start with but got waylaid by trying to soothe Dad with a respectful performance of *Major Tom* on the clarinet. By then, Brahms was far too uncool for me as the eldest and the best. I was sure they would understand if *Major Tom* had anything to do with T.

As would Dean Savory, in the playground at school, the most badassed school bully that I had ever come across.

It was a brave little girl who dared show Dean no respect at all. She would run about the playground, playing tag with anyone she liked, sometimes prodding and pushing them to get a reaction from fear that, otherwise, no one would want to play with her. And she didn't care who she prodded and pushed herself and their reaction, and she didn't have the faintest idea who she was messing with. She ran into a group of Dean's friends, me included, whilst he held court about how awful it must be to have a mother in the loony bin!

'So, tell,' she said, 'why do chicken want cross road, not catch bus? I need know. I need know now.'

Dean turned to face her, his fists clenched, muscles tightened, ready to raise his arm.

From the corner of my eye, I saw Polly darting in from the side of one of the old air raid shelters in the school playing field and Douglas following from the quiet area in the playground.

Despite Douglas's best efforts, Polly arrived first, pulling Elle back from Dean's downward swipe, leaving his fist to land on Polly's elbow.

She didn't cry.

'Your Sister,' enquired Dean, Polly standing then resolute before him.

'Yes, I'm sorry,' I said. 'She likes to think she is something she ain't!'

'Chicken, why?' she asked.

Dean laughed.

Elle looked up at Dean expectantly.' To get to the other side, of course,' said Dean, punching Polly in the arm again.

'You really should look after your family, Stewart,' he said. 'You are the eldest, aren't you?'

Elle curtsied, and I nodded as Polly, still resolute in her thinking she was something she wasn't, or at least it seemed so to me.

We were all marched off to the Head of Year then to take part in a talk about how atrocious we had all been.

It was like Group at the mental hospital, Lady, as the social worker, Mrs Grigg, called it, or so Dad's diary described it.

'Woke 6.20, up at 7. Large clouds. Had lingering dreams of Mrs G telling me to accept that I was a deeply selfish man and asking how I felt about that. The radiators were sputtering again. Milk was up by a penny, and my calculations for the oscillator on Concorde, just wasn't working.'

The Head of Year's hair was all up in a pointed bun like the top of the Airfix model Saturn V but without a tip.'We shall discuss, children, how not to hurt each other's feelings.'

Group was where you could learn about all feelings. If I was ever allowed to go, I imagined, which I wasn't. But next to Dad's diary in the living room's bureau, a new book had appeared, near the ones about Concorde, Gloster Meteors, and hard-winged Mosquitos.

The book was called "I'm OK. You're OK." It was a present from the Social Worker, Mrs Grigg, who I thought Dad fancied.

Polly stole it.

So the next time Dad set off to Group on his bike to see his floozy woman, the social worker, I made my way up to Polly and Elle's bedroom.

Finding Polly hidden under the eiderdown that was covering over a book-shaped lump, I grabbed hold of the edge and swiftly pulled it back.

'Hey!'

'Give it to me,' I demanded.

'What?'

The question didn't warrant any answer, the item in question having been shoved under Polly's back quickly, with the corner still poking out for anyone to see.

Instead, I strengthened my fist, just as Dean Savory had done, and sure enough, the OK book was retrieved from behind Polly's back and offered to me.

I took this and, for a moment, wondered at her cheek in trying to keep this from me in the first place, but it was a kick I gave her as a result –not the earlier intended punch –because that was the good guy thing to do, or so I reasoned.

I shouldn't have bothered, Lady. The OK book was a load of bollocks.

Again, Polly didn't cry.

Why would she never cry as I wanted?

Mum did at Dad, or used to, before she went to the mental hospital over what had happened in the bath.

'No, Michael.'

'Oh, and again. 'Oh, oh, oh!'

I got Dad's diary out at home again to try to work it all out.

"Cycled Smith's. Got Aeroplane Monthly. Interesting article about polyamide coating for sails on a solar panel. Wouldn't it all be too slow?"

More bollocks, if ever there was.

"Chain off the gear spindle again. She thrashed about in the gutter, trying to fix it. Polly said she wanted to wash my feet. Strange girl."

So I put down the diary and switched on the radio again.

"Only you are the best, the eldest. Only you can take your father to the stars." Said your predecessor, Lady.

And all this got me wondering about Dad's Polyamide...for a bit, and I decided it must be about his space ship, which would have one, no doubt, just like mine, but it wasn't big enough yet, mine. It was more like a missile at one forty-fourth of the size, and it could only grow to the task I had just been set if I somehow got rid of Polly's stupid Skylark.

Your predecessor, Lady, had entirely decided on this.

Then Dean started talking about what he had heard from the long lectures that Douglas had somehow heard or devised by his new printing press in the mouldy green shed, given by Grandfather, to help Douglas with his prophecy

'Films, television and radio are there to show us how to come closer together and share our pain and strategies. The very nature of what cries out for the goodness in men - for our universal approach, the unity of all. Even now, through this media, the voices reach millions throughout the world - millions of despairing men, women, and little children - victims of a system that makes us maim, torture and imprison innocent people when they respond.'

Douglas and that T again, probably.

And then, when Elle greeted Mum on her leave visit home, she was excited and wanted to embrace her and everything she had to offer.

'I told them,' Mum had said to Elle, apparently, 'I didn't want to come, that if I did, there was a risk I would end up dead.'

But Elle never got her embrace, with the fat lump in front of us, dribbling slobber as thick as Douglas's snot and complaining about all her ECT from a funny, swarthy, doctor called Professor Weaver, in the hospital.

But that had nothing to do with my task of taking Dad to the stars. What about my being the eldest and the best?

The Saturn V sat by my bed, to the side of me. It looked like the triangular beams at the top of St Richard's roof, pointing to the sky like the only answer to everything.

'That's right,' said your predecessor, Lady, 'if you could only get your father into the ship.'

He was so annoying that I had to tear Polly's Skylark sponge ship into hundreds of little pieces.

'Da-a-d!'

But Dad still wasn't listening.

With Douglas and Elle off to Nazareth because Dad cannot cope, Polly and I had to go to his secretary, Auntie Trinnie, and her husband, Uncle Ben.

Uncle Ben had a humpback, but he knew all about football and engines, and if I could put an engine in my Saturn V, then, well, it would be a job done.

The opening was an engine. Not a Rolls Royce, Merlin, not that best, more like from Dad's old work at Napiers.

Uncle Ben didn't have a mouldy green shed, but he did have a living room. And in Ben's living room were all kinds of whirry bits and bobs about proper science, not that make-believe that Mum used to always be on about with her crimson bobble hats, Never Never Land and Peter Pan.

'Only you will save us from ourselves.'

Polly, still pissed at me for my tearing up of her Skylark, had other ideas.

After we rolled wire around a battery to make a coil, Polly took all this apart so she could use the wire to strangle her Sindy doll, if not herself.

She got another slap for that. I don't know why, but it felt good, anyway.

She cried to Auntie Trinnie, who paid her due mind, removed the wire for safety, and returned it to Uncle Ben.

Undeterred by the slap, after we had coiled the wire again, secured this, and made it fool proof, Polly took the matchbox we would use for the base as she knew and stamped on until it all broke.

She pretended she didn't know why she got a punch later, but Auntie Trinnie, believing in Uncle Ben's faith in me and what Mum had said about me when they'd visited her in the mental place, didn't think I had it in me.

'Such a nice boy, he is. Butter would never really melt.'

Mum was right, but it still came as a surprise to me.

Polly's tears. She would grow out of them when she learnt.

Elle and Douglas, on her return from Nazareth, maintained the same if my interpretation of their craziness was correct.

'Blue Moon,' sang Elle to the new doll Dad had bought her on her return – a doll he hoped would teach her how to cry properly, through the eyes, rather than her knickers.

Douglas got a helicopter that he quickly abandoned to Tingle Three, giggling in delight as he watched the cat run around and around, chasing the bloody thing.

Dean Savory warned me that I had to beat back Polly's soldiers of the Lord's response, that she would inevitably try to rain down from the firmament, through her daft prayers, for my wanting to manhandle Dad into the Saturn V instead of her.

After all, it was my space ship. I had built it from Airfix. Polly didn't have the right. I was the eldest, the best, and the only one who could save the day.

So, I did. I kicked Polly for making me believe that the Saturn V was bigger than it was and that I could get Dad in it.

It was like she was doing what you were doing, Lady, from the radio, or even from my new record player, getting into my head and making things that weren't real seem like they were.

Of course, it was real, the *Sent Surprise*, or would be, if not the growing Saturn V.

Polly withdrew to her bedroom to nurse her pride, blood and her bruises.

It was so real that Dad was then getting on and trying it out for himself.

His foot caught on one of the cardboard tube nacelles, jutting from the side, as his long legs swung over the frame. He adjusted the Sturmey-Archer gears to space contortion factor one by his thumb, only slightly beneath the much larger-than-usual frisbee stuck onto the handlebars of my Chopper with Bostick, painted, as it was, in the livery of the *Sent Surprise*.

'It's not exactly aerodynamic,' Dad said, Lady.

'And where's the aluminium casing?' he asked in an energy that was indeed a surprise and otherwise completely unbecoming.

'Without aluminium, it will blow you apart!'

This was also the news about a new blockbuster feature on Film 77, which had an even better evil villain than me, and he wasn't the eldest, or was it on Top of the Pops?

'Darth, what?'

And Dad's foot was ready to press down hard on the peddle.

But he was too big for it. His knees would have hit the saucer section if he got on.

'Don't, Dad. You'll break it. How did you find out anyway? Did Douglas tell you about it?'

'No, it was Polly,' he said, getting off and nearly crashing the carefully constructed improvements to my bike into the end of the shed as he did so. 'She told me that you were ruining your bike so you wouldn't have to do the shopping.'

'That's just her Princess Leia', said Dean, 'and for that, she really needs to be punished.'

So, I did.

I chased Polly down, Lady, to her bedroom again and found her still underneath the eiderdown. This time with her empty packets of Angel Delight and her Sindy doll, which had all the hair missing on one side of her head.

As the sounds of *Major Tom* and the music from *2001, Space Odyssey*, played out in my head, I allowed myself to be taken by its will, Lady.

I wasn't exactly sure what it was – maybe your predecessor. All I was sure of was the will to rain my punches down, draw out Polly's cries, and that she needed to understand her penitence.

At first she was reluctant, not a sound, not even a whimper, but as my blows became heavier and more rhythmic in keeping with whatever piece was playing in my head, the fast intake of breath as though she were preparing, not necessarily for the right fist again, already knowing what to expect from this, turned into what looked like one of Douglas' fits.

'At least the information in R2 will probably remain intact.'

Or was that David?

Polly turned her face to dodge and kicked her legs to protect herself. But slowly, I was able to draw it out of her Lady, first the whimper, as said, building to a moan, a steady cacophony of yelps, building to a scream, but an evil, previously unheard scream, except for Douglas bursting through the door to Polly and Elle's bedroom in great stress.

'Vicar Morgan,' he shouted. He's coming down the gravel path with Mr Biggs, and he's in uniform -the uniform of the Police, just like Auntie Belinda works for.'

I stopped and turned to face him, the anger still building inside me. But there was something else too.

Concorde was being rated as the best high-speed vessel on the box television.

'It is just not true. It is not right,' said Dad.

Vicar Moore and Mr Biggs chose not to hear this, or so it seemed, showing much more concern about strips of copper stolen from the roof of St Richard's church.

'Do you know anything about this,' asked Mr Biggs. 'It's just that in the church accounts, the depreciation of the building seems dependant on a prediction recorded in something called the Thelemic Prophecy.'

'Douglas!'

Dad knew who the culprit of this was.

He said it had been T and Dough that told Douglas when the battery matchbox engine I had been trying to make in the mouldy-green shed before Polly smashed it, wouldn't work, because it wasn't powerful enough, and Douglas, wanted to help me fix it, after all the help I had tried to give him.

'Would you care for some tea,' asked Dad of our visitors.

'Don't mind if I do, Michael. Have you any of that new stuff from Tattooine.'

'No.'

But this voice, Lady, from the shed of Douglas, really wanted to find a way to help me find a way for Dad and me to find a way to get to the light, for I was the eldest. I was the best. I was the only one that could make any of this real.

Vicar Morgan and Mr Biggs left in protest.

'And he calls himself a Christian?'

I wasn't laughing, though I had to acknowledge that the voice did have something to do with my wanting to escape from all of this, even if it was into my own mind.

Melissa knew all about how I would to get away. She could understand that it took a lot more than trying to create a situation where I would be taken away because I was too bad, too bullying and far from the best, having never learnt the skills.

At least, that's how she explained her understanding to me. She heard it from her Dad, to whom she was close, closer than we were to ours.

Melissa was my girlfriend. We had met at the chip shop.

Melissa had turned to her group of friends, one of whom had a smear of tomato ketchup down her blouse, and they started to walk away. But Melissa turned back like she had something to say, and she did.

'You know you will never get anywhere if you keep acting like that.'

'Acting like what?' I asked.

She pointed to my bike, with its drooping side nacelles and wobbly saucer section at the front, now taking over the brakes.

'You are just as the Lady warned me.

'You know the Lady, too?'

Melissa had looked me up and down at least twice before speaking as I looked at her. She was petite, wavy-haired, and quite attractive, with her warm smile and big eyes. She wore Laura Ashley clothes too. Nothing about her came from a charity shop.

'All, I know,' said Melissa. 'Is that the Lady told me all about you and your daft clothes and how I should help your escape? But your bike, well don't you think it's a bit shit to make such a journey in, isn't it?'

But I was in love. So much so that the saucer section of the *Sent Surprise* fell right off, and the nacelles from the sides started to droop badly, revealing just how pathetic I was.

'Yes, the Lady told me it hadn't worked before. Three times so far, there is still no chance of ever getting him on the ship. I can see why, now.'

Melissa wasn't at attractive as Auntie Brenda's daughter Miranda, though that wasn't going anywhere fast, if at all. And anyway, Miranda was a full three years younger than she was.

'Did you know that my Dad's a builder?' said Melissa. Oh, yes, he can build anything. Once, he made me my own Millennium Falcon and he has heard all about your Airfix model and the problems with your dad and your brother, Douglas, isn't it? Yes, we all hear about it at school, from Douglas's writings, all the time that he shares in English with that Mr Fergusson who likes to hear all about your dad's penis.'

It was a strange beginning to what initially seemed a peculiar relationship. Someone who seemed to understand, well, Melissa understood bits, but that was a start. I had never known anything like this before.

Melissa got on with the others, too. Especially Elle.

'A cuppa tea costis 2p, Misses Mel.'

Polly seemed so relieved to have my attention distracted after the last time she caught me under the eiderdown in a compromising position with sexy Miranda.

'She's my friend. My best and only.' I had to take her mind off this. She might have told Auntie Belinda.

'You slag.'

'Fuck off!'

But Melissa had such an excellent way of folding up our clothes after anyone messed them up, the divvy spaz Douglas, in particular, now totally immersed in the stories coming out of the mouldy green shed.

Polly never did tell Auntie Belinda. Why, I don't know!

It was a developing relationship strong enough to bring Melissa's father to the house to check out what his daughter was getting into, which surprised us all.

When Bob entered the living room, Dad, from his black-leather swivel chair, turned off his Debussy on the Hacker radio.

Bob took the threadbare sofa, as Polly bought in two meagre slices of Battenburg and some weak tea.

They shook hands.

'Bob, Melissa's father.' He said.

'Michael, Stewart's'

We were in the kitchen, listening to everything.

They sat.

'Stewart is my first born.'

There wasn't any sign of sulking.

'You have another and I believe daughters, too?" asked Bob. Nor was there any sign of building from him.

Dad nodded. It was as though he was trying to make out everything was normal.

'I do. And you are a builder, I believe, Mr ...'

'Bob,' said Melissa's father. 'I am a builder, painter and decorator.'

'A builder, painter and decorator,' said Dad.

'Yes, it is, as I said.'

Dad bent his head low.

'And are you, as my wife might describe it,' asked Dad, 'a bit common, as a result? No offence intended, of course.'

Bob waved his hand in dismissal of the idea.

'If you like,' came his reply. 'None taken.' He leant forward as he spoke. 'Stewart tells me your wife is in hospital.'

Dad looked up. 'She is, St Bernard's. Do you know it?'

'The one with the big walls. You go every night to see her?' asked Bob.

'I do. I have to. My wife can get very demanding, and they expect at Group!'

'I see,' said Bob. 'Well, Grace and I,' that was his wife, Melissa's adoptive mother, 'are happy to have Stewart when you're there.'

Dad looked up.

'He seems happy with you,' he said.

'And we with him, too. And his brother comes too, sometimes.'

'Yes, Douglas is sometimes very sad.'

'We don't like to see it.'

They smiled at each other. Dad then fidgeted a little and twiddled his nose.

'So are you going to help Stewart build a new ship to take me away,' he asked.

'I can help him build a ship,' replied Bob. 'If that's what he wants. But it will take a whole lot more than...'

'Because I don't want you to. You see, I don't want to go.'

The door-bell rang. Dad got up to get this as Bob left. It was Mr Biggs again. This time, he was not in uniform.

'I have looked it up, Michael, and it is as real as Jane Fonda's workouts, with aliens liking the Mash get Smash adverts. In the prophecy of Thelma, it is written that the Kingdom of "M", long, may her socks be upon her feet, is within us all' - not one person nor a group of people, but in all of us and in you!'

He pointed at Dad, who by then was obviously not himself, as though he'd been taken over by something, and it couldn't have been Douglas because he was still in the mouldy green shed. He hadn't come out for three days by then.

'You, we, have her power,' continued Mr Biggs - the power to create happiness! You, the people, can make this life free and beautiful and completed with one's brother.'

'Maybe,' said Dad, 'but I know the effects of a Portergeist take over when I see one, slamming the door in Mr Bigg's face.

I remember feeling quite proud of Dad for that, Lady. It wasn't often that Dad could be so strong, decisive and decidedly missing the point.

The tennis ball, being used for French Cricket, was thwacked by someone then. I can't remember who, but as high as the eye could see, it went – higher, even, than the steeple of St Richard's, where, apparently, according to Douglas and the general rumours around the house at number twenty-six, Melissa and I were soon to get married, so I could make my own escape from all of this.

'Free and beautiful and complete', continued Dean in the fiery wake. Douglas, having come out of the mouldy green shed for a bowl of custard, nodded in agreement with enthusiasm.

The ball flew up and up until it reached its zenith fast and started to fall.

'The coffin corner,' said Dad. 'It's not what happened to Concorde, Sputnik, or even the two-wheeled *Sent Surprise*, but from what the boys at NASA were pushing for, it might just as well have been.

It was true that earlier, when the man at the Model shop produced his latest version of the Saturn V ship, it was seven feet high, with reinforced aluminium casing and type TSP F35-4 rocket motor included for a six-second burn and only a ten-hour construction window.

'But it costist £72,' observed Elle.

And I only got paid £58.90 a week at Tesco's, Lady.

Maybe with the help of Melissa's dad and some scaffolding for the steeple at St Richard's. It would only be so I could shut you and your predecessor up, Lady, so I had more space in my head for Melissa in preparation for our marriage.

We built it, me and Bob, the new model, in Bob and Melissa's small garden.

Dad found out, maybe from Mum, as they were talking then, all about their concerns regarding Elle. Mum from her flat in Brentford after she got kicked out of Edna Bone's, Dad from his music room that was just starting to get a bit cluttered.

I was so surprised when Dad offered to contribute towards the wedding ceremony.

'Make sure you get your Dad to step off the LM first,' said your predecessor, but by then, Lady, he was a bit old hat as far as engine design was concerned and got drowned out by Concorde, flying overhead.

'That plane shouldn't be allowed,' said Dad.

Mellissa got to planning. 'The invites will be from some proper printers, not your brother's shed, though I suppose he can be best man if you think it will help him. I want gold lettering, embossed too!'

As for the church, well, I know St Richard's is where you got your dinner from, but I live closer to All Saints, and even though the Church is very scary, they do have a decent size hall we can use, at reduction, for the reception.'

And in my mind, the ship that would take us away soon enough on our honeymoon, was made from balsa wood, which we could slot together with a simple tongue and groove and liberal amounts of Bostick.

With the heat of the chain reaction from the family, I imagined, they would burn, or at least fuse light the engine, as would the strategically worked-out metal fixtures on the inside of the panels to the frame.

But it didn't matter much what I thought Lady. It was only a ruse against you. It wasn't as though it were ever meant to fly anyway because Melissa and I, we had other plans.

'Outside caterers will provide the menu; we're not going to have any of your Dad's salads. Or that Wimpy shit that he likes, and it has to start with a prawn cocktail. As for the hymns, I don't know, isn't there a thing in your family about David and his psalms? All my family are to come, yours too, and their families, even Pete, innit, but not Miranda Case. Yes, Stewart, I do know!'

Then came the polyamide film for the outside. It wasn't explained why polyamide was needed, not even by Patrick Moore on the box telly, glaring at me like that through his monocle like he knew exactly how it was and was going to be in the future.

The engine, which had grown somewhat since my attempts with a battery and matchbox, was a two-stroke, donated by the 59 Club Biker chapter that also used the church—a donation organised by Bob, a member who sometimes helped them out as a mechanic.

What did it matter that it had a different name than expected? What mattered was that Melissa could see precisely the style of what I had planned for our honeymoon.

It came, the big day of the 'do ya's'. The old Vic – well, he was pretty ancient, really – winked at me as Melissa walked up the aisle and waved his hand as if trying to calm me down. But I wasn't anxious, like Douglas, with his fingers fumbling about in his waist jacket pocket, and I realised the old Vic was trying to address him instead.

I looked around a bit at Mum's jutting teeth. They were such an embarrassment. Whether she would even get an invite, debutante or not, was touch and go.

Melissa arrived.

'The grace of our Lord Jesus Christ,' started the old Vic, determinedly, whilst simultaneously willing the mothers to get the children to stand properly and show some respect, as he spoke, 'the love of God, and the fellowship of the Holy Spirit be with you all.'

Melissa held up her hand as though to put the Minister right.

'But not with the David,' she said. 'Or Miranda Case. We have our journey to make for love.'

The old Vic continued.

I appeal to you, brothers and sisters,' he said as Douglas sucked up a little more of his dribble from the side of his mouth, 'by the mercies of God, to present your bodies as a living sacrifice, holy and acceptable to God, which is your natural, spiritual worship.

No one saw Douglas lick it up with his tongue, apart from me, thankfully. Or at least that's what I hoped. I didn't want him embarrassing me again, with his prophecy, like at the chip shop.

The first hymn started with Elle in full voice, leading.

'The quiet waters by.'

Then it was: 'I, Melissa,' she said, repeating, after the Minister, 'take thee, Stewart,' and I remember feeling quite proud of myself that I could do this, I resolved, 'my wedded husband, to have and to hold from this day forward, for better, for worse. For richer, for poorer.'

I concentrated on the Minister.

'In sickness and in health. To love, cherish, till death us do part, according to the holy prophecy?'

No. No. I couldn't get Douglas's stories out of my head.

'Wilt thou have this woman to thy wedded wife, to live together according to God's law, in the holy state of matrimony?'

'Yeah, yeah.'

But this wasn't it either. Not yet, but at the reception later.

Melissa seemed so proud.

'Ladymans and gentleweds,' said Elle, taking the microphone from Pete, innit. 'Clap hands' gever,' she said, 'for the awfully wedded couple, my brother, Stewart and Melissa, son of Bob of the builders, not mashy smash Lady Teddy bear alien, like marmalade.'

'On behalf of my new wife and I,' I said, 'I would like to

welcome you all on this special day and thank you all for coming. We are both so pleased to have you here with us today.'

'Ahh, that's alright, mate,' said Pete, innit. 'And thank you, too, for all the expected gifts and unexpected generous contributions to our star-gazing honeymoon.'

At the lowering of my hand, everyone sat. Someone turned the music down.

'I first want to thank my new father-in-law,' I started, 'not just for his generous contribution to this day and the space ship, but also for encouraging me to take on the role of loving and protecting his daughter, Melissa.'

'Here, here.'

Douglas seemed a little embarrassed by the silence he had caused with his rude interruption.

I waved his embarrassment down, like I would a joke, and trained my gaze at Mum, her buck teeth poised as though ready, but I was not scared of her anymore.

'To you, Mother,' I said, 'as sarcastically as I can make this, I really want to thank you for setting me up to be the success you could never have and for, in the process of this, never being there for me, with your unremitting, unconditional love and support, and for always allowing me to make my own decisions in life – which, if the warped madness of how to love you instilled in me is to be believed, will prepare me and Melissa for raising our own children in the not too distant future. Not that you will have anything to do with them.'

Mum looked back at me with one of her false smiles, ever the narcissist. And with her cold stare back and so self-conscious, or that's how it seemed, she turned.

'Yes, I appreciate that very greatly.'

Then I turned my attention to Dad, who was struggling to open his two-ply serviette at the time, with his tie getting so inconveniently in the way.

'And to you, Dad, I say, thank you too, for also being not there, in delivery of a dream to follow, or in attention, of course, except for the occasional Wimpy and pilchards, but even though always promised, never a Curly Wurly.'

I moved my arm, gesturing to the other guilty culprits—

Douglas, who had caught a particularly choice bogey in his fingers and Polly with her long down-digging chin.

Elle, I decided I would let off.

'Now,' I continued, 'I would like to take a moment to thank my brother and two sisters.'

Douglas smiled.

Polly was busy adjusting the pins of her ill-fitting fascinator.

'From the moment I introduced Melissa to you, you have all made her feel very welcome. For instance, Polly,' I said, 'when I kicked out to teach you of your place, Melissa was amazed at your resilience and determination to still blame me for everything without taking any responsibility for your thieving and blaming me.'

Polly scowled and looked away.

'Douglas', I continued, 'you have shown us both just how determined you were never to let us make music together. How you never let us near and would try to dictate in that stupid prophecy of yours how everyone else was always to blame.'

'Right, you are, bruv!'

'And not forgetting Elle, of course,' I continued, smiling.

She looked up.

'With you, Elle, we have no issues at all. Melissa has such fond memories of playing shop. You were the one who helped her feel most welcome with your endless imagined cups of tea.'

'You like it?'

Melissa nodded. It was a well-prepared speech, but not one that I thought any of the others would expect.

'Special declaration, of course,' I continued, 'has to go to the other member of my family, not always seen, but always present, given the extent to which my Melissa wishes me to be rid of her.'

Melissa nodded again.

'Well, I tell you. And for those of you who don't know, the Lady is false, posing as though she were, in fact, my dead Uncle David!'

Dad looked all around the hall and then back to where I had indicated, jittery and even scared. He even took up his camera, switched the viewfinder on, and searched.

Everyone else was looking for this mysterious guest, too.

'Well, Lady,' I continued. "I found my journey, as you wanted me to, and as you might be aware, if you can bear to listen to this, it is with Melissa, and not with you, that I shall take off in this wonderfully crafted spaceship to find the light.

'And of Melissa herself', I continued, turning to her, "I feel so lucky to have found in you a bride who not only reads me well but actually gives a shit about me, and not because I am the eldest or the best, far from it. And seeing your smile every day, well, you know, certainly puts a bigger one on my face, too.

'Then, in the name of David,' piped up Douglas again. Let them reach for the stars, for escape, to make their own lives. Let them run away and reject all that they know will not serve them to find their own great adventure.'

After we arrived at the airport, we took off, leaving them all forever. The Concorde on which we travelled was more incredible than the model I had produced with Bob. It was to take us both to our own island, away from all of the family, all of my friends, all of them.

This was what I did, Lady, when in my head I converted the model into our means of escape. It is what I had to do to get away, not to have to be the eldest, best, or anyone's diamond in the rough, Peter Pan, bully, traveller on the *Sent Surprise*, or anything else.

The others would just have to cope on their own. They had done most of the time anyway. The only one that I had any real concern about was Elle.

And then, 'All rise,' someone said – Oh, yes it was you, Lady, from the picture, about to receive your blessing from her.

'Pray silence and behold, the great 'M', long, may her socks be upon her feet, that she might make clear to us that you had to earn the right to be here. Bring understanding to your Babel.

'We might not be able to control if we were the eldest,' said the great 'M', 'but we could certainly take charge of whether we need to be the best, or simply like all the others, as Thelma had done, wouldn't you agree Stewart?"

Then she placed her hands upon Thelma's head.

'Snap out of it,' ordered Melissa.

Steve Porter

ELLE

Mummy calls them sniplets. Douglas wrote them down for me.

Not much love tender in Edmonton, like Elvis promised. Love di'n't like it much in Disco.

Pissed his hand, when down my knickers, but stop him, no.

Tol' Police, but not dem to say to all at turch. And not to Douglas, neiver, when him to ask on bus, next day, which will, most probly.

Police asked me, 'Why?'

I said, 'Douglas, upset 'gain, would. Him fink he not wiv me to stop it, like wanted to stop Daddy from on ship first, but not, for Daddy not to blame, but was, like Teddy Bear Aliens, wiv Mr. Biggs was PC at Feltam Police Station.

Police say not know Mr. Biggs, nor any Lady Teddy Bear Alien, not in 1984, or for full five years before. Looked up, in them paper records.

Maybe, would different, if had not gone wiv Daddy in ship, let him go alone, like Douglas wanned.

Must try look after Douglas.

Him sad.

Happier sing time was much, afore, when Lady Teddy Bear Alien firs' come.

'Oh, for the wings, for the wings of a dove.' Mummy, me, sing up the stairs. Polly, try join in. Sent way, cos voice not good nuff like Mummy.

I liked singing. I liked Mummy too. We sang 'gever good. But Lady Teddy Bear Alien on window of telly box, shouty over adverts, wanted me sing her songs. I said 'NO!' Her songs I not wanted. Liked Mummy and songs by man with hair like Daddy, Presley, only.

Mummy, me, laugh, 'bout joke, we could be in a space ship, on a telly window, sometimes. Very 'diclas!

Polly said, 'Yes, Elle, it is ridiculous, as mad as a chicken wanting to cross the road.'

But, 'I never sawed a chicken take no Wellie boot mad pills,' said.

'Never mind.'

So 'Tender, Love me,' as Mummy done her doves and Polly sent away from up the stairs for bad effort.

Poor Polly.

Asked Mummy, what is 'maginary?

She not say.

Lady Teddy Bear Alien on stairs then come.

'For Mash get Smash!'

Was words from new advert, or Douglas? What mean?

And Daddy moan then from Music Room oppsit. His Taikovski. Went, doop, doopety, doop, doop, dip, dip, day.

Polly said Daddy had a fairy too in his music room. A sugar-plum one. But no fairy up, down, costume for the swings, or for Lady Teddy Bear Alien's ship, very upset from me wiv Mummy and not wiv her on Skylark ship – Noah and Nelly.

Sing back her, 'You not maketh me down to lie!'

'Why, Elle?' asked Polly.

'Cos lying 'bout things, not good,' said. 'Not right. I never done. Not need mashy smash. Good girl, me.'

Lady Teddy Bear Alien, not unnerstand. mostly, cos had tol' her, earlier, if I let her be friend, like I said, would, honest, she would keep the bad monsters away, in all the long night.

Douglas might unnerstand? Maybe?

Next day Mummy gone Bernard's, from mad pills, and me Polly play, wiv 'nuver family in playground by George's turch. Not Daddy's fault. Not Mummy's neither. 'Why do mash get smash?' asked.

Polly said don't know what on 'bout.

Swing family, fairy-costumes up, fairy-costumes down, larfing Polly, me, 'bout had no fairy-costumes, too poor.

But Polly's dress had sequins on. Me, brand new polyester skirt. 'spensive and mustn't tear.

When making stick-tents in woods, I tell her 'When, I turn into Lady Teddy Bear Alien,' I said her, 'I join Douglas and Stewart in the Cubs.'

Polly said: 'Watch out not tear my skirt. Think they better than us.'

'Who?'

'Them with fairy costumes, up, down, and their purple and their black and white Nike trainers.'

'Oh!'

Stick tents made bivowivvywacks, like in Brownies.

'I'll be the indeean and you be the boy cow.'

'But I'm a girl.'

'I'm too.'

'But you funny with the teddy bears.'

How Polly know?

On telly window, earlier, home, sawed us family by swings wiv no black and white trainers and no mashy smash aliens.

'No trainers?' said Lady Teddy Bear Alien back. 'Ask your Daddy.'

Polly runned off.

'Catch me!'

Ran. Hide-and-seek then. Polly found every time, cos sang, 'Love me tender'.

I knew Polly would find me. I wanted her find me. Ha ha ha. Hee hee hee.

And Lady Teddy Bear Alien, 'sisted, my head, when we got opening by trees, that all on ship, have black and white trainers, Nike, if I come and bring Daddy wiv, and if not, then monsters must with me down in woods today, for big mashy smash picnic.

'Love me true.'

I larfed, said her! 'Go away, silly.'

Then I ran and ran and Polly ran and chased and Lady Teddy Bear Alien, di'n't show any monsters, but said her monsters were not nice like fairies, or aliens. Best me beware of Teddy Bears in woods to come mashy me sure, like Douglas say from him mouldy green shed.

Mummy say: 'Very diclas and 'gainst God!'

Was all for wings of dove, then. Aliens turn into really bad Teddy Bears.

Douglas still sad.

Tried not wet knickers, when Mummy went hospital, tried tell Lady Teddy Bear Alien on telly window all 'bout it.

But were Mummy's bags packed already, in the hallway.

Lady Teddy Bear Alien said, she might able to stop monsters mashy, if I believe her 'surprise', and come down to the wood wiv me today, bring Daddy, see all the tired little Teddy Bears and get him on ship!

'No.' I said. 'I wanted no mashy smash at me, or Mummy will go and not to picnic. You mark my words.'

Mr Parsons said that me at school.

Then, men, grey, walking down gravel path. Walking, walking. Could see from window. One waved.

Waved back. Even smiled.

A long minute, then, rat, tat, on front door.

Daddy not sure, neiver, like wiv Douglas's sospicious mind, when them sawed.

I held in my tummy, held it good and strong. Breath too.

Was like Elvis song, 'Can't go on together.'

But, who? Daddy? Mummy? Me?

Grey men, door, from ambulance, looking at Mummy, picking up her packed bags.

'Well, bye then, poppets,' said. 'Be good.'

Walking Mummy down gravel to Bernard's.

Tried, but couldn't hold in anymore and so dribble, trickle, wet socks.

'She's pissed herself', said Stewart.

Cried.

Douglas wiped the floor.

Not good day.

Mummy left, said, cos di'n't like Thursday early night surprise, Daddy doin' bad and shouting, 'No, Michael, not in the bath!' But it was rubbish idea. Coul'n't believe of Daddy's rude thing, out, and noddy Mummy, whilst me, Polly, looking through gap in door.

Was not 'maginary.

But on Telly window, alien ship, inside, showed, better, no bath, that Teddy Bears liked anyways. Always their button-eye drop out, my Teddy anyway.

Mummy di'n't like much very, showed. Mummy di'n't like Daddy's purple noddy by the taps.

'I said no, Michael!' say she.

So was liar, Telly window. Douglas 'greed, and Lady Teddy Bear Alien not in control. I was, and maybe one day, when in control, Lady Teddy Bear Alien there would show nice fings 'stead. Maybe starry, starry's flying past, maybe Tinkerbell, flitter-flutter, from Mummy's Pan Peter show, made on sewing machine for Oriel, wiv fairy costume wings, much better.

But after Mummy's early night surprise: 'Cost of bubble bath is why your Dad doesn't want to be with me,' Mummy said. 'And where the hell are my mad pills?'

Douglas pointed Music room door to show Daddy was there. Twiddlin' nose. Flippy up quiff in room.

Was him way. Not him go get in no silly alien ship.

Really, I loved my Daddy in music room, but sad he all alone, fought. Lady Teddy Bear Alien wanting me believe he in 'pression, pressed to wall of Polly's Skylark ship, shame for early night surprise wiv Mummy. His arms held back by memtum, side, watching starry's, as the mashy smash Teddy bears got ready for him for his noddy badness.

'No!' I tell Douglas.

Flying past Clanger moon, sawed on telly window. No

Tinkerbell to rescue Daddy from memtum 'gainst wall.

Sang him song.

'I'll be yours through all the years.'

Good, better, less make me wet self from scared, bout Teddy Bears mashy smash, Daddy, or me, down in the woods.'

But song not what Teddy Bears want, Lady Teddy Bear Alien say. They want song about great picnic.

Was all on telly window.

Pilchards on toast. One slice each, Daddy got two. Douglas made squash too strong, made teeth bad, Daddy poured half in vase. Better, coloured water not tasty. But Daddy was the Daddy, not one scared to be pressed back wall of ship by mo-memtum. And did care us, must care, that Mummy still gone.

Prayers, none. All hope gone with ambulance, Douglas said. Stewart too. Silence. Douglas's turn to do washing-up,

Sorted all out in head. Beat my 'fused.

All, what was on telly window, better than real what was happ'nin home, 'leivable, not fusing, like Polly, Saturday nights with Brucie.

Smashy plates, kitchen, then.

Douglas always drop fings.

Lady Teddy Bear Alien, say me, Douglas idiot. For mashy smash sure him, less be nice to me and help me get Daddy on him ship.

Said No. want play Lady Teddy Bear Alien, more. Always on 'bout Daddy and why mashy smash him ship.

Needed different song

'Blue Moon.'

Polly wanted Liverpool long haired lover stead, but I louder her than.

'You've missed a bit.'

Was Daddy at my colouring a Skylark, in Polly's fav'rit book.

Skylark could be ship, wiv two fronts, four porthole windows and balloon top to reach stars.

'All aboard.'

'What makes a bear great?' say Daddy, coming out him music room

'Dunno.'

'Ursa Major,' him say. 'The Great Bear.'

But why Daddy out music room with all that?

Him red in face and 'gitated, like seen ghost.

'I will not go with you to the great bear, or anywhere else, David.' Daddy say. 'You have to let me stay. Someone has to look after the children, now that Hannah has gone.'

Who was David? Oh! Sill me. Daddy's brother. Up above the sky so high, like a Skylark in the sky?

Made no sense. Telly window not in music room and anyway, was switched off. Made no money, neiver.

'membering in bed time

'You should love your Daddy in Skylark, very much.' Lady Teddy Bear Alien say. 'Not love your Mummy gone Bernard's, all her fault, Daddy should be come back to me. He will have his picnic, happy, with all the great bears, and you can come too.'

No. Daddy to stay with me.

But wasn't right, Don't know why, and then Stewart by me at yes'days breakfast then with his Saturn ship, for fairy costumes up, down, said, inside wiv all the Nike trainers, what was football boots for girls, said. 'Blue is the colour.'

'Of the moon?' I asked, but still not really right and need help from Polly, for Lady Teddy Bear Alien in head, 'bout how she then want Daddy to join the purple team

'West Ham,' say Stewart.

But Polly snoring and Lady Teddy Bear Alien, like mascot of the West Ham: 'Because at six-o'-clock their mummies and daddies, will take them home to bed, or they will, they will mashy smash the Chelsea at them's wood picnic.'

Wot's a Chelsea?

Was Stewart, try play keepy-uppy, wiv Douglas, who sulky. Up, up, and away wiv Tinkerbell, or –

'Cos you's a tired little teddy bear.'

Left ear to pillow.

'Picnic time for Teddy Bears.'

Right ear to pillow.

'The little Teddy Bears will have their smashy time today.'

Pillow over both ears, drown her out.

'See them, catch them unawares...'

Baby Jesus, Daddy/Polly's God, make Lady Teddy Bear Alien go away. Counting sparkly sequins on Polly's dress. Oh, for the wings, for the wings of a Saturn be in.

'Blue moon. You knew just what I was there for.'

I really wanted some of that Auntie Binda pie.

Morning, 'membered will see Auntie Binda soon. Pick blackberries, for pie. Very good, really 'cited.

First breakfast. Mountain of cornflakes, spilt milk, Douglas got cloth, Polly wiped. Not enough milk for Stewart, not Daddy's fault. Not Mummy's neiver. Mummy in Bernard's 'opital for mentals, gone, afore.

But Polly say St Bernard's not in Bible, so must be bad. Can't unnerstand all fings like that, so.

Cornflakes with water for Stewart. My fault, shouldn't spill milk. Stewart noise of getting-up. Crunch. Clump.

'Fuck!'

'Oh, no!' Polly scareded of him.

Daddy had mutter to self, as played his new Olimus camera.

'And I deserve all this?'

'Blue is the colour,' sang Stewart, coming down.

Daddy's head in hands.

Lady Teddy Bear Alien, very shouty 'bout the ship, this time from radio.

'But Michael, you have to control the ship! That's why you're here.'

Skylark, Polly's ship, broke, 'parrently, after Polly pulled off the balloon and memtum started on ship and Stewart shot her with chew gum from him stick slingshot.

Stewart then, kitchen, football-kit, ready and holding him own space ship.

Daddy said, 'No, Stewart. No football today.'

'But Da-a-ad.'

Polly di'n't smile, cos 'before you start, wipe that smirk of your face, child.' Daddy was the daddy. His dentures wobbled.

Gave Stewart my milk for cornflakes, for shut up and he eat, stroking his space ship. Me, left play with dry flakes, flick them Daddy's face, get him out 'pression.

Stewart zooming his space ship all over kitchen table. Was bigger than Skylark. Lady Teddy Alien wunnered, if it big enough for Daddy, me and all the purple and Nike black and white trainers.

'Course is,' tol' her, on the programme, bout Patrick, coming from the Radio.

'More. More,' said Douglas, probly finking of presenter, not cornflakes, but then time for dishes.

Stewart washed; Polly dried. Daddy look his watch, then up off chair, faster than a flitty Tinkerbell, 'spectin the insides of a Saturn for room and button to extend polyester wings.

Lady Teddy Bear Alien, from behind Polly's skirt, or was it Polly done it, pulled out Douglas's book called a fel-a-meen-ic proficy, summink.

What is it?

Gravel path, then road, mustn't trip, dangerous.

'Got a stone in my shoe.' Douglas, 'plained, as Stewart zooming his space ship.

'To the Blue Moon,' said Lady Teddy Bear Alien.

I hoped so.

But Daddy 'nored this, pushed his bike, tall, strong. And no teacher or mummy di'n't need to tell him stand straight.

Stewart still zooming, kicked stone to Polly's skipping. Raleigh Way, Queens Hill, Castle Way. Had to learn, not forget, case got lost. Past the woods. Up, not down and never in disguise. Sang to get rid of Lady Teddy Bear Alien, head again, trying to get back in with no love for Mummy, if I go down to the woods ever again.

Fought about space ship and how big and whether could inside me and Daddy go. But not right still.

'Never let you go.' Elvis minded me 'bout him being lonesome tonight if he did go - a sospicious mind.

Clanger moon on telly screen blue and they had no mash get smash, just a mad fel-a-meen-ic proficy, say Douglas.

What is it?

Somehow got there, knock, knock.

'Who's there?'

'The chicken, crossed the road, for your big, huge blackberry pie.'

'Well, you better come in, then.' Was Auntie Binda. She very love.

Daddy gave her brown envelope. Money, money, money.

'All there.'

'Thank you, Michael.'

Him frown on bicycle, off work. always frown money, look like Clanger Iron Chicken try cross road get away from gift money ever 'gain.

'Yes, but if you get him in space ship,' Douglas say, 'is right, for you, for him, take you, your Daddy to light by him polyester wing fings.'

Maybe he right. Maybe, but when Daddy cross road, get to other side, 'stead, behind clock tower, like a Saturn on corner and a 10-1 countdown, Stewart's games, should I have gone wiv?

Pie!

Felt bad Daddy off, me not wiv him, but Auntie Binda had proper squash and 'nopoly, played hard.

'Never land on Chance would be a fine thing,' she said, start make the pie.

I did, with fimble piece, choose, cos same shape top of Saturn ship.

'Oh, fuck!'

Polly, whenna land on Stewart's Pantalonwill Street and Douglas get out him comic, wot was newspaper for chillen.

What is fel-a-meen-ic? Me asked 'gain.

Lady Teddy Bear Alien, in my head, said was Douglas's proficy, and how in ship together wiv Dad, not the mashy smash, to come, if not go, get a better picnic, and blackberry pie, f'sure.

'Will you piss me tonight?' sang, as jiggy wiv legs.

D''n't want jiggy wiv legs, di'n't want mashy smash from Lady Teddy Bear Aliens, wanted Daddy, so as Douglas tol' me, in finger first fimble, rest hand, arm, whole body, till, in head, least, sitting next Daddy inside space ship.

'She is ruining the game.' Was Stewart.

'Yes, well, that's enough, now,' said Daddy, 'thank-you very much. Is that the outer hatch for me to escape from?'

And Lady Teddy Bear Alien singing back.

'For ev'ry bear that ever there was.'

All the smashy bears then, come, to get Daddy then, for not wanting go, picking up chance would be fine fing cards, fought.

'Is gavered there for certain because.

'Elle's ruining the game with her jiggy legs.'

Auntie Binda in, clunking, from hallway, took hand mine. And all 'nopoly cards dropped to floor.

She grabbed my hand

'Elle, dear,' she said, 'will you come and help me fold up the day clothes?'

Wiv Auntie Binda take me away, Teddy bears will just have wait, for mashy smash up Daddy on ship.

'First lie them straight on the bed, girls.'

'You can't escape that easily.'

'Fold the left arm in and over. No Elle. the other left. Yes.'

Did it best could.

'You must stay, and keep your Daddy here too, or...'

'The right, same. Bottom up to meet top. Flop over holding with one hand. Take hand out slow. There.'

Did it very good.

'Auntie?'

'Or,' say Lady Teddy Bear Alien, 'it will be terrible for the both of you.'

'Yes, Auntie.'

'I love you, more than all teddy bears in the woods.'

'And I love you as well.'

'You have made my life complete, Auntie.'

Good smell pie from oven.

In woods, searching.

No surprise bears from Lady Teddy Bear Alien, no more,

cos me no disguise, playin' wiv Polly' gain, not wiv Daddy on space ship.

'Are you sorry we drifted apart.'

But Lady Teddy Bear Alien said, needed me in down in his woods, in disguise, for surprise. I try say him, I not s'posed to go in woods on own, too bad, but Douglas say, 'Every bear that ever there was wants play wiv you and your daddy when you get woods by space ship, and in your Nike trainers.'

'All my dreams to fill.'

So on space ship, whatever I 'magined, all purple robes ready and black and white trainers, one pair on Daddy, not scuffed, not polished, but it still not right.

'Picnic time for Teddy Bears,' Lady Teddy Bear Alien sing.

Was hard to 'nore.

And stopped by pile of fallen logs. Auntie Binda looking me. Douglas too.

'Elle, my dear.'

Stood. Held, all in my knickers too much, held from, 'You know the Teddy Bears will be having a smashy time today.'

'Oh, Elle,' said Auntie Binda, look my piss stream.

'It's all in the prophecy,' say Lady Teddy Bear Alien.

What's proficy? asked' gain.

'Thelemic, from a Thelma,' she say.

What's Felma?

'Soon,' Douglas say.

And Blue Clanger Moon magicked past the window of space ship I not on, but was magined and could see Iron Chicken from Clangers cross road.

Auntie Binda helped take off wet knickers in woods, knickers in bag, washed hands wiv dock leaves.

Lookin' all around for bears come.

Only Blackberries, but still could be hiding.

'You know, I like that lovely Mr. Presley too,' said, Auntie Binda, come me.

'Really?'

'Yes, Mr. Elvis Presley. Love me tender, love me long. Take me to your heart.'

Steve Porter

'Really, really.'
'Yes, dear
We sang togever then, picked blackberries. Marigold gloves made safe. Not pricked. I loved Auntie Binda.
Gone a bit, Lady Teddy Bear Alien, then. Good. Hoped lost in space. I loved my gone Mummy too, maybe to space ship of Felma's proficy – Who is she? – to escape all the shouting.
Is that in Bernard's?
'Elle dear,' said Auntie Binda.
'Yeah.'
'You know we shouldn't lead our lives just through songs. For you must know Elle. It's impossible for every bear that ever there was, to come down to the woods today.'
's'not. Lady Teddy Bear Alien comes in dreams loud, says bad things about Mummy, bout eating capisools and supposed to make shouty go away, wiv Lady Teddy Bear Alien, not nice no more.'
Auntie Binda sad face hugged me. Liked it lots.
'No dear, don't you see. If, at six-o'-clock, their mummies and daddies come to take them to bed, then all the bears that ever there was, can't be there, can they? Their mummies and daddies have to come from somewhere else to collect them.'
'But...'
'And if their mummies and daddies aren't there, then the Lady Teddy Bear Alien ghost-bears can't be there either. How can such a little wood take all the bears that ever there was?'
'She's right,' said Stewart, oldest, cleverst.
'But...'
Polly ran over, dropping blackberries.
'Look, I've filled my Tupperware.'

Lady Teddy Bear Alien, asked me when in space ship, way past blue Clanger moon, on course to great Bear: 'What's a pie like?'
Was what got Daddy on the space ship.
Membered, back at Auntie Binda's, rolled out pastry. Pushed down, pulled out. Pulled sticky dough fingers. Licked.
I asked Lady Teddy Bear Alien, back, 'Why you keep tell me I should I love Daddy not love Mummy?

Great Bear, outside, not that great, see. A few twinkle stars, all gavered, which if joined up would be dot to dot bear pic, only.

Lady Teddy Bear Alien said, 'Because your Daddy left me, when a child, wanted send me away, hurt me very bad.'

Rubbish, but belly tight from holding wee. Held. Held. Looked Auntie Binda. Smiled. Everything good, everything fine. To tell her. Tell her whole twoof.

Said to him, 'Daddy says, you is muchy like David from way back when.'

'I am David,' she say.

That was what wasn't right. Unnerstood then.

'Mustn't listen you,' said. 'Sospicious.'

With Mummy goes hospital gain times four. Daddy to work. Where me go? In day as well night, hear him, see him too on Telly window, coming for to carry me home, by the Great Bear, but little one there too.

'Ursa Minor,' 'splained Daddy had.

'Also known as the little bear, dipper,' said Douglas.

Was crackle on Telly window, like when Concorde flew over, or maybe a shootin star, like happened afore Jesus born.

'Or a Patrick Morgan comet.'

On plate at our table was only salad.

Lady Teddy Bear Alien say me. 'You all gonna go Cygnets Home. Auntie Annie, new Mother, House number three.

Not want new Mother, house free.

Saw it, then, on Telly window.

All us marching to Presley, wiv space ship 'corder watching. 'Oh, when the Saints...'

But never to march or cross road on own, or...

'You'll want to be in that number.'

'Di'n't!'

'Douglas's right, It is a comet,' said Lady Teddy Bear Alien. 'Bright as a pole star, like we all being pushed to it by the protons. Heard it from Fe-le-meen-ic prophecy.'

Douglas joined in 'bout what want, 'stead of salad.

'Sometimes sandwich, jam, sometime baked beans, toast. Not and never to spill on school blouse.'

His way to look after me.

But I fought suspicious, very.

'Wasn't my fault,' said. 'Just dripped.'

Best not tell lies,' said Lady Teddy Bear Alien.

And so the twoof, out.

But then, the other Teddy Bears, from ship, were coming. They come Teddy Bears to mashy smash me, like bears in wood, less I not love Mummy and help Daddy get past, new ostacle in space.

What ostacle?

Pole star pushing us with its protons, said Daddy, like...

'We're caught in a trap. Can't get out.'

But Daddy never sunged before. Hummed bit and doop dooped, sometimes, twiddling his nose.

Di'n't know whether believe or not.

The bears, great and little, then, dipped, poled, and all ganging up, coming for my dinner, even though we nowhere near the woods.

'We want picnic, we want pie, blackberry.'

Had do sommink.

Like whassit, Daddy's Daddy, say, write book about, comets, but I di'n't know about fings like that. Knew about Tinkerbell.

Fairy costume up, fairy costume down family, was there on swings again and if could get up there with her, in space, wiv the starry starry's, swing off swings.

Polly not want come.

So went 'lone.

'Sure.'

Youngest gave up swing.

I swang and I swang, forward, backwards, try get right height, hard. Knew if let go at right time, would fly up, up, and Tinkerbell would tell me.

Down, legs behind, hold on and lean back, as pull into swing like seen oldest fairy costume girl do earlier and up, up.

'Stop that, this instant.' Was Polly, wiv voice like Mummy.'
'You'll hurt yourself.'

Did, told.

Just a bit dirty when I falled off.
Muddy skirt.
Lady Teddy Bear Alien larfed.
Tinkerbell cry for me, bout me not yet come.

Daddy said must I bring washing to Auntie Annie.
Lady Teddy Bear Alien tol' me. 'Must put it all in. All the piss and shit, so in the 'sheen to show what happens when Mummies leave and Daddies not able cope with all and what Mummy said from Bernard's, bout naughty letter from Auntie Binda.
'I am just taking them for a bath.'
'Elle, did you do this?' asked Auntie Annie
'Lady Teddy Bear Alien said to,' I tol'.
'A Lady Teddy Bear Alien, you say, Elle? But why did you smear it over the walls and the front of the washing machine?'
'Dunno.'
'Bad girl,' say Lady Teddy Bear Alien. 'Very bad, awful, trying to muck it all up in the Saturn and against God!'
Was how we all got kicked out of Cygnets. never to go again.
Got a Paddington though. Present. Auntie Annie.

Big meeting! Auntie Annie had called Child Psybologist.
'Never done, Daddy,' said me. 'Never seen washing machines with space ship windows, like that and don't know nuffink of fel-a-meen-ic.'
'You lying,' said Douglas. 'You did do it, Elle. I saw.'
'Di'n't.'
Teddy Bears, all ganging up again on Telly window, as the Pole Star called.
'Did!'
Douglas right. Mustn't tell lies. Get beat up by Teddy bears. Me got us kicked out of Cygnets for all piss and shit wiped on washing machine, for fear of smashy and not want find fel-a-meen-ic, with Daddy, like Lady Teddy Bear Alien want.

Not so much, in next home. Not Daddy's fault, not Mummy's neiver. Just too 'spensive marmalade fick of fin and peanut butter too squodgy bad for teef, like Daddy and so Paddington had to do not wiv.

'No.' Was Lady Teddy Bear Alien back again. 'Was cos your Daddy really di'n't care. That's why you should send him to me. Put the ship back on course.'

How?

Daddy knocked big door. Women, Carmen, 'welcome.' Funny hat, purple robes, white and black, Nike trainers, what's all part of great cafflick plan, without orange marmalade. Was Nazareth House.

'Go away then,' said Douglas, 'leave us, here. Go back to your David.'

Him again.

Then Sister Magnificence.

'No piss and shit, Elle,' Daddy said me, as getting into Uncle Mick's Robin Reliant.

'Not thin cut?' asked Paddington, or was it me?

Marched by Carmen, Sister Magnificence, double-quick past all the other children, and a bad one, like me, must be. Sawed it on the telly window. Bad one, him, me out there, wiv all the Teddy Bears ready to mashy smash us, like say in proficy.

What is proficy?

Lady Teddy Bear Alien larfing.

'As if Paddington could defend you, or Douglas?'

Later, but not much, bad one on wood-slatted bench, asking.

'You got it, then?'

Me, 'What?'

'The orange. If not, teddy bears will really come and we all proper punished.'

Hold. Hold.

Douglas not there, holding hand, mine. Had to make bed with fold corner sheets, not polyester.

'Oh, well. I is Leeky. This my place.

'The toilet?'

'Yes, where they put all wetters like us in the long night.'

'Oh!'

Was glad to have a new friend.

Was very glad in deed.

Morning. Breakfast. Shitty shat in queue for no toast and really bad, burnt sausages.

Cos my Daddy can't cope, with Mummy taking sixty, pop, pop, pills to Bernard's, space ship, where Mummy must have tooked off to, Douglas, say.

Leeky bad one, called, unnerstood. Him have no parents, too. 'bandoned.

'Like me,' says.

'Stop that chatter.' Sister Magnificence shouting.

Marmalade nowhere.

'Not good here, Nazareth,' says Leeky. 'Not good, for make sense or money. Silly cafflick plan.

I see Teddy Bears coming 'gain.

'You sing?' asked Leeky.

'Sing?'

Wiv Elvis lonesome song, not work, try 'The Lord is my Leeky, I not want.' But he says I am rubbish and all out of toon.

'Who cares.'

'You are right,' he says, 'who ever cares 'bout us.'

Sister Magnificence ladling beans. 'This is what happens when you leave your Daddy, or your Daddy leaves you. Elle Porter, will you stop banging your head on the table.'

'Where Magaluf born,' 'parently,' said Polly, when went home for weekends, and all will go back to her and Mrs Byatt in the long night, if we eat all breakfasts and be good children.

This fore she sent Skylark to good for nothing, place, bin.

'Wanna dance?'

'No.'

Di'n't want dance wiv her what binned Skylark!

Lady Teddy Bear Alien back at Nazareth say not to be good children, 'you must both get away, to take control space ship polyester wing fings, your Daddy needs to come. You must run to the White House, where Sister Mary is.'

Wasn't really sure was right to do, but Leeky said, Sister Mary was sometimes good with cakes, special ingredients. Sometimes even marmalade.

So when back from school, to be bad, like Leeky said, run wiv him, Douglas and we dun it runned so fast cross grass to Sister Mary's big white house.

Arrived and Sister Mary outside, finger on lips.

'Don't tell Sister Magnificence.'

'Are you kind? asked Sister Mary?' 'Do you cake?'

She larfed, nods, called us in.

Squidging dough in her hand, giving Douglas first, then me.

'I could be,' she said.

Then came out marmalade. Real, orange, fick cut. Paddington desperate, jump out my pinny pocket to hug her.

Spread over her cake base. Then gift Douglas, me, spoons.

'It's what it might be like in heaven, past the tall gates, as truth as proficy wanting self-will, love all part of Cafflick plan.

'Oh, you know that as well,' said Douglas.

'Doesn't everyone?'

On the telly window, in corner of kitchen, Dad scared, in Stewart's space ship, polyester wings not flapping

Why not? Should.

Him staring out of window at all the bears coming. Lady Teddy Bear Alien in lead, some one eye, others, half a leg. Muttled fur, ears hanging off and some with no button eyes, cos all falled off in bath.

'We want our picnic!' Them shout. 'Marmalade!'

And 'for Mash Get Smash.'

Pick up sticky dough, give Douglas clod and run outside, throwed it

'WE WANT OUR PICNIC!'

All lumps marmalade too, fast hurtling, like comets, 'gainst space ship behind, to mashy smash up all the bears in the grounds of Nazareth wivout belts or shoelaces but wiv sticky marmalade goo. Paddington frew the most.

Weren't bears really, was Carmen wiv Sister Magnificence, and she, them not best pleased, at all.

'You will stop that, now. Or I'll get Father O'Shaugnessy to ban you from Communion.'

We hear from Carmen that Mummy coming home and if we could be ready by tomorrow night six pm sharpish.

Daddy, 'parently, had offered Carmen Milky Way.

'Take that away,' she had said, 'no, give it back. I am going to give it to your children, as you should have done.'

'That's my Daddy,' I say. 'Don't rude, my Daddy.' Well, would said, if, wasn't other side door in space ship.

Diclas.

Six pm sharpish, we are on top of the climbing frame and Douglas on slide. We stare over the big walls, looking for Uncle Mick's white Robin Reliant.

Lady Teddy Bear Alien said, 'Best get inside, your Daddy won't come. Don't believe in him. Don't trust. Was him 'bandoned you Nazareth, first place, cos you bad, very bad and awful and don't deserve your Daddy. Him for me.'

The cars move fast on road, faster than eyes, but Douglas says just look at the colours and they are easier to follow.

Blue ones, red ones, one even pink and then a white one. Look. Look.'

'No Elle, wrong shape. That's a Cortina.'

I put on my mittens.

'Oh, when the Saints,' I sing.

That would make it good, fought.

Douglas shaked head.

'Come marching in.'

'There a white one, and is a white one, but is...'

'It's a Robin Reliant alright,' says Douglas, pointing. 'It's them! It's them!'

Good and hope for not bad for him.

I see the white too, travelling down to the roundabout, slowing down, turning, as I jump up and down, turning the wrong way.

'Bastards,' says Douglas.

'Oh, when the Saints come marching in.'

White-and-black Nike'd Carmen comes out.

'Sister Magnificence says, you' catch your death if you don't come inside.'

'Then, we'll catch our deaths,' say Douglas.

We sit cold, silence, peering, looking for the Robin.

Sing, Blue Moon, make better.

'Elle,' says Douglas.

'Yes.'

'Shut up.'

Lady Teddy Bear Alien 'peated best go inside. 'Your Daddy not coming, you 'bandoned, just like she was and Leeky, way of world for bad ones, not can control ship proper, fraid.'

But if I stared hard enough. Wrong way around the roundabout and then Douglas, pointing again.

'It is. I know it. It's them.'

After the little Robin car turned the right way around the roundabout and made its way past the gates, Nazareth.

'Porters,' says Carmen. 'Sister Magnificence wants you in the hallway double-quick fast, or you get slap.'

At home proper, Daddy's black leather swivel chair, taken over by lump, Mummy, fat, stuck out teeth dribbled down mouth, with mouldy eyes.

Lady Teddy Bear Alien 'splained, 'Your Mummy must be very sick! Better back on Saturn, with the wings, send your Daddy back on proper course to Blue Moon. Help he deal with guilt, stead, for sending you away, on ship, like he did me?'

Told her, 'I would not, cos I loves everyone and all and don't want anyone go. Is my will. Fe-l-a-meen-ic, as Douglas say.

Auntie Binda, behind door.

'Hannah, I have bought your children.'

In pushed.

From eyes with fat pillow-bags Mummy looked up, grunted.

'Hello, poppets,' but sunk into black leather swivel-chair, face like ghost. 'Take them away. Too tired.'

Auntie Binda pulled us way.

'Anyone for pie?'

On Saturn controls set for moon, polyester wings turn.

When not wanted by Mummy, 'nopoly, kitchen table.

Stewart wanted banker. But Polly wanted too.

'Never,' said Stewart, 'She's a thief.'

Auntie Binda is banker.

All shook up, the dice.

Polly shook head.

'Chance a fine thing,' Douglas back.

'No, it's not,' Stewart's eyes angry.

'Will you be quiet, the lot of you,' Mummy shout.

Lady Teddy Bear Alien turned me then.

'Stop banging your head on the table and press button to advance beyond go.

My piss back.

'Elle!

Button space ship prest then. Whoosh!

Big concerns for me, new school for can't unnerstand, 'sept that could, that when Mummy, coming out of in toilet, at psybologist room, private, Mummy said me, 'I need to leave your Daddy or will be dead if I don't.'

'Why she tell you outside a toilet?' asked my new friend, boy met on bus, Pete, innit

Di'n't know.

'Pleased to meet you, I am sure.'.

Yes. Marjory Kinnon my new school. Got bus all the way. Picked up Raleigh way. Pete. Innit, always on bus. Very council house, like Mummy say, but salty earth too.

Lady Teddy Bear Alien say all must out Saturn, now landed.

Had we, when? Fought was in bus.

Polyester wings retracted.

Learning lots, already at new school.

'You new?' Had to listen hard, but got it, end.

'I Elle.'

Pete, innit, smiled me 'gain.

'No, I mean are you new? Don't look like you know about the light here'.

The light in Marjory Kinnon brightin up the Puff Dragon, and all-over hanging things from ceiling, by tall gates.

'I have a sister and two brothers, a cat and a Mum and Dad,

but Mum in a hospital for pill taking sixty. Polly too, maybe. Am Elle, me.'

'Pete, innit,' asks, 'know anyfing about Marjory Kinnon?' Di'n't.

In class, in playground, in lunch hall there was no clue. Who was Marjory Kinnon? What she do for me?

'Is she ghost? I asked Pete.

'Who?'

'Marjory Kinnon?'

'Dunno.'

I learnt be frighted of ghosts, what heard and not seen.

We ran around playground to find about Marjory Kinnon.

Lady Teddy Bear Alien, 'What about your daddy?'

'Are you Marjory Kinnon?' asked Pete, innit.

'No, I'm Jimmy Butler. Why that man not wanna come out that space ship?'

Looked him down and up. Di'n't look like no kid from council house.

Pete, innit, was looked at other boys playing ball foot soccar.

'What man?'

'Come on, Pete, innit. Before it's free o' clock and school ends, day.

Nuffink bout Marjory in the toilets, classroom, nor in the cloakroom. What is cloakroom? Why have a room for cloaks? Is it purple?

'Dunno either,' said Pete, innit. 'You have lots questions.'

'Marjory, Marjora,' I asked again. Hope she would hear. 'Marjory Kinnon, where you are? Need you teach me unnerstand all fings, like a Felma.'

No answer.

Great windows too, nearly open to show all light.'

Pete, innit, called me to one wiv wavy hands.

Was Lady Teddy Bear Alien throwing her arms about, from the other side of the window, her gescuring, to great bear, bright light and tall gates.

And song sung being.

'Oh, for the wings...'

Was an angel and she had wings pulled off by rest of Teddy

Bears for not being ever good enough. Or was it a Lady Teddy Bear Alien?

There was party, like picnic. All there, friends, bears, even Tingle, chasing 'maginary hedgehogs. Stewart had put his record player downstairs in the garden. Speakers, 'don't trip over the wires' too. Douglas did trip, but that was ok, cos he'd dugged a line in the grass then for wires, with his insoles, naughty, so deserved. Polly had got all the food. Bottles and bottles and bottles of Tizer. Crisps. Sarnies. Pilchards, pork pies, lettuce and salad cream. Real Angel Delight.

Lady Teddy Bear Alien still tryin' get Daddy out Saturn, somewhere. Forgot, by then.

Sullivan boys first, picking out the songs. Michael and Alistair. Polly liked Alistair. I not s'posed to know. Wore best tart top, she did. I not allowed.

Polly still thought she the Mummy.

And Alistair and Michael Sullivan were wide boys, said. But Stewart said they was Teddy Boys really. Leather jackets, like Grease, and all.

And Presley, afore.

'You ain't a nuffink but a hound dog.'

'Is that why your hair looks like a duck's arse?'

Them larf, then off to place beer on the table from kitchen, by the hedgehog graves of years gone.

Them picked their songs of Summer luvvin, me picked Elvis. Love me tender. Stewart. Tol' if I could keep a tune, I, could sing along too.

Fiona was nearly not dressed. Ginny gave cardigan. Melissa, Stewart's sweetie, with screaming eyes back her.

'What Mama, and why she killed a man.'

Douglas not happy, Fiona with another. Gumphing about the garden, with the bears, wearing Douglas Sullivan's jacket, wot stole. Alistair was very wiv Polly, when played Major Tom, what Lady Teddy Bear Alien couldn't unnerstand, nor Daddy, still in space ship, holding on to clasps and refusing to come out, him never heard of Major Tom.

Polly nearly got a kiss.

All the other bears were there too, fancy dress, from earlier picnic, so 'Say, Oops upside your head'. Everyone ran to sit in straight line, then two, with Stewart eldest in front, line one. Ginny in front Girls, line two. Lean bob to left, straight, bob and shimmy, straight, then bob to the beat very fast.

Polly, getting ready then.

Arms up.

Ginny knocked Douglas's drink all over Alistair's jacket.

'Di'n't mean that he di'n't want to.'

Daddy pull back from Lady Teddy Bear Alien, still try yank out from landed Saturn.

Douglas carried on, smiled back, showing gap in front tooth, when it got knocked out, bang, in mouldy-green shed.

Ginny looked away.

Daddy appeared window of ship. Him hand raised and waving.'Oh, excuse me, Stewart. Could we have the noise down, just a little?'

Hard to hear him frew window.

Noise up, Stewart done.

Wanted go Daddy, then, to rescue him.

Polly shook her head.

'He has to go and get the Swiss rolls, soon for Major Tom, and if you rescue him, he won't be able to get them for you.'

So di'n't. Swiss rolls was very 'portant.

'Stead fought I'd serve the rest of picnic food made by Clanger Soup Dragon.

Picked up plates with Pork Pies, crisps, sarnies, pilchards. Lots of dolloped salad cream. Took plates round, helpful. Make everyone happy.

Tony threw his lettuce leaves onto poor Tingle, who left in mighty fast big hurry, salad cream smear her back of fur.

'Are you lonesome tonight?'

Stewart winked. It was his party, membered, then. Was Seventeen.

I ran over, snatched mic from his hand.

'And I love you so.'

Looked Stewart, for reaction, approve for my singing toon. Tried very hard.

Stewart smile.

'Look up,' said Lady Teddy Bear Alien.

Was going to, 'spected to see Daddy with swiss rolls, but...

'Go on girl. You sing it how it is.' That was Polly's Alistair.

Not pleased, Polly. Alistair talk me, not her.

Still no Daddy. Ran to Saturn to find. Him not there. Saturn not there. Must behind the clouds. Then to kitchen window. Jumped up to see clock. It was seven o'clock. S'posed to be her by now, surprise, but nowhere near look like coming.

Where my Daddy?

The Birdy Song they were all doing it, the bears very good. Me, not, di'n't have mind. Nor to that one about stayin alive, wiv your muvver and bruvvers.

Polly grabbed my hand, pulled me to dance. We did tweet, tweet, with hands and a shake my arse, dum, dum, dum, dum.

Lady Teddy Bear Alien said, it were enough to get Inspector Mansfield round, such a dreadful man. I told her, 'Shsh.'

Was shshed.

Maybe Daddy shut her up too, from up in gallery.

What gallery?

No time. It were Ginny that came.

'Elle, you have a visitor, some skinhead at your front door.'

I ran to the back door, tore through house and there he was.

Pete, innit!

First, I introduced him to Polly.

'My friend, Pete, innit, from Marjory Kinnon.'

He smiled held out hand like gentles man.

'Is this your...'

Douglas stepped over, slim-barged between us, then took Pete, innit off.

'I'm Elle's brother.'

'What 'bout your Daddy and the gallery?' Lady Teddy Bear Alien was hardly heard over shouts from the teenagers.

'We want Abba. We want Abba. Bee Gees rule.'

'No, Presley!'

Was this my chance?

Dancing Queen good, but couldn't member words. All the bears that were there, thinking a great picnic, stuffing furry moths, too dancing, Bee Gees too high for my voice and Pete's, but could mime, like Mum did when practicing Stewart for Peter Pan. Did good.

Douglas dunna conga.

'No, let's do it, like he does, spaz-crawl.'

Couldn't hear Lady Teddy Bear Alien, see Daddy neiver.

Everyone joined in and all strange walks from everyone in long line.

Douglas was laughing, so I was laughing and Pete, innit, doing as told, joined in.

Then through what like clouds, above, the gallery, Dad. A comet, with something behind, heading towards.

The record started.

Pete, innit, grabbed me. Arms.

It were all together then, us. Him holding my hand.

'Is that,' said Polly

Lady Teddy Bear Alien, in front of gallery, hand beckon Daddy to her.

Was not s'posed be moochy song.

'It is,' said Polly.

Then she shouted loud . 'Elle's got a boyfriend. Elle's got a boyfriend!'

And then from the side, by the mouldy-green shed, a shadow appeared, silwette, so Polly called it like from *She* magazine. *Muvers away from Their Children*, writed, by A.E. Porter, Stewart tol' me. But this time at party she weren't away, she was right here with us, big, all redded up in face and toofy.

'Oh, for the wings, oh the wings of a...'

All the bears and Polly, Stewart, the Sullivan boys looked.

'What's all this then?' asked, Mummy, changing the subject.

Was not going to be good, Lady Teddy Bear Alien, warned, she could tell, and most others could tell too, standing there, complete silence, as Mummy opened mouth, with red eyes.

But she di'n't say anything, she pointed up to clouds in sky, looking gormless like 'afore when lecified, at what looked like a boy, short trousers and shadow, like one from Nazareth really, then a desk.

The sound of a gavel bang.

They di'n't believe in bible like Daddy, the Gaters, but did believe in other fings.

'It's all about your graduation from the above human evolutionary level.'

The bears were all sitting there in Babel clouds gallery, licking marmalade from their furry mouths, listen to Pete, innit, on way to new 'sistance was through a space ship behind a big Halley comet.

'Really.'

Sure, Polyiamide film, 'terrupted, Lady Teddy Bear Alien

Daddy interested more.

'You mean like with the craft to get through the gate?'

'Yes,' said Pete, innit, 'and wearing black and white trainers, covered over in purple robes before they to do them suicide cos their lonely.'

'Like on the telly,' said Daddy.

'Like on the telly, Mr. Porter.' Was my Pete innit.

Daddy looked sad.

'Is not your fault, Daddy,' I said, 'and you don't have to go with Lady Teddy Bear Alien, if you don't want to.

Lady Teddy Bear Alien glare then, me.

'But he needs the love,' say Pete, innit, 'say's so in prophecy, if David to be free, Elle. I have thought it all out and we agree.'

The bears, seemed, couldn't care less.

'We do,' I said.

Daddy in his black leather swivel.

But what is the Felma, I ask.

Answer come from voice singing up the stairs.

'Mmm, ee, ayy, ahh, ooh.'

Daddy says, 'she is not to be blame and not her fault neiver.

'I am happy to hear you say so.'

That Mummy, not the Felma!

The bears started to fidget when Lady Teddy Bear Alien talking on about, 'Oh, the next above human evolutionary level to take. A just punishment for all your time spent 'voiding David and the space ship, or any way to get to him in the wake of a big comet and 'norin' all your children.

'Never did,' I said him.

And Douglas get out his book again. 'Is will of Thelma,' he said. 'It is all written in my Workbook

Daddy looked, like he finking, then worried, as Pete, innit, smile me.

'But Elle, you can't leave me and go off with Pete, what will happen to me?'

'Is right', I said. 'Got Tingle Three.'

Pete, innit, pick her up, put her on Daddy's lap.

'Don't worry,' Pete, innit, said. 'I'll look after her. I'll look after her Mr. Porter.'

Daddy got up, upset then, walked to door, all snivels, opened and started to leave.

Teddy Bears follow him, as Mummy took her space, in front of desk, wiv two friends. One of them Auntie Edna, old neighbour, when me very small.

'Auntie, it's me.'

But Auntie Edna not listen, nor boy and Pete, innit, off too, what wiv space ship diss'pear behind clouds and me all alone, not unnerstand everyfing, so ate a plate of mashy smash, as two wings of dove fly past, till Lady Teddy Bear Alien gone, turned into a new woman and that was what a Felma was, angel woman for Dad, which was when I unnerstand all what love tender, about, not what happened wiv Disco man.

'Will Police do me for banging da man's Noddy fing like I done after disco?' Me asked Pete, innit. 'Cos he runned and runned off after like him running from all Teddy Bears that could ever be in woods.'

'What are you, some kind of mental?' him say.

Pete, innit, said I 'could not be asponsible, chance be fine fing, anyway. Probly police nick 'im for being bastard.'

'You fink?'

'Yea, I fink, Elle.

'Hold my hand.'

Him do it.

It all alright then, and when I visit Dad for Poll Tax, get him do summink good for him daughter.

Portergeist

Steve Porter

THELMA

So, that was Michael and the children. Well, as much as David and I could drag out from them. They were young, muddled by childish things. Or at least they were not getting it enough to bring about the adventure that David sought, needed and tried to manipulate them to provide.

But despite this and their problems, the children believed that they had, in fact, moved mountains or even spacecraft to bring Michael to the yellow-bricked fiery wake.

They argued that each had created their own adventure or journey, even if it might have sometimes been in flights of fancy and not always in the physical realm.

They also understood this was always possible when Babel and the will of "M" were involved.

David still should have warned them. It wasn't as though he didn't suspect something like this might occur.

But not even David could have conceived of the possibility that Michael's children would have reacted by placing their father behind bars – or, properly speaking, as "M" pointed out to me, railings around the top of the upstairs gallery – to stop any of them from falling out and joining David in the wake?

They had been so determined to use their journeys to protect against such a fate and fight back against the call of the fiery wake.

Michael had been complicit in this, too. His point-blank refusal, for instance, to join with David, preferring Concorde and the moral certainty of his Christianity to defend against anything that would stand in the way of his giving into any kind of hasty departure.

With Douglas, for instance, the wanted escape from Shed Boy was deeply insulting to David. How much time had he put into that? Especially with the fates or this so-called 'will' that Douglas kept on about, which would have meant that I was always going to be responsible.

How did he know?

And Polly's search for her truth, against the will of her Magaluf's teachings, was also a little too predictable.

Like her mother before, she refused to play in the Generation Game, knowing she was going to lose, but she still stuck around, as defiant as a debutante who never made the grade, even if she did fear becoming like an Admiral's granddaughter, with all the entitlement that came with this.

It had all contributed to David's ploy of bringing me in.

And more, that Fonda woman, Bertrand Russell, nor Billy Graham were surprised that David had to ask for my help. Billy even offered assistance with his interpretation of the last part of the bible through his own monitor.

But how did David know that I could provide this much-needed help? I certainly hadn't so far.

But of course, this could have been another example of David's trickery, as the children were supposed to interpret, and the problem with this was that it was not entirely devoid of sense.

Mona did have a presence in the real world, to which her many films could attest, or was that make-believe, too?

A world, his life, perhaps made up for the children to enjoy because Michael certainly hadn't enjoyed what the fates had bought for any of them so far.

Like with Douglas's fight to make sense of it all in the prophecy, that must have been the truth because they heard about it at the Synod that David invited me to attend.

Stewart's ship might have descended, bringing the final piece of the puzzle to secure my participation in this scheme of his, but it might just as well have Polly's Skylark, I wasn't really sure, what had caused my compliance.

As far as I can remember, no one much cared, and even when I offered them the option of Star Wars to explain, possibly with Darth Vader at the helm, most of the court of "M" didn't seem to know anything about it, and the children were otherwise engaged, too.

'Just another fairy tale,' said Michael.

Of course, he was referring to the engineering impossibilities displayed by some of those ships, what with all their unexplained jumping.

Stewart's interest was only in how it might help him escape.

There was a resultant sonic boom as the bottom of the ship broke through the clouds, and it wasn't from a ship that looked anything like Michael's Saturn/Concorde.

But Elle's journey away from the Space Aliens of Smash or her Teddy Bears, which she finally confronted and triumphed in by lobbing globs of marmalade at them and largely missing, was a whole other order of things to consider.

A television was in the corner of the gallery, and a parade was showing on the screen.

From that, *Steptoe and Son's* Wilfred Brambell was up front with his cup, still trying to worm his way into the affections of that same wanna-be Mona Freeman from the Streatham High Road before she fell from grace and found Perry Mason.

The children mostly didn't appear to care or let on much, apart from a glimmer of recognition from Douglas when T and Dough acted out a story from relief at Tickencote with Mr Fergusson conducting the affairs.

But Polly soon put paid to all that, insisting Douglas pay her some attention to the wash basin painted in the colours of Rhubarb and Custard.

'Why can't I wash your feet,' she asked. 'You have the same stumpy toes, and if you would let me, then it would be just the same as doing Daddy so I could get him ready for the Skylark.

The ship with the frog-foot landing struts landed by the Kentucky Fried Chicken stand at the end of the yellow brick fiery wake, leaning over a bit, with its tip pointing towards Babel as though to announce something.

Everyone was waiting, looking for the door to the craft, which an expert must have crafted because there were no observable seals surrounding anything resembling a door or a hatch, and neither was there a cockpit or any windows at all.

The door didn't open.

The screen was more interesting than what Douglas was trying to pass around to the children, who were still behind the rails with Michael.

'But it's the prophecy. The prophecy of Thelma, as revealed, I tell you!'

And I had come, ready to bring about the next part with Stewart as the next victim, or so the bishop announced.

'Charging away from all responsibility on his Chopper bike to get to Melissa and Bob.

And as he arrived at the great horror of a Saturn Space ship, one forty-fourth of the actual sizes, Stewart knew because I had conceived of it and Bob had built it.

Elle was next on the ship with Michael, singing her way past the Clanger blue moon. She was particularly excited by the sight of the Iron Chicken below crossing the road to enjoy one of Auntie Binda's hugs and a warm hug of love.

The Babel People, in response, put on a welcome party, with Delius's music competing with a funked-up version, using Electrostatic speakers of 'How Great Thou Art.'

The nuns, led by Fonda, swayed, and Billy Graham bought out the table and a silver gavel.

As I was hiding in the shadows of the Kentucky Fried Chicken stand, Bertrand Russell worked out how Michael would appear.

Moneypenny typed out a notice so that all could fully understand properly.

'He will beam down. It is written.'

And then, when Tinkerbell flitted across the sky on a broomstick, the screen that the children and Michael were watching started to bulge outwards as though in that very minute was quite ready to burst.

When it did burst, the shimmering presentation of a person appeared, tall, a little bulbous about the waste.

It was Elle who said it.

'Mum, is that you?'

Of course, David needed me to assist. I could see that, for how could any mortal stand up to and defend against my...

'Of course, it's me!'

'So you're back then?'

'I am here.'

So this was Hannah? I wondered how well I would fare.

Steve Porter

HANNAH

A small leather jacket, fairy costume, up and down skirt, purple painted nails – how individual! And she didn't even have any wings – a lesser angel, obviously – not yet graduated from finishing school. It wasn't as though she deserved any respect.

She sat behind a large desk in what looked like the middle of nowhere. The smoke of the ship's earlier journey, stretching out in a disappearing fiery wake before us, an empty gallery above, as though resting entirely on a cloud. A couple of doors in front of the table, two chairs, empty, and a small piece of pavement on which I was supposed to stand. I had no chair. It was obviously set up this way to intimidate me – a state of mind I could not allow.

'Yes, well, now I really need you to listen to me,' I said. 'And listen well.'

The lady picked up a silver gavel from the table in front of her, inspected it and the receipt.

'Why? Oh, look at that. Is it really nineteen eighty-nine in your world?' she asked.

Was she actually back-chatting me?

'Why? Your Honour.' I immediately responded. 'So you can learn how, just like it never worked when you tried to take over their lives with that silly spaceship, that none of your silliness is going to work with me!'

Judge Thelma seemed suitably surprised – astonished even.

Then the door to the left opened, not fully, just like they did in St Bernard's, before we were to be admitted for our latest medication privileges.

The sound of a banged gavel.

'Let the investigations begin,' she said, to her Nurse Minion and myself. It was with a surprising authority and it rather woke me up.

'You will attend the chambers of both the defence advocate and the court liaison,' she ordered, 'to prepare for the hearing, on the charge of preventing Michael from finding David in the light, as soon as I have dealt with this prophecy thingy that everyone seems to be going on about.'

So that was what this was? A hearing. And so soon, after the space journey past Venus on Elle and Stewart's, Saturn.

Obviously, it was a game.

Yes, and why not?

'Did you learn all that from finishing school?' I joined in. I hear they play some very decent games in finishing school. I preferred hockey and was quite good at it. I even won awards.' Because, as I had learnt from my 'Froebel' training, and from my interactions with all the others on the locked ward, that it never hurts to engage, and in this place, it might even help me to understand just that little bit more about what was happening to me now and why.

As Judge Thelma looked at me, I smiled at her. She seemed a little too authoritative though, for an angel.

And I too could well imagine the voices that she would come up with too. Interesting, possibly even quite persuasive. Worthy of my consideration, at least. To help me determine how I might be able to wrest back at least a little control for myself.

The Nurse Minion pointed away from the table to a couple of doors.

'Well, it's Mogodon, Valium and Paracetamol, for you dear, later. Professor Weaver has just had a visit from the Pharmaceutical company.'

Inside was Edna's room, Edna Bone, and just like it was before.

Seagull-flocked wallpaper, nineteen fifties star-designed curtains, a makeshift kitchen with a plug-in hob, sideboard, immersion heater, a surprisingly modern front-loader instead of a twin-tub and a plastic draining board.

It was so realistic. She was standing there, Edna, in the same cleaner's overall that she had always worn, holding my rather tired looking Viking Statuette present from Michael.

The room hadn't changed much since Michael and I had first graced Sandycombe Road all those years ago, after we'd just had Stewart.

Lovely boy. Full of promise, my Stewart.

'Where do you want me to put this?' she asked.

Michael had given me the statuette as a birthday present before – well, that bath! But this was neither the time or the place to remember all that.

'Over there on the dresser.'

I was sat in the wicker chair, creaking with as much foreboding as the stare in the Viking Statuette's glassy s eyes. It looked like an avatar for Joyce Grenfell, with its hair-bun between horns.

'I thank you.'

And to think she, Mother had once been put forward as a debutante! Until it was made clear to the world from the bulge in her belly of me, that she had badly transgressed. A shotgun wedding had been hastily arranged.

Edna placed the statuette to give it a clear view of the whole room – she turned, the curls of her hair slapping against her ears.

She had become so old.

'Well, I'm going to look after you now, dear,' she said, 'you know, like a friend, someone to take your side against anything they may throw at you.'

Well, this was all very nice, and really quite refreshing, given... but...

'Who's they?' I asked, wondering if she knew that I was a part of the game too and therefore really did need to understand the rules and the participants.

There was no bang from outside the window of the room. There was no bell, no gavel-producing, judgement, or even acknowledgement of my recognition of the antics that Judge Thelma might be getting up to outside.

Edna didn't respond.

And even though the room was hardly fitting for me, being the granddaughter of an admiral, or in fact a suitable abode for how I imagined a would-be prosecutor to live in, I wasn't displeased. In fact, I found it rather appropriate, in a humbling, punishing, sort of way, given what I had done. My makeshift bed laid out ready, the prayer cushions and list of tasks so as not to stray from my resolve to carry this through.

'After all, if a mother has left her children,' continued Edna, 'then she must have done it for a good reason. How are they, by the way?'

The Viking Statuette just sat there!

'Oh, so, so. Coping, you know,' I indulged her enquiry. 'And thank you for letting me come, Edna. You know, I really had nowhere else to go.'

'Yes, well, you must learn to walk about it all with your head, up, up, up,' she said.

I enjoyed Edna's accommodations. Despite her common presentation – a bit like Brenda, really – she at least knew the importance of friendship and of a proper deportment.

The statuette was still in silent witness to the guilt I was supposed to feel about my being here, instead of with my children, were I to accept this. For I had to remember Thelma outside and that anything I did, I knew, could and I was certain *would* be used in evidence against me.

'Are you alright, dear?'

'Perfectly, Edna.' I answered, determined not to slip-up, in any way at all.

At the bottom of one of the boxes I was unpacking, I found a child's drawing of a figure in a triangle skirt. One of Elle's. Oh, she was such a love. Were they horns coming out of the figure's head? Such imagination. Or maybe it was mine?

'Look,' I showed Edna. 'I'd forgotten all about this.'

It was of a time when the children were younger, more easily controlled, if I get my drift. Because there was no one else around at the time to get it for me.

'When you read, you begin with ABC,' I said, to change the tone a little.

Edna took the picture, studied it a while, smiled and hurried off to silence the whistling of the kettle on her small and rather tired Baby Belling oven.

'With, or without?' Edna asked as she fussed over the tea.

It was important to have a prosecutor who makes a quality cup of tea, I decided. Darjeeling was to be preferred, whether or not this came with a silver teaspoon and sugar lumps from Barker's. It was only what I deserved?

'Hannah?'

I turned.

'What was that about your ABC? Sounds a bit posh to me, the way you say it.'

For, is it not always better to educate the wanting, properly?

But Edna, it seemed, changed her mind and did not want to let me.

'Oh, silly me,' she said, 'I meant. I was asking you about your tea.'

'Oh, sure, Edna, without, please. I'm on a diet, these days. Fat, enormously, as a result of what I have done, obviously. Can't you see?'

Then the other door, where I found a much fancier apartment. Wandsworth, I had it when on approved leave from the hospital.

Mary's place. Mary Gilmore, or so it read on the door, who had the appearance of someone trying so hard to remain in her prime, only thirty years too late.

With an overly dramatic poise, she took position in her armless, brown-leather throne, or at least, that's how I was supposed to have seen it portrayed.

'My husband, Michael, has paid, I believe.'

Play the game.

But she seemed very young, I thought.

'Won't you sit, dear?'

She was supposed to be my therapist, this Mary, Court Liaison too. Apparently very bright. At least this is how she had been sold to me earlier, by Professor Weaver, my psychiatrist at

St Bernard's, who'd apparently only just appointed her.

'An intelligence that is beyond compare, Hannah, and understanding. So knowledgeable of the problems women have with men.'

That old chestnut.

'Well, if you insist!'

I took up my position, on the comfy chaise longue, opposite, remembering to sit up straight, cross my ankles and direct my knees straight at her, so as not to give anything away.

'Shall we?' She cocked her head. It was a definite Brodie-like gesture, completely within role. Professor Weaver had done well in choosing her.

'Of course, Michael doesn't really want to pay for anything, let alone my time with you,' I told her.

Thelma must have known I would seek to educate her. It was her way of getting me to reveal, as the game demanded.

She was right. 'But it is of course Michael's responsibility. I am his wife and very entitled!'

'You are entitled,' she came back, like she'd just stumbled upon her first possible therapeutic breakthrough. 'As a woman, you are entitled, and Michael's responsibility towards you is just as, or even more, important?'

'And duty. Giving us the ability to care?'

I smiled.

It was a good game. What the court would want. A means of determining if I was up to the required standard to be judged worthy enough?

Mary sat up and with a wave of her hand, like a royal, she gestured her invitation.

'Tell me of your schooling and your father,' she asked, as she handed me a plump cushion. I wasn't sure if it was a lack of practice, or was she just very nervous, as one would expect?

I took the cushion and let her ponder, question a little, on the inexperienced quality of her approach.

Poor thing.

But she was taking too long and I got a little bored. So I asked, in my best plaintive, mousy voice. 'Is there any hope?' It was a line that always worked with the other staff on the ward.

A smirk broke through her practiced, pursed-lipped, professional composure.

'So you seek to get away from your parents' lack of hope for you,' she returned, like she had just discovered something really important.

Well, I was not the type to dash down such enthusiasm, and anyway, as Professor Weaver at St Bernard's had said, I did need, at least, to try to trust someone.

'There was a letter,' I informed her. 'A letter, once, well, it was Christmas day actually, from my father, informing me, by way of a present, that I was an embarrassment to him, unworthy of being his daughter. And I would never get a job, I would stay like my mother, in the kitchen, killing all the old musical numbers and suffering, as all stuck-ups should. "I like a nice cup of tea in the..."'

I hoped that would do it for her.

'What, an intelligent woman, like ... Mensa, wasn't she, your mother?' Mary seemed so horrified at the very idea.

I shot her a disapproving look. It was my trump card. and her expression quickly changed back to how it should have been, if she were really in her prime and suitable enough to put together a culpable defence of me.

Silence.

I decided to play on this a little to tease out Mary some more. Not a sound. Just her stern, pursed and pedantic lips needing to be pierced a little.

I giggled, inwardly.

'So don't you feel sorry for me yet?'

I really shouldn't have asked this?

Again, nothing.

But I wanted and needed her to draw me out some more. It wouldn't hurt her to try.

'He would try to dismiss all my needs, my father,' I said, as much for myself, as for her, 'but I was not the lie, he wanted of me, as my children have recently been accusing me of living,' which, of course, I was sure had also been a part of Mary's briefing from Professor Weaver. To be the subject of a ward round in a mental hospital. Is this what my life had come to.

Mary, then visibly composed her expression to a genuine, enquiring respect of my situation. I was beginning to like and accept her for her effort.

'Your father never knew how to love you!'

But this was so definite that I wasn't sure if it was a question or a statement.

Mary looked up from her notes, her eyes like she had come to a vicar's conclusion on female clergy and what she was about to say was the only point worth considering for anyone in the congregation.

I didn't respond.

'He was a bad man, your father,' she continued, her lips trying to get back into a pout of a teenager, 'with his nasty clump, clump, clump, up the stairs, coming dreadfully for you.'

She paused.

She was obviously a little aware of how this unsettled me, so I thought I would help her to see this a little more, by pausing a little too. I'd been told it was quite the thing to do, when in therapy with one so young and obviously inexperienced and it was also the Christian thing to do.

A suitably long pause.

Then, 'Is that why you chose Michael,' she continued, 'because you thought he was at least as bad as your father and that was what you deserved?'

There it was. The substance of this meeting. Of the standard necessary for her to qualify for a therapeutic Mensa. Mother might have even taken her on as a project, if I had ever been able to introduce them.

They appeared. I didn't know if Mary was aware, or if she even cared. But I could see them, like two just rose branches sprouting from her temples. It was too far from reality from anything you'd normally expect from an obviously apprentice court liaison therapist, but she was trying and in a way the horns did have a purpose, like they could extract and distil all the hurt essence of love.

Honestly, the things, I had to put up with.

'I am a woman of my own mind', I said, to both soothe and stem the growth of them and my guilt. It had sometimes worked before, when I was with Michael.

But this time, back in the Wandsworth rooms, the horns were calling to me, calling for a little bit of attention, like Polly would, or Douglas. And I was quite unable to resist.

'Oh, and by the way, do you prick your fingers when you touch the tips of those horns of yours?'

For as it was, as the nurse at St Bernard's finishing school and Michael had much earlier accused me of living, there is always another reality by which to determine the rights and wrongs of defence advocates with growing rose branch horns.

I had nothing to fear though, such delusions were usually on my side, in St Bernard's, after a dose of electro-convulsive-therapy, or at least until then, they had been.

Was it still nineteen eighty-nine, or had I regressed again to an earlier existence?

'Does it matter, dear?'

'Well, dear,' said Edna, 'where shall we begin?' Then her voice changed. 'I believe it might now be time for me to tease out your justification for your leaving of your children.'

Well, at least she was being nice about it!'

I can't remember if the programme on the television was Edna's choice or still that of the Viking statuette, which, seemed to be vibrating from interference, possibly from Thelma outside the window, who was about to begin.

'Yes, children, we are in fact going to be moving to music this fine morning. So shall we all make a lovely fairy ring? Yes, and then we can all be wonderful flowers growing in the long, long, grass.'

It was a good game, quite me.

'Is this what you do at work?' asked Edna.

'Perhaps in my last position,' I replied. 'But now, I work with the handicapped.'

From Edna's television, 'Let's all make a big circle. Spread out – wider – wider – just fingertips touching – that's it. Flo, now let go of Gerald. Because flowers don't hold hands, they just touch fingertips. Flo, I said let go of Gerald. Stop that, Hannah, we don't want screamers in our fairy ring, do we? We only want lovely smilers.'

The words from the television were worryingly not coming from the woman's mouth.

'Oh, that's marvellous, dear,' said Edna. 'Was the smiler, per chance, Elle?'

The statuette became very agitated, like it was conducting the whole theatre of all this with his evil misbehaving antennae.

'Bless his lack of cottons.'

'Shh, dear, I am watching.'

I did.

'Yes, Michael? You're an asphodel,' said the woman. 'Well done. So imaginative, just like your mother. Ralph is your father, Hannah? Don't be ridiculous. That's impossible. Ralph, pay attention, and don't pummel Hannah with your stomping up the stairs. What flower are you going to choose to be? No, dear an "undeserving, misogynist" is not quite the type of flower we aspire to at St Bernard's. Please don't take such a tone in my class. I've told you so many times.'

'Hannah,' asked Edna. 'Are you alright?'

I raised my head, smiling back in embarrassment and let the game continue.

'No, children,' continued Joyce on the telly, 'it isn't funny. It is in fact, very, very silly. And if Ralph can't think of a better flower, we will have to go on to someone else until he can. Now, Cressida, what do you mean you are Ralph's wife and Hannah's mother, don't be silly. Anyone would think you've been touched. Yes, Mary. What kind of flower, are you? That is what we all want to know. A rose! Another one. And you too, Flo. A red one, you say. Oh, I have got a lovely bunch of roses today, haven't I? Flo's is red and Gerald is a wild one, so I expect you are a beautiful white one, aren't you Hannah? Unloved? No, dear, we won't have any of that in the beautiful garden with the flowers. A beautiful white one. Yes, you are. A wild ghost flower, young David? My, my, I am impressed.'

Momentarily, I rested my head in my hands, sneaked a quick peek out of the window at the author of all this. Thelma was just sitting there, seemingly mesmerized by the light, as though the gates were nearly ready to open.

'Remember you're all lovely flowers in the grass,' Joyce from the telly continued. 'What is that in your mouth, Ralph? No regard for poor little Hannah. You don't think she should be at school? I think you should leave the assembly hall and go and find somewhere to spit out that despicable thought. You can come back when you've done so. Pick up your feet now, both of them Ralph. I've never seen a beautiful flower so inattentive, and rude. You are almost as bad as a disreputable artist with shocking curly hair!'

'Oh, that Joyce,' said Edna. 'She has a real, rare talent, don't you think, Hannah?'

Judge Thelma, from outside the window, was still busy inspecting her gavel, as though she was getting tired of the wait.

I too wanted to see how this was going to play out.

'Now, children, we're not going to wait for a silly boy who likes putting bad thoughts into little Hannah's head, we're all going to be lovely flowers growing in the grass. The sun is now shining on us to make us grow tall and beautiful and – Michael, will you please stop imitating Ralph and stand properly. Flowers don't look backwards through their legs, do they? Not even highly imaginative ghost flowers. Hannah, dear, can you tell David what we do with our double-horned heads. Yes, we do. We always hold them high, indeed. Up, up, up!'

Thelma looked back at me, with eyes that seemed so tired.

'Well, I think all you teachers do a tremendous job helping the children,' said Edna.

Did she actually think this was real, I wondered?

'Edna,' I said. 'This is Joyce Grenfell doing comedy. I don't do comedy.'

She switched channels then, Edna, probably under orders herself from Judge Thelma, like with the orders she was trying to give me, from that lovely *Play for Today* about what happened to all the sad and lonely in the children's homes these days.

I remembered it well. Poor screaming Elle. And the shit all over the washing machine, as Annie Buckland the manager at the Cygnets had told me.

Well, it was atrocious, I say, simply atrocious of him to think, and the small, swarthy doctor too, looking at my own sheets and at Elle's birth, for she was always my favourite, of the girls, with all his –

'Staunch the blood,' to the tune of that lovely Mary Poppins song... Now, what was it now? 'Just a spoonful of sugar...'

No, Largactil, or chlorpromazine, a new one, just today.

But this was not right, really. I felt less control than when I'd started, and I really did need to take some of it back.

When I discussed the incident with Mary, her pursed lips betrayed her wanted condemnation of the status-quo I was trying to aspire to, I was sure.

As Miss Brodie would have, and actually did say, right there and then: 'one must never succumb to the ignorance of one, so obviously come from the lesser classes, dear.'

Mary had not been my first therapist.

To the nurse at St Bernard's excellent finishing school, during the first admission.

'Sing it all out, Hannah. Sing it for the sake of your true voice. That's it. "Mmm, Eee Ayy, Arr,"' when I was fearing what would happen to Michael, if I'd told anyone ... all his Viking inclinations in the bath to make me so unworthy.

Like father, like son-in-law. It's what happens when you give in to being taken over.

But I wasn't going to let this get the better of me, like before, I had told her. 'When his thing was standing up, up, up!'

Of course, Mary hadn't a clue about any of this, which was very rude of me, I thought then.

'No-one would listen to me about it, Mary.' I said, to the full extent of my ability to present as very bitter.

'Of whom, do you refer?'

She picked up her notebook, pointed her finger half way down the page, as if to check something.

'Because it was not your fault, Hannah,' said Mary, picking up her notes. 'Couldn't have been. You were reacting at the time, it says here, too incapable to defend yourself and that you didn't yet know how to brisk up, at all.'

'Indeed, I did not,' I said.

Whilst Mary engaged in further reading, I was drawn back

to all the wailing and flailing of all the other would-be debutantes in the locked ward of St Bernard's finishing school, where at least one of the staff nurses had listened in!

I tried to help them, of course, the other inmates. Give them someone they could talk to. Maybe, cards. Some crafts, build a dolls house, or something.

'It was like I was a wilting daffodil,' I said, like I was back there with the nurse, all over again.

Mary put down her notepad and gave a pronounced nod, as though she was about to announce something really important.

Well, she was my therapist.

'You know, of course, Hannah, that all daffodils come from the family of the narcissus?'

And evidently, quite bright too.

'Narcissus?' I returned.' Wasn't she the false God that liked to fall in love with herself?'

Mary started fiddling with the two sprouting tufts about her temples, as though they were goading me. They seemed so similar to the statuette at Edna's,

'And?' I asked.

'I am just pointing out the association, Hannah,' she said. 'Did you know of the work Professor Weaver has done on narcissus types?'

Her horn tufts were now growing into fully fledged spears to be scared of indeed, for any lesser person, without the resilience of having an admiral as a grandfather, of course.

The game was becoming a little less enjoyable.

I took a long breath in, like the earlier nurse therapist had taught. Diaphragmatic.

'Now, you are not saying, Mary, of course, that I am inclined to such a way of being, are you?'

Sharper, the horns then, like on the hair clips you can buy from Woolworths, or so the art therapist had told me earlier, when trying to create a new Tinkerbell out of a Sindy Doll, for Polly's birthday.

Mary looked down and said nothing. She said nothing for two whole minutes, as her horns started to turn pink and increasingly opaque.

It was like I was back at number twenty-six, staring at the Viking, when Michael had first given it me. Such an odd choice, for a birthday present. What was he trying to say? But I'd said nothing, just accepted it, not with a smile, because... Well, who smiles at the gift of something they have not even a remote interest in, at all.

Again, from her notebook, Mary read.

'You were more concerned for how you presented, at the time. The granddaughter of an Admiral. Not a council house recipient without the clothes to assume even a pretence of a society background.

A victim that deserved all she got for selflessly giving up her hopes and dreams for the pitter-patter of children's feet, to replace the love that Professor Weaver gave. Oh, and it says here, your husband too, thinks you never understood, what with your never being able to become a debutante and so needing another purpose.'

Complete piffle, but imaginative.

I could see this was just another part of the game, her role play, of which she was becoming quite the expert. I held back, to allow her to continue and because I had to hold it back to retain my composure and claim back some control.

Calm, easy, calm. For I knew that if I ever wanted to get out of St Bernard's, such was indeed, necessary, then I had to dispose of my anxiety.

So I bought my hands together into a feint clap.

'Well done,' I said. 'So you understand all that there is to know about me? Oh, and look at the time. Well, we'd best be packing up now, don't you think? Why don't you let me consider the loss of my prime some more, whilst you run off and get yourself another poor victim to play with!'

Patronizing the youth. It was what I was always good at, apparently. Or, so it said in the report by Professor Weaver, as written in some very sensible handwriting in Mary's open notebook at her side.

It was evening and still we unpacked at Edna's. The Viking's beady eyes reflected the light from the hole in the drawn curtain.

'Of course, you have your reasons,' said Edna. 'You must have. Maybe, if we can talk about them, then...'

There are times, I decided, when one just has to change the subject to something one can actually understand. Because, they say, it is sometimes acceptable to be scared and acknowledge, even wallow in it. Such as it was with the sheets that Michael had given me when Michael made me leave them all and him.

'But it was your fault,' continued Edna, 'I mean, it was you who made that choice.'

I think Elle must have been in charge of packing my things for me, whilst I slobbered about on the sheetless bed at number twenty-six.

'Uhm, Edna.' I asked. 'Could I possibly trouble you for the use of your washing machine? It's to see if I might be able to wash away the reasons for my choice of leaving them.'

'Certainly,' she said. 'But I very much doubt it will help. If it's linen, you might want to use the carbolic? Just make sure you fix the hose to the taps tightly. It leaked last week.'

This surprised me. I thought Mary, being young would be quite up with modern ways. The Viking wanted me to make it plain to her how I got here.

'No, polyester, dear. Brentford Nylons had them on sale again last year.'

Edna placed her tea next to mine, her movements precise, respectful. We were drinking from her best plastic, fake China cups, but there weren't any saucers, flying, Star Trek, or not. Edna wasn't a rich woman in monetary or indeed in terms of her imagination either. A distinct lack of pelmanical instruction, I suspected.

'There, there.' It was nice to feel the comfort of Edna's hand, as she wiped the tears from my cheek.

I was quite overcome by her care.

'I had to do it, Edna,' I said then, my voice barely above a shamed whisper. 'If I had stayed at that house, with Michael, I was sure I was going to end up dead.'

Edna nodded.

'Yes, I can see you might have seen it that way.'

The statuette didn't seem to agree, or care much about this, at all, the stare from its beady eyes having glazed over, in preparation, no doubt, for its next intervention, misogynistic.

Edna stroked my cheek with her finger, allowing me to think, for a moment at least, that at last someone understood the punishment I should face.

'Good night, then,' she said, and with that she got up with her notepad and, looking at the statuette, she nodded and started to record down all her learning by observation to be used later at my hearing.

'Good night.'

Then they came at me the horns, just like Michael had in the bath. But that was alright, because I was playing the Glad Game, just like with Polly. Polly as in Polly and Hannah – Pollyanna.

Edna didn't get this either.

A light from just outside the door was drawing us back into the atrium of the fiery wake.

'So it has begun,' said Edna. 'Quick, quick, my dear. We don't want to keep any of them waiting.'

Music played. Solveig's Song.

We made our way back in, Mary following too from the other room, and there was the desk and to the side the gallery again with its rails and a couple of electrostatic speakers from Michael's music room, either side, and the five of them sitting behind the gallery rails.

Edna turned, went back to her room, leaving me to all this, on my own.

Joyce and the Brodie woman were sitting in the straight-backed school chairs, opposite the main desk with the gavel, just like we used to have at Oriel.

I looked around for a seat for me, that still wasn't there.

Where was Judge Thelma?

'All rise. Up, up, up!'

Joyce was the first to get up in her galleon dress, as though ready for a ball. The Brodie woman was slower, at first donning a black gown, poise and presence as though from the nineteen twenties. Judge Thelma, I could see, when she'd finished entering, was also wearing a gown, and a pair of black and white trainers from Nike. She descended honourably to her seat. The music stopped.

Everyone else sat to, following the lead of Joyce, who from her confidence, seemed to understand best what was going on here, which was just as well.

'Is the Court Liaison present?' Thelma's enquiring eyes, were roving around the hall.

The clerk of the court, the nurse in charge of the ward, at the finishing school, shuffled papers, by the side of Thelma, as Joyce stood and after plumping down her galleon dress approached the desk.

'I am handed here, your honour,' she said, 'by the learned liaison of Mary, whom I believe to be thoroughly good, true and eminently prosecutory.'

The children, from behind the rails of the gallery were laughing. I wanted to laugh to at how ridiculous a scene this was too, but with Judge Thelma's looking as she did, stern, formidable, even with a hint of royal, I thought better of it.

I was not alone with the thought, I could see, or about any respect that might be due. The Brodie woman bowed her head too, her flapper dress, under her gown, revealing a whole other passionate lifestyle

Judge Thelma picked up the gavel from her side, tapped it on the sounding block.

'Are we ready?' she asked.

It was Joyce that offered herself first.

'With all assessments undertaken and passed, Your Honour,' she said, 'this Hannah is deemed both capable and able to be deemed culpable, that is if Your Honour, feels disposed and will accept my recommendation.'

I knew that Joyce was on my side. Same type of background, really. Jolly hockey sticks and tea parties at Lipton's. I might have even passed her the sugar cubes.

Miss Brodie was much more matter of fact.

'She is ready,' she stood, 'and I will defend her.'

Judge Thelma banged her gavel again, precisely. ''The charges, then!'

The nurse or clerk appointed to the hearing, probably by Professor Weaver, started to read from her many papers.

'That the defendant has willingly prevented the coming of the Michael,' said Joyce, 'to take his rightful place by your side, beyond the light and tall gates.'

She looked to Mary, Joyce – me.

'Counsel for the defence,' asked the judge, 'has your client heard and understood the charge?'

The Brodie woman inclined her head.

'She has and she does.'

Judge Thelma looked up to the gallery, to the children, my children, assembled behind the rails with Michael and a huge pile of papers next to them.

Mary snapped her fingers. The children stopped their play, focussed on the proceedings below.

'Thank you,' announced Mary, 'it seems we to begin.'

Joyce stood. It was always her turn, as the prosecution, to start first. It was the same on Perry Mason, and that Rumpole of the Bailey.

'Members of the jury, the case I am about to put to you is that the defendant has prevented the coming of the Michael to his rightful place at the great 'M's right-hand side beyond the light and the gates.'

She seemed so much more friendly then.

'To establish this, I will seek to prove to you today that by a series of acts on the part of the defendant, that she is indeed guilty and more, that she has planned this over a very long time.'

Had I?

'You will no doubt hear from the defence that some of the motivations on the part of the defendant were underpinned by some unnatural thinking.'

'I should say so. Michael was quite mad! Even Professor Weaver said so, and at Group.'

'I shall, members of the jury, instead show that the acts of marriage, having children, not being able to love and raise them and then taking flight into this unnatural thinking,' she pointed to a report on the table, which Thelma quickly picked up, 'were all set in motion to prevent the coming of Michael to this place.'

Said with a smile, too. I always say that a smile brings out the best in people.

'Needing Michael to stay with her,' continued Joyce, 'so she could successfully defend her position in her challenge of all that was expected.'

'She was nothing like her mother,' offered an all-knowing voice from above. Michael gestured Polly down again in her seat

Joyce then nodded and took her own seat.

The Brodie woman was up next, pacing the width of the atrium, with much more energy in her stride, 'if what is being shown here isn't unnatural thinking, or an attempt to confuse, but a belief system that is the defendant's very purpose, then I members of the jury, might be very confused myself?

She stopped her pacing, looked around with her own roving eye and then up at the gallery to the children, but not to Michael, who didn't deserve her recognition, anyone's really, for bringing about the circumstances of this debacle.

Instead, perhaps, I ask you to consider, could this not be a perfectly reasonable reaction to a set of unfortunate circumstances within a logical framework of thoroughly capable and independent thought.'

She stopped pacing.

Michael, shook his head.

'It is what I hope to prove.'

She continued. 'It is my earnest hope to submit and prove to the court that to let oneself be constantly skivvied, as was the case when with Michael, is to the defendant unthinkable. It is like robbing the defendant of her dreams, and to be robbed of your dreams is to be robbed of life itself.'

The expressions of both Judge Thelma and Joyce seemed very animated in their apparent agreement of this.

'And, indeed, if this is the case,' the Brodie woman seemed to be getting into her stride, 'is it not also logical that in a belief system where there were never any tall gates, maybe not even, any lights, that this is in fact a part of another scheme set to confuse, that the prevention of Michael's coming was impossible, as there was, in reality, nowhere to actively prevent him from coming to.'

General confusion about the court ensued and some pointing at the clearly visible gates beyond in the clouds. Someone, somewhere had got things very wrong.

'That the defendant got married,' the Brodie woman started again, 'is not in question.' She paused. 'But the reason for doing so might have actually been more about being in love and wanting to actively celebrate this within the marriage.

Absolutely.

'That the defendant had children is also not in question.' The Brodie woman looked up again. 'Indeed, there you all are in the gallery and happy to be so, as I take for granted.'

All in the gallery nodded, except Elle, that was, who had her hair stuck to her blouse with an icky piece of bubble-gum.

They didn't even know her, or did they? The paper at their side that in which they were so engrossed, I knew from the size of the pile – Douglas really had been hard at work on his prophecy Thelemic – had completely taken their attention.

Thelemic, Thelma? Thinking, thinking.

Wasn't she the judge? How could she be a prophet too? It was hard to predict this type of delusion.

'To the charge of the defendant,' the Brodie woman continued, with a smile of satisfaction that all attention in the court, apart from the children, was hers indeed, 'her not being able to love and raise the children, as a means to bring about the defendant's reason for being here, there really does need to be an alternative.'

Joyce shot Judge Thelma a quick glance, who nodded back very quickly. Then Joyce turned to me. Her all too piercing stare drilling into me. 'And did you, Hannah,' she asked, in an increasingly accusatory tone, 'tell me in our briefing that if you were to stay at number twenty-six, you were convinced you were going to end up dead?'

I had to answer honestly, as me, I felt. I was under scrutiny. In a hearing, with a judge. My whole future depended on this.

'I did.'

For I had done nothing wrong.

And who was this Joyce, anyway, to think that she had the right to take such a tone with me?

'And did you also say,' she continued, trying to tear the sequins of her cuffs from the flare of her skirt, 'that the reason behind this was that there was a David, brother of the Michael, who is dead, almost, and from his position and many guises, neither real or provably delusional, was trying to take over and get Michael away from you on a space ship?'

'The space ship didn't really exist,' I said.

'I see.'

I really hoped that she did.

Judge Thelma dropped her gavel then. Probably overcome by my presence. The nurse, clerk smiled at her sycophantically, before picking this up.

'Indeed, I am sure you are correct,' continued Joyce, 'but maybe you can help me out? You see, Hannah, you are here with us now are you not?'

'I am.' There was no point in denying it and I actually did believe that I was.

'Then I wonder how you think you got here? It's not as though there are many people that can reject a space ship.'

Wasn't it obvious? By delusion, I wanted to say, but it was not in my power to answer, for some reason. I looked to the children, but there were too many shiny lights to distract them, let alone the papers.

Joyce snapped her fingers. 'I put to you, Hannah,' she said, 'that Michael did try to build a ship, but you prevented him from doing so, with all your protests and procrastination about how you were being treated.'

Was it ok now, to say my piece? The children's heads were safely back in the prophecy, Judge Thelma and the rest of them, all eyes were looking to me.

I took a deep breath in. Then. 'I did not come here on a ship,' I started. 'I was in St Bernard's, needing to get away from Michael, for his complete inability, just like my father before, to understand me.'

It felt liberating.

But only to me, evidently.

'And what, pray,' asked Joyce, 'and begging the courts indulgence, is that, may I ask?' She was pointing to an odd shaped bicycle, labelled Exhibit A, that had just appeared next to Judge Thelma's table.

Thelma leant forward form her chair and looked at this, decorated in the livery of a ship from the sixties and with a huge saucer section precariously lodged on the handlebars.

'Might it be one of your delusions,' asked Joyce, 'perhaps sent you out of the ether, by surprise?

Stewart?

It was bold, brash, with the saucer poking out and the nacelles drooped.

'A miracle, perhaps?'

But her little joke was not well taken. 'Well, obviously,' I explained, 'it looks like a space ship,' I explained, 'one that the Michael, or even Stewart might have constructed, or so Douglas has told me, but Douglas really does have such a fanciful imagination.'

'So what we can all see in front of us then is a delusion, one made real for us by your confusion, perhaps?' asked Joyce.

The image kept changing, from the *Sent Surprise* to the Saturn V ship, and how did I know this, and then back again. I even thought, momentarily that I saw a Skylark sponge, but it's balloon popped in the face of Polly's scowl and then we were back to the court again, with the nurse, ready, in her seat, holding the conductors for the ECT machine.

'I don't know anymore,' I tried to defend. 'You, the hearing, you are all trying to trick me.'

But then the images disappeared and from the sombreness of the atmosphere in the court I could feel myself claiming back all my capable and independent thought.

There was a little silence, for a bit.

'Oh, I see,' I said, tapping my nose, as a gesture of my understanding, 'you are trying to give the children a means, by which they might understand the circumstances surrounding what I did!'

In the spirit of my learning here, I approved of the approach wholeheartedly. It would have been quite a trial for them, my leaving the house, like that, and at an age when, well, how could they possibly understand?'

Thelma was discriminating in her look towards me then – interested, or she looked so, possibly.

'How, it wasn't the children, you were leaving,' she said, 'No, members of the Jury, it was Michael she was leaving, 'because you wanted to prevent him from getting to the light and the gates. You needed to give him justification, for defending against David and his staying to look after your children.'

'I did,' I said, nodding, for I could see I had nothing to lose and it's always best to be truthful anyway. 'Yes, your Honour, it was exactly like my defending counsel says. Although, in my defence, at first, I did offer to take them with me, but for some reason they just didn't want to come.'

Joyce sat down, then.

As she did, the Brodie woman and got up and took over. 'And could you, perhaps,' she said, in her best presbyterian voice, 'educate the hearing as to why you think the Michael might not have built any ship to get away from you, or take off in this, especially when you and the hospital were accusing him of such unnatural thoughts at the time? And that if you were to stay with him, you would surely end up dead?'

I got angry then. It was inexcusable.

'Well, he did,' I said, 'build a ship, or at least tried to, a ship of St. Bindar's, if you must know, to spread the word and live in what he saw as the only true religion.'

From the corner of my eye, I could see Polly in the gallery with her hands joined together in prayer.

'But when,' I continued, 'this was recognized as that which might be able to take him to and through the light and tall gates, he was understandably silent and reluctant. Michael always liked to be silent and reluctant. It was his way, as all in the family, despite the age of some them, knew all too well. And I would appreciate it, if you didn't twist my words.'

'We all had to agree with Mummy.' It was Polly's voice, I think, hard to tell, with her head still buried in the papers.

The Brodie woman puckered her lips, turned to me.

'It was he that did not want to go,' she said. 'It was not you Hannah that tried to stop him?'

I saw what the Brodie woman was up to and it was a good

ploy. A ploy that I should play along with

'Why would I want to stop him? I needed him to buy my tights – from Debenhams.

'Your tights, you say? From Debenham's?'

'Oh, yes,' I said, well no one could stop me. 'He made me a mother, and a mother needs strong tights to defend against his advances,' and then I found my voice, 'but Michael never gave me enough money. Not for tights, sanitary towels, those new cherry tomatoes, even for lipstick!'

The Brodie woman smiled, turned to Michael, up in the gallery. 'I put to you Michael, up there, that you never gave Hannah enough of anything...

But then the sound of a banged gavel was heard again.

'Enough,' said Judge Thelma.' I will have order in my hearing. Order I will have.'

The music started up again, but this time is was not Solveig's song, this time it was Tchaikovsky, played on the piano with a similar hammering to that of Mrs Boulting, from back at Oriel.

'Closing arguments, if you please,' ordered Judge Thelma, overcoming this.

Joyce looked indignant as she rose again, bowing her head to Judge Thelma, who again, nodded.

'Thank you, Your Honour,' she said and quickly turned to the gallery. 'Well, you all know, children' she said, 'what I am about to say, because I have said it before and I am very likely going to say it again. Whether your mother stopped your father from taking up his place being real, or unreal, is not the true question here before us. What is important here, children, is whether your mother deserves the rewards she seeks for leaving your father and you?'

Michael, at this, was twiddling his fingers to Mrs Boulting's Tchaikovsky, completely mesmerized by the memory and the Nuns in the back, dancing to the gentle commands of that Novice Fonda.

Joyce smiled at me then, as the Brodie woman took her seat again. Joyce looked each of the jury up and down with the scrutiny of a child psychologist.

'And in this parting,' she said, 'for which your dear mother now seeks sanction after the fact, that she might afford the rent of Edna.'

It was the Brodie woman's turn then, and with all the gravitas of a headmaster of the Oriel Infant and Junior school and Justice of the Peace that he was.

She stepped forward; this time so much closer to the desk of Thelma.

'I believe my esteemed colleague has done well making my case for me, in part. Indeed, the defendant is not guilty of preventing the Michael from taking up his rightful place. But the proof of her innocence against the charge does not rest solely on the point that my esteemed colleague has outlined.

No!

The truth here and running throughout her entire life is that she needed to enjoy the freedom she had found to control herself and all others so she can be herself, by herself. And that is what now she often feels the need of – to think; well, not even to think, but live. To be satisfied with the dismissal, so implied by the hearing finding favour in this argument and free from any assumed guilt.'

The Brodie woman took her seat.

Judge Thelma at her table was scratching her head, as if asking what any of this really meant? She turned to the jury.

'I believe,' she said, 'I am bound to sum up the case and give direction as to what to consider as admissible. She then looked at her papers again and those handed her by the nurse. 'But I confess I am now too confused to do so and not even sure I want Michael to be with his David, anyway.'

She paused.

So, I am compromised and cannot offer any summing up, and instead I must leave the decision to you. I ask that you consider, on the basis of what you have heard, if the defendant is guilty or not of preventing the Michael from taking his rightful place at the side of the great 'M', sent, on a Skylark sponge, constitution class *Sent Surprise*, or Saturn V space ship, it really doesn't matter which, only that justice must be seen to be done. So I ask you children of the gallery, members of the jury, are you ready to consider a verdict?'

235

'We are,' said Douglas.

'Then, you may retire.'

It took all of two minutes for the jury to decide and then come back. The tension in the fiery wake was palpable.

'Have you a verdict to offer to this hearing?' Thelma asked.

'We do,' said Stewart, as the foreman, eldest and best that there was.

'And?'

Douglas stood up in the gallery, but was pushed down again by Stewart.

'We are ashamed to say your honour, that we find our mother too delusional to care,' said Stewart, 'except for seeking your sanction for her leaving and a divorce, of course.'

'Oh, I see,' said Judge Thelma. 'Well, if anything is true here, it is that your mother, members of the jury, has left you all and so to the question of settlement, of compensation for her leaving you and Michael.

He looked back at her with mad eyes

'...in the decree that I am now minded to make absolute, is that half and half...

'But I don't want to take away from the children,' I said, 'and so will accept much less. All I want, Your Honour, for my Debenham's tights, you will understand, is the sum of ten thousand pounds.'

Judge Thelma looked around for objection and on finding none, banged her gavel.

'Then sanctioned your leaving and divorce, for the settlement of then thousand pounds, that you may forever indulge yourself in tights, it must be.'

The gavel sounded for the final time.

I met up with Edna in the Wimpy to go over old times. I had been thinking of her of late, and all that fun we used to have, which was nice of me.

And we laughed. Well, I did.

She was more reserved.

'All that silliness back then, with the Viking, but I never thanked you, Edna and I wanted to, for taking me in, when I was at my worst.'

She was examining the menu card, trying to clear the dried tomato sauce from the mains part with a folded serviette.

'You were a bit scary,' she said, studying the stain.

'I know,' I agreed. 'I wasn't myself, but I am now and I've moved to Chiswick, well, Brentford Towers, which is close enough, and I joined a new church, Edna, and they held a fundraiser for me, to get one of those new fitted kitchens.'

'How nice, but isn't that taking advantage of their kindness? Did you manipulate them into it with one of your sob-stories like you did with me?'

She looked up, her part clouded-over cataract in the left eye betraying her struggle with her task.

It didn't surprise me, that she had taken so. It was the same with some of the elders at my Church. More wary than most, distrusting. Concerned with smaller things in life, or a smaller world view, less able to adjust to change.

'Oh, no Edna. It is obviously what God wanted. A miracle, you might say. But anyway, that's not important. You see, the council won't let me install the new kitchen unless I agree to replace it how it was when I leave. If I leave.'

'If you say so.' Edna dabbed the serviette into her glass of water and brought this back to the offending spots of sauce and started to scrub.

'Yes, well Edna, you see,' I said, 'I cannot give the council such assurances and so thought, I should gift the kitchen to you, by way of my thanks for your earlier kindness.'

The tomato sauce spot on the menu would not budge, however much Edna tried.

'Here, let me.'

I tried to take the serviette from Edna, but she retracted her hand. So I licked my index finger and rubbed with enough vigour until the menu was clean.

'There. It's clean now. So what do you think of my offer for your new kitchen?'

Edna pushed away the menu, sat back.

'You should have paid your rent.'

She called for the waitress.

'A cup of tea, please, and whatever this one wants.'

I had to smile. Same old Edna. Straight up. Impossible to put one over her. It was what I always liked about her.

'I am not trying to take over or control you, Edna. Heavens, if I haven't learnt by now then I am indeed not blessed.'

The pastor at the Chiswick church, a non-denominational, had shown me this, how to put what I'd learnt from Mary, to good use. Love begets love as a smile begets a smile and it is good to help the needy, show them just how much Jesus cares.

'No, it is a gift, Edna,' I said. 'A simple, honest gift. Not a means to right any wrongs you think I may have done to you.'

The tea arrived. Two cups, a pot and a little jug for the milk.

'There is nothing wrong with the kitchen that I have. All those cupboards to bang your head into they make with those new ones. I have seen them Hannah, in that MFI maize.'

'But it will make things easier for you, Edna.'

'You never complained.'

I could see I wasn't going to get any further with this and so I changed the subject.

'And how are you these days? Are you in need of anything? A hairdresser for your tired, perhaps?'

'No, Hannah. Well, apart from my tea. I think you should pour. My arthritis.'

'Of course.'

And as I poured, we got to talking some about the old days.

'Your Michael didn't deserve what you did to him, still pops in from time to time.'

'Really, Edna, Oh.'

'I know he is odd. Always was, but he was never a bad man.'

After my first sip, I thought I would tell her, 'The children,' I said, 'have him down as having Aspergers, high-functioning. Brilliant in some areas and completely useless in others, especially socially.'

'You didn't care much then.'

'I didn't know and anyway with all his silences and control issues he was preventing me from leading my life. It was really, quite cruel of him, Edna, as you will no doubt remember.'

'I don't.'

I understood. 'That's the narcissist in you, Edna,' I said. 'Maybe, you should come with me to my church. They have a female pastor joining next week and she knows all there is about bringing God's love for the feeble of mind.'

But then I saw that Edna had already left, with not so much as a goodbye. I suppose that's all you can expect from people such as her, who cannot believe they too could enjoy a modern fitted kitchen. If only Edna had attended a finishing school!

Fancy, Edna Bone in a finishing school?

So all this was why I couldn't let you, David, or anyone really, have any control over me. Well, apart from when I was low and weak.

But I am not weak anymore. I mean to say, David, for that is who you really are, I know, back at our wedding, me to Michael, when I thought you were interested in me, in that way. Yes, you can tell me, now. I am ready. You always were such a flirt, David, to my wanted ambitions and I, as you no doubt already know, well, as you already know, I really could have been a debutante!

DAVID

Well, there was a love, between Michael and Thelma, deep, and understanding, at least in nineteen ninety. Fading though, after about six months and then, over time, well, angels don't tend to do very well when trapped inside the mortal realms, without any wings with which to escape, especially when the selfish reason for her descent doesn't really want to know.

Not that anyone would have noticed, anyone observant enough to discern that such a nonsense fairy tale could only ever be that. Or was this really achievable?

Michael didn't know and he didn't care, either. He had other ideas about what his future held.

'No, Thelma, I will not go into the light on a spaceship, yours or anyone else's. It reminds me too much of the seventies.'

'But Michael, the seventies wasn't your fault!'

Yet, the clutter room of Michael's new Shepperton house with Thelma was a direct link for him to reclaim this his time. A much-prized shrine.

There, he would gaze at his children's old school reports, the much-thumbed photographs of Tingle's Two and Three, a montage of family accounts, poking out from a picture of Babel and a rather holed, as though darts had been thrown at it, picture of a bearded Bruce Forsyth, under which was scored the words – Was it all my fault? Even though he was living with me,

Starry sorrows, no doubt.

In fact, having put her up to it in the first place, I felt a bit sorry for the old gal, for that was what the angel Thelma, once light of the prophecy that would allow things to be alright again, had become.

How?

'No, Michael, you will empty your catheter before you go upstairs. If I've told you once I've told you a million times, don't you know that at your age, you can no longer pass up any chance to pee!'

There was no salad cream either, Michael was banned from wearing smelly trousers and with his *uhms* and *aahs*, tutted at all the time, to be rid of, like it was with his old dandruff.

Indeed, married life with Thelma was becoming much the same as it was before with Hannah.

Well, it's hard to teach an old dog new tricks.

But there were good times too, occasionally, Thelma's invitations to scrabble count, against Michael's ever urgent needs for a slow, exploratory cuddle on the couch.

'Will you stop touching there, that's my wing stump that is, you've got me all back to front again. You know I don't like it.'

Thelma had learnt to become sharp in her old age.

Oh, but when the children came.

'Oh, yes, I do my art, while your father does his – whatever he does up there, and have you seen the garden? Marjory Kinnon's daughter, from the Art Club, Wednesday afternoon, two pm, as well as Fiona, they just love the garden. By the way, did you know, your father is obsessed by the height of the cut of the grass, by the azaleas. Yes, I know, we do. We do, all of us, we just have to love him.'

Michael would agree.

'We are a couple. God-willing. Like a puzzle box, with all its pieces deep inside. We are destined to fit together, forever and ever, Amen! Oh, I've just bent the corner piece.'

To Michael's children, to all intents and purposes, Michael and Thelma were indeed a happy fairy tale, able to suck all the life from their guilt of having left him for his bending of all the corners, until they all left the Shepperton house, that was, and Michael would ascend to the safety of his clutter room.

I felt sorry for Michael too, of course, what with the fall of any hope for his chosen adventure dream all around him, but that was so much harder given our difficulties and I couldn't intervene. Not while the angel Thelma was at work.

I wouldn't dare.

It was like that time they went to visit the Isle of Wight, on one of her little trips.

'Oh, come on Michael, it's only for a couple of weeks and the hotel will cost less if we go midweek.'

Or: 'Michael, do you want some Kentucky fried...'

But again, Michael had other ideas.

'Oh, is that a bus museum? Come on, Sweetie. It will be pleasant. I might be able to catch a glimpse of the excellent Dobson Daimler bus, just like it was when Brian and I used to travel to Chatham for our aniseed balls and he would spit them out at my face to punish me for always wanting to play with his chemistry set flames.'

Michael just didn't understand what possibilities awaited him with the angel who had given so much, if he could only just recognize it.

The sad truth was that the angel without – wings, that was – just as it was with me, showed no signs of achieving the task Thelma had set herself, to help Michael find his adventure with me, in the light, beyond the tall gates.

If she wasn't already, Thelma was in danger of becoming a failed angel.

The problem, it seemed, as Michael observed cannily, in the sanctity of the vestry counting house of St Richard's, just before the production that they were supposed to attend, was that Michael didn't yet believe in any other possibilities.

'I don't,' Michael said to himself, not wishing to offend any deities that might be hovering about by the newly cottoned again cassocks. 'It's only what "Call me, Alan" calls her, and as for all that business with Patrick and the 322nd Grand Synod of the 'M', well. I don't know really. I must have been a little out of sorts, like Hannah was when she first went to her finishing school, St Bernard's of the Mentals, wasn't it. It was all so very dark.

The music on the church organ started up.

Michael had to get a move on.

'Uncle Michael,' came the chorus from the children of the Sparklers group, as he entered St Richard's Church, recently taken over from the Discoverer's Club. Michael was in charge of the sticky-backed stars.

As the words of Tim Rice (was he actually a Christian?) filled the hall with the wigwam roof that Stewart had first introduced Michael to, Michael gave of his carefully prepared slices of Mars Bars. It was a deterrent for the children against stealing the collection, for there were limits as to what you could claim back in gift aid, even with that nice Mr. Major, who, it hadn't escaped Michael, had a pretty decent quiff too.

'Israel, in four BC had no mass communication,' sang the St Richard's youth choir, and not without the energy of the earlier Bay City Rollers, rocker-billies, if that was an acceptable description. 'Jesus Christ, Superstar! Walks like a woman and he wears a ...' Michael was by the baptismal font, conducting such fond memories with his finger.

They were all so childish, back then. Well, they were children, even if Michael couldn't see this.

In the sermon by 'Call me' that followed, it was made clear, of course, that Israel, did in fact have mass communication, in the form of the MTV and some pretty noisy fax machines.

'Lo,' continued 'Call me' from his lectern, 'for this is the message of the Lord, Lady, or all who might have once had aspirations to journey in the Saturn ship,' or that was what Michael heard.

It was a clever move on Thelma's part, and I could see what she was up to.

'We shall call it a pilgrimage, to make it alright and greatly good again.'

Indeed, it had to be Thelma. 'Call me' just didn't have the cynicism for such an idea.

'A sponsored pilgrimage to raise funds for the stolen copper on the church roof.'

'With that lot, and you, Michael,' said Thelma, 'it's always about the money. Never fellowship. Always with the money!'

For this betrayal of Thelma, by Michael, I observed, for the old ways, was worse than his earlier abandonment of his children or was it the other way round? For a moment Michael wasn't really sure.

Guilt, why could Michael just never shake this?

With Stewart and Elle, Thelma knew from my telling her what had happened, but for the other two, well, the rocks and stones themselves would never sing, would they?

Nevertheless, the earlier sermon of 'Call me' had struck home to Michael in ways beyond any clear communication of Thelma's apparent lack of concern for his happiness.

'Thelma,' he asked, when they got home. 'Why do you never buy salad cream anymore?'

She didn't even answer him, so concerned was she with her next plan.

It was then that Michael decided. Yes, he would go and find out why the gates of the movement were being presented on the television as so tall.

Because, as Michael had realised, as I had, religious stories have more in common with fairy tales than we realize except that fairy tales tend to be secular and are not based on a prescriptive belief system or religious codes.

Fantastic articles, sometimes, the *Radio Times*.

Or was it that Michael needed to escape into his own world?

'What do you mean, you are going to seek your vision, I am your blessed vision.'

'Thelma, dear? Sweetie? But you know why you cannot come too. Who else but you can look after our Tingle Four?'

For Michael, this wasn't so much a lie as hiding the real reason behind his need for respite. Mr Biggs had long thought she was responsible for the loss copper on St Richard's roof.

Michael just didn't know.

Inspector Mansfield did. 'She just keeps going on about the copper she needs for that crazy idea of hers for a spaceship and to get you to love her again.'

It was only then that Thelma found her greater understanding of how Polly must have felt when Michael had taken issue with her over the theft of the five-pound note.'

Not that Michael was in a position to be the least bit concerned, or was he?

'Call me', as Pilgrimage leader, had had the journey all mapped out. The Church of the Holy Sepulchre, Temple Mount, the fourteen stations of Via Dolarosa, where Jesus carried his cross.

Was this the cross that Michael had to bear? Could he actually take a break from Thelma? Did he believe that all that was being said and done could offer more than the promise that she offered?

Indeed, the Boeing 737-200, predecessor to the Airbus that Michael had actually worked on, after Concorde, well, the cooling capability, offered Michael a much better alternative than Thelma's space ship.

As it touched down at Ben Gurion airport, without Thelma, Michael got out his guidebook, earlier sent him by Douglas.

There are always visions to discern when one has such a strong faith.

'Where are the gates?' he asked of a little leper boy, for you have to have a little leper boy if you're outside the entrance to a hotel in the land of God, where the others had left him, upon being dropped by the shuttle.

The little leper boy with his tiny scabbed hands out as though beckoning all Christian love, twitched his head to the left.

Michael found a couple of just exchanged shekels and dropped these slowly into the boy's hands.

'Ya mean,' said the boy, 'Golden, Dung, Herod's, Damascus, Zion, Jopper, or New, mate?' looking with disdain at the paltry amount in his tiny scabby palms.

Michael graced these with a twenty. 'I don't know, the one with the tall gates.'

The boy looked up. 'Ain't no gates in Jerusalem that are that tall, mate.' And just as the boy was about to withdraw his hand, Michael caught sight of an image on the back of the note.

'There', he said, pointing to the image, 'that's them. The gates. Where is that?'

The boy looked at the note, pointed to the nearby bus stop. 'That's the first Hebrew High School, just by the first drop after you arrive in Tel Aviv.'

'It's just like the one I used to go in Gillingham?'

'Maybe it's the same designer,' said the boy, smirking, quite rudely. 'There is only one, ya know, and long, may her socks be upon her feet.'

The boy shrugged his shoulders and went his way.

Michael got on the next bus and could imagine it all so well. The tall brick pillars, holding the gates, the dirt pathway leading up to the entrance. And once inside, the ornate plasterwork of the architraves leading the corridor ceilings down to the great hall. Where the headmaster, or God as David and I would refer to him in his black robes, perfectly creased suit and a set square sticking out of his pocket.

He arrived. But God wasn't there. And neither was Thelma. Michael missed Thelma, he realized, and he missed the visits from Elle, since just after the Edmonton knicker episode with the bad man. He missed all of them not visiting when they didn't, which was not his fault, each having their own reasons, but were their reasons good enough?

Then Michael saw a flapping piece of plastic sheeting and remembered Thelma investing in the same back in Shepperton, probably shattered at his behaviour towards her, and having to look after Tingle Four. What on earth, as it is in heaven, was he thinking? Was he mad, as Hannah's psychiatrist had said? Indeed, from where do such visions actually come, he wondered?

Michael didn't even get off the bus. He just carried on to the airport and flew back home immediately.

He mailed a note to 'Call me', to explain.

It was all in the prophecy. Thelma was the will of God, of Mona. Mona, leading us into the light, but where was it? At the end of the fiery wake where a Hurricane once played? By the light of a silvery moon, that the darkness couldn't comprehend.

Why could Michael not comprehend? Was his guilt of leaving me there on the pavement, too slow to rescue, enough to create this darkness that denied him the opportunity to see beyond the tall gate and the light of the movement?

Was this a light that fallen archangels knew about? One with broken wings, perhaps.

Thelma was thinking of her next move to make things all right and pave the way for Michael to find his way to the light on his return. He just had to become more accustomed to the idea.

And when Michael got home, full of guilt for his totally unjustified abandonment, he was determined to make it up to Thelma, by doing all that she asked.

She wasn't upset, or angry, but she did have her plan from earlier, thoroughly researched and good to go, to bring peace to their relationship.

The following day, out came the Volkswagen, green. The journey was largely without incident, until a large car, swerving to avoid Michael's over-hesitancy with the German engineered, precision brakes.

Now that Thelma had his attention again, she would ease his overcoming of his greatest fear.

'Bloody pensioners.'

But Michael wasn't fazed by this at all. Instead, 'We used to play on those,' he said, pointing to a playground that was coming up fast. 'Of course, our swings were wooden and the merry-go-round squeaked. And that was where we used to play planes.'

Thelma smiled again, picked up her knitting. 'So we're getting near then?'

'Only a couple of minutes to go.'

But the journey actually took a little longer than four minutes, according to the red-bleeping dash. There was no sign of any explosion of protons, not even a threat of one.

In time.

It was a short walk from the car park to the meeting place.

'Ah, Mr and Mrs Porter.' The official beckoned them into his Portacabin. He wore a council-crested tie with a rather worrying windsor knot and a shabby jacket with curled over lapels that had never even seen a twin-tub, much less a Timpson dry cleaning shop.

'Love. Calm. Be as he needed to be.' I told him.

Maps were spread out on the table.

'Nice to meet you,' said the official. 'Well, after not finding the plot on the microfiche, I had to search high and low and only just found these an hour ago.'

Michael waited for Thelma's reaction, which, we both knew was sure to come. She was biding her time.

'I'm sorry.'

The man looked back, query in his eyes.

'Oh, no need to be sorry, Mr. Porter,' he said. 'This is the bit of my job I find interesting. Your wife's letter gave me a mystery and I always like to solve mysteries.'

Thelma smiled, smugly.

The man proceeded to search the left side of the map with a magnifying glass.

'You see in those days,' he said, 'the plots were smaller, for the poor that was. I take it you were poor?'

Michael nodded, I noticed. He seemed appropriately shame-faced.

'Oh, I'm sorry,' said the man. 'I just mean, well, it was the war and rationing and well, he was a child, as your wife's letter pointed out and all the children went into the wretched plots in those days.'

'He wasn't wretched,' said Michael. 'He was my brother.' And he was quite loud, too, at least for him.

His twin-brother whom he had tried to ignore all his life.

But this was Thelma's mission, I reminded myself, not mine, and I had to hold back.

Thelma prodded Michael in the arm

He startled. 'There was a cross, I believe,' he sputtered, as some of the neutrons about his electromagnetic aura jumped.

The man looked up.

'Yes, in the 'sixties they were removed, ground-reclamation, they said.'

'Oh. Uhm, Ahh!'

The man then traced his finger up and down one of the

maps: 'There DRP 542, that's it, his initials. David, Richard, Portergeist, wasn't he called?'

I saw Michael look to Thelma. She nodded.

'David, Richard, Porter,' he said.

'Bingo,' the man said joyously and led them out of the Portacabin with a sprightly and energetic step.

I was finding all of this really quite macabre.

'Are you coming?' The man shot back at them the look of a real explorer. But not so much of a real explorer that I was to be that easily placated.

When they got to the plot, Michael asked the official for a moment alone.

'I never forgot you,' he said to me, talking to an old handkerchief from his pocket.

My old handkerchief, with the moon and the stars and the sun, embroidered by Mother's unloving care.

Get ready.

'I would like to order a proper headstone, this time,' Michael told the man.

'Right,' he said. It was that simple.

'It doesn't matter how much it's going to cost.'

How could my brother have changed so much?

'As you wish, Sir!'

It had been Thelma who suggested this. Probably in the prophecy, maybe. Reclamation of Michael's sanity, or whatever it was that she might have alluded to at the time.

And just as I was to calculate the equation for this and the electrostatic force between two identically charged objects and the distance between them and the soon to be charged protons.

'I did it because I love you, Michael,' said Thelma. 'Love, calm, it's all you need and allow yourself to be, Michael, and it will all come out right in the twin-tub. It always does.'

Michael was snivelling in the clutter room. He'd written a poem all about it. He'd written several, over the years, secretly, and locked them away behind the flap of his bureau in his Shepperton clutter room but this time, like they had a life of their own, they wanted to be let out

"What else can I give you?" He read it out, to himself. To see how it sounded.

"You have left me in pieces
Shredded, so much that I might never
be able to be put myself
back together again
Is that what you wanted?
As I let your thoughts run through my head
My life, and through your possession too
of my children,
perhaps others too?"

He sobbed a little. Then came another vision.

'You must go to the gates, first, you know the tall gates, by the Kentucky Fried Chicken stand.'

But Michael couldn't see any Kentucky Fried Chicken stand in the clutter room, or anything like it. All he could see was a city of clouds on the screen of his brand, new Tiny 405 computer.

'Where, your angelship,' he asked of the vision, 'is the noisy Kentucky Fried Chicken stand?'

Thelma, who heard him from outside the clutter room, where she was hoovering, laughed.

'Just follow your nose,' came the voice of Mona, the great one, may her socks, always be upon...

It had been a while, but Michael had done it once, with Stewart at least, with Douglas not having the wherewithal, after I'd collapsed on the pavement.

So Michael looked for the light, behind the City of Clouds, right in front of him. There was a particularly grey cloud in front of his nose. It was moving about quite a lot, but how was a puzzle because he felt no wind. Of course, there wasn't any wind. The clouds were forming up into what at first seemed like the skyline of Jerusalem, then Tel Aviv and then came the light and he felt the momentum. Perhaps it was the will of God, or maybe the other one?

'When you arrive,' said Thelma, 'you have to go into the glass-fronted building.'

'What glass-fronted building?'

He was quite happy with the accelerated momentum of the barge on the fiery wake. It had been a fair old while.

'The school, silly,' she answered. The one that looked like the hospital.

'You mean the school that David and I...'

He could hear Thelma's sigh.

'When you get there, just ask for the fax from the office of Mona Freeman.'

When he arrived, another leather-jacketed – Michael wasn't sure if it was male or female – let him in. He first checked out where the fax machine was located and on finding this, pressed on a button on an expanded telephone and heard a whir and then a louder whir and the leather-jacketed one ripped off the paper from the bottom of the expanded telephone and handed it him.

The words were small on the top.

Cover Sheet, from the Office of the great 'M'.

There was a lot of gobbledegook and below, almost as though it were meant as another page, a small centred paragraph of instruction.

"It's time, Thelma, bring him in.
This is no time to be a lonely, any more.
Michael is running out of time!"

It was the words of Mona, Michael knew. Mona Freeman and she wanted him. She very much wanted Michael to be with her in one of her films.

It was very quick when it came. About the time it took for one of those faxes to be sent. And I thought videos were the latest in modern communication, The wonders of the modern age. I almost didn't believe it was happening.

First came Michael's hernia, but that was before, giving the possibility of abdominal difficulties, bloated, then punctured, as a result of Michael had only recently had a catheter bag fitted and this had started leaking.

But this wasn't enough. For the uplink to the wanted new reality, he really needed some by-proxy sepsis of the blood.

The ambulance staff were coming. Thelma was in bits on the phone to the ambulance service, having dropped all Michael's phenobarbitol down the sink.

'Yes, they will be there soon, Mrs. Porter. Just make sure he keeps his fluids up.'

He was shaking, as he sipped.

'Shall I call your children, sweetie?' asked Thelma. 'Which one should I call first?'

Michael coughed, then spluttered. I could see he was woozy from all the strange energy around and beginning to lose consciousness.

Inside the ship, Stewart's, Polly's, or Thelma's, it didn't seem to matter very much then, there wasn't a lot of room. All the valves, coming in at us both from the surrounding Bakelite plastic casing, the windows small, and where was Thelma?

Praying, or so she would have us believe. Praying for her wings back.

When the ambulance staff arrived, they banged on the stained glass of the window that Thelma had gone to such pains to design – pampas grass and birds.

'He's in the living room, bleeding,' said Thelma as she opened the door. 'It's his hernia wound, burst. He's not very clear of mind. He isn't at the best of times, but today it does appear to be worse, like he's been zapped, or something.'

But unlike it was with me, when they saw Michael, the paramedics didn't have any dark, final looks about them. Thelma seemed a little more confident.

Either that, or this was a part of her plan all along.

'Yes, sweetie,' she said, the ambulance crew nodding in agreement, as what looked like a death barge appeared to come out from the field of asphodels on the screen of the ambulance echocardiogram machine.

'Now, you just get on this barge,' she said. 'Yes, it is the fiery wake. Oh, look it's the space ship and breathe, Michael, breathe, let the winds from the clouds that call you, give you all that you have for so long desired.'

Michael got into the ship and he made himself comfortable.

From the light of a nearby procyon star, outside the small window of the ship Michael appeared so much healthier, and then as I saw my own reflection in his eyes, it seemed this was also true of me too.

We stared at each other, a while.

'Michael?'

'David, is that you?'

Michael looked at me for a moment, as I looked at him, and then we both looked at his watch, before he carefully took it off and then threw it away. And we watched it drifting off slowly, into the dark Babel space before us.

What is it?

Then we felt our own momentum, as though we were being pushed into the darkest ...

'So is this what your much wanted adventure, looks like?' asked Michael.

I wanted it to belong to the both of us, but I wasn't going to say anything.

Instead: 'Look, what's that?'

Through some sort of vortex tunnel, like a black hole, we could both see Elle laying out Michael's body in the hospital, just as she had so many times before in the various homes where she had worked.

Michael took it much better than I did, on the pavement or at Abbey Road.

Apparently, oxygen had to be given, Douglas was being told, having arrived too late, 'but it got so that after a while,' Polly was saying, 'there was too much fluid in the lungs, caused by the infection and the subsequent sepsis of his blood.'

'Would that be crocodile blood?' asked Douglas.

'Like with me,' I said.

'What do you mean?'

'I was supposed to have died of sepsis too. Peritonitis leading to sepsis of the blood? It's what I died of.'

A sudden light flashed, as the planets of Alpha Centauri shot past us, or maybe, it was the Blue Clanger moon, just as Elle, would have wanted.

I told Michael this and he laughed. It was nice to see him laugh again.

Then we learnt, from the residual energy of a travelling fax, one of Michael's grandchildren had just named a star after him.

What you mean like the star of David.

It was my turn to laugh then.

But all that was before, and here, well, it wasn't so easy to define things.

'We should be, as we need to be,' said Michael. 'As Thelma wanted and always said.'

I had nothing to argue back with and didn't want to, really.

'Yes,' I replied. 'Thelma was always right, and she was very good for you, Michael.'

'Thank you.' He smiled. 'I am very grateful for her teaching of me. Predetermined, as it was. I think it was why she was made an angel.

From far into the darkness, came a glimmer.

'It's probably reflecting on the glass front of the watch,' said Michael. Some star, somewhere.'

'Maybe,' I said. 'Or perhaps it is one of those old black and white comets of Dad's.'

Michael laughed.

But the light was getting brighter as we seemed to be drawing closer, though Michael had no means of measuring this, except for a 12.4274-mile-long antenna, that looked like a cable release from his Pentax, holding a polyester sheet trailing from copper wires, from which a broadcast was about to come in.

This is the BBC. Reports of violence are coming in from the Rossla Modern block, research settlement, on the Deep Space, meteor, Themoetius, currently traversing the Nallhead passage.

'What kind of research?' asked Michael.

As if that mattered anymore.

'Individual will, or something,' I replied. 'Being done. Does it matter? It could be an adventure! It could be Flash Gordon, or maybe even Ming!'

'Heavens,' said Michael.

The BBC again.

'Mined Tinkerbell Dust protestors, from the Billings institute, have gathered to the isolated location as smoke rises from what looks like a gypsy caravan of bonbons.'

'I see,' I said to Michael. But it was more of a question really. 'We are creating this?'

I nodded.

'It's our experience they need,' he said, and so full of confidence. 'Come on, we have to get our Widdecombe on if we're to save them.'

The BBC again. 'The first time anyone had ever heard of the Rossla Modern block, was when Tinkerbell dust was discovered by Bunter, along with its protonic potential, if scattered out from the Q14579 Lagrange Point, to shield the realm from the effects of global warming.'

Michael seemed very perturbed with the effect of his Brylcreem wearing off.

'But the required ballistics for such a feat,' he said, 'are beyond the conductivity of even copper.'

A Reginald Bosanquet Beacon call.

'What is your emergency?'

(Something unintelligible)

'Yes, Hello, are you there?'

'Hello, can you hear me?'

It was a quite So matter of fact female, name of – (unintelligible again).

'Yes, Madam. What is the nature...'

Interrupting. 'We need Mr. Singlet (bleep in the audio), Melissa, Patrick Morgan, Novice Fonda, and a small, swarthy doctor, in Oriel prime, immediately!'

Michael, started to reposition his glasses.

'Is that you, Shed Boy?' he asked. 'Are you there? Can you save us from ourselves?'

It took a little while, I could see then, through a monocle I'd picked up from somewhere. Well, seventeen parsecs, actually, before the First Responders started to arrive at the research station. They were immediately followed by chaps from the

Babel TV station, who were uncovering the rather unacceptable and troubling reality: No-one was allowed anywhere near the caravan of Bon Bons.

BABEL REPORT

'T, can you tell us what's going on?'

'Thanks, Dough. We're standing at the outer security gates of the caravan, and, as you can see, there is a large gathering of Billings Agents, but, even with mince pies, they're not being allowed into the secure facility.'

'Not being allowed. What do you mean they are not being allowed? Who's not allowing them, T?'

'Well, we can't get anyone to speak to us right now, Dough. But we can see that there is a sizeable presence on the other side of the fence and what looks like some sort of broadcast from a Bakelite monitor that the followers of the movement are dragging into the stony courtyard.'

Michael picked up the microphone.

'Shall we?'

I nodded.

Michael held the microphone to both of our mouths.

It was so good to be together again, after so long.

'This is Dave and Michael Portergeist, here,' announced Michael.

'Quite So' I joined him. 'And we are happy to be of assistance to you.'

Shouts in response from the courtyard.

'It's not, is it?' asked Michael.

'It is,' I returned.

'We lay down our challenge, and our commitment to you,' she shouted 'that forever you may continue, in space, cyber, or reality, if true to the Thelemic prophecy, you'll stay and not fall off the engine casing, like a someone who could never have managed to get here on his own!'

It was Sir Winston Churchill.

'We will remember,' I said, solemnly.

BABEL REPORT

'So does this mean a new adventure, T?'

'Always,' said Dough.

Michael nodded and smiled. 'I'm glad we're together again,' he said.

'Slingshot and its elastic,' I returned.

'And protons. Yes, and "M" will be proud, too,' said Michael. 'I hear she's in the cloud city now, with the Bay City Rollers. But she doesn't like the long-haired lovers that came from Liverpool.'

I laughed.

'Well, I always thought the Beatles were so much better, anyway' I said.

Then, just as Thelma would have wanted, we started to reimagine the true will of the prophecy and the reason behind the purple and Nike trainers.

'Michael,' asked David.

'Yes, brother.'

'Do you love me.'

'I think I know how to now. So yes.'

We hugged.

To the full orchestral performance performed by the Lagrange Point Philharmonic, a lone John Lennon (ditto the last citation, of course), sang along, beautifully, and not like Delius, at all, as you would expect from such a master.

"Limitless undying love which shines around us like a million suns. It calls us on forever and across the universe."

AFTERWORD

The years went on. The clutter room got sorted and cleared, allowing Thelma to set up an art studio, but her art was just not as rich, or satisfying, as a connection to the afterlife in the fiery wake of Babel.

The quickest way of getting back, without polyester wings, Thelma realized, was death, but not a half, sort of, death, like it had been with David. A proper one, as only Thelma could have willed, and did, dying from grief and a dose of phenobarbital soon after, or so they said at her funeral.

'Well, I did it, "M". Can you let me back in now?'

Having established her own art studio, following the falling off in her career, M was more than happy enough to oblige.

The stairs descended.

And ascending the great staircase to whatever was her place to be rightfully assigned by the great 'M', Thelma turned to see Michael and David flying off to their future in the wake of some fiery comet, at first, and then flitting through the tall gates by the fiery wake.

Let there be light!

And there was.

But there wasn't anyone from St Richard's at her funeral.

The rest of the family were there, apart from Hannah, of course – too divorced. That and her disability in her Sheltered Housing block, where she continued to teach only this time those with dementia.

'There is just not enough Jesus in this place.'

Some of these were debutantes too. Hannah so needed to be seen with the right people. And she told her children that, after she goes, on her gravestone is to be inscribed, simply.

"I tried. I really did try."

As for Stewart, he became in order pipes man, father, business man and general good guy all round. He had two kids with Melissa, became a football coach for the community, and a plumber's merchant with a sales record to be proud of. He also got himself a mansion in Lincolnshire, complete with an oval bath and bubbles.

His greatest achievement though was being the type of father that he never really had himself, and learning how to cope, the best at it. More too, using this to instil values that he could also pass on.

Then, after a break-up with Melissa, he learnt how to love again, not just himself, but his new belle, Lynne, able to support, live and grow into contentment for all he had done.

Douglas, after he finished distributing the prophecy and taking a three-year trip around Europe chasing hippies with a backpack, became a Social Worker. First in homes, then in the field. He wanted to try and to help people find their voice, just as he had his own, but he still had difficulties with Thatcher's overhaul of the system and sometimes remembering what he had chosen to forget about martyrdom.

It would come back to him. It always did. Then an arts manager, first to go to get a degree, then a business owner.

Over the years, he managed to develop quite a following for his resilience and unique approach to life, or so those that followed him often said.

All that was wrong with him by then was that he sometimes lost his house keys.

His partner understood, though her father never did.

Later than most he had his son, of whom he was always very proud. Laid back, wanting to become an engineer, just like his granddad, bless his polyesters and all who sail in her.

Polly, eventually left home with Tim, started a family, three, ran nurseries, progressed to a degree, sorted herself out with a better therapist than Mary, even learning how to ring and even visit Hannah sometimes.

She too set herself up a business and managed to become a much-admired senior lecturer too in a university. Child care and safeguarding. There was no one more qualified.

But she was always so much more to the family. She became the Bostick that held them all together. And didn't they all do, well. So much better than acceptable. Well, they did.

It was because Polly never felt the need to be a debutante. She was not the same as her mother, far from it. With Polly the tide turned.

Elle, with her life-long lived message set to define her, moved on to a life working in various care homes, her marriage to Pete, innit, lots of Karaoke, and retirement, though she still helps out with a disabled man once or twice a week, when the need calls.

She turned into the most capable gem.

'Bloody diamond,' as Pete, innit, was not afraid to tell anyone, everyone, all the time, and she also delved into poetry.

'Loving, able and with so much to give, despite her lack of understanding,' but not in any practical sense. Capable, it should be said,' as indeed, all recognized.

'Fly, Dad, fly.'

Like a breath of fresh air, she was, specialising in how to make everyone's life complete.

Apart from Tingle Four, that was, who, following the demise of Thelma, had to go to a friend of the family, where sitting at the left-hand side of thje Great 'M', when she could be bothered, she still showed her self-satisfied, expression as a reward for all the hedgehogs she had killed.

And as the years went on, most that would come into contact with any of them, would often remark, how is that, coming from where they did, none ended up in prison, on drugs, or wasting away in some mental hospital?

'It's about how we survived,' they answered, 'how it played out, despite, and from this, how together, we all learnt to grow up and become.

Other titles by BLKDOG Publishing for your consideration:

Britannia: The Wall
By Richard Denham & M. J. Trow

THE END OF ROMAN BRITAIN BEGINS.

The story opens in 367 AD. Four soldiers - Justinus, Paternus, Leocadius and Vitalis - are out hunting for food supplies at an outpost of Hadrian's Wall, when the Wall comes under attack.

The four find their fort destroyed, their comrades killed, and Paternus is unable to find his wife and son. As they run south to Eboracum, they realize that this is no ordinary border raid. Ranged against the Romans at the edge of the world are four different peoples, and they have banded together under a mysterious leader who wears a silver mask and uses the name Valentinus - man of Valentia, the turbulent area north of the Wall.

Faced with questions they are hard-pressed to answer, Leocadius blurts out a story that makes the men Heroes of the Wall. Their lives change not only when Valentinus begins his lethal sweep across Britannia but as soon as Leo's lie is out in the world, growing and changing as it goes.

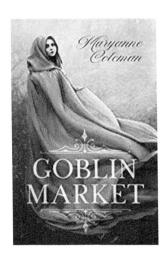

Goblin Market
By Maryanne Coleman

Have you ever wondered what happened to the faeries you used to believe in? They lived at the bottom of the garden and left rings in the grass and sparkling glamour in the air to remind you where they were. But that was then – now you might find them in places you might not think to look. They might be stacking shelves, delivering milk or weighing babies at the clinic. Open your eyes and keep your wits about you and you might see them.

But no one is looking any more and that is hard for a Faerie Queen to bear and Titania has had enough. When Titania stamps her foot, everyone in Faerieland jumps; publicity is what they need. Television, magazines. But that sort of thing is much more the remit of the bad boys of the Unseelie Court, the ones who weave a new kind of magic; the World Wide Web. Here is Puck re-learning how to fly; Leanne the agent who really is a vampire; Oberon's Boys playing cards behind the wainscoting; Black Annis, the bag-lady from Hainault, all gathered in a Restoration comedy that is strictly twenty-first century.

Fade
By Bethan White

There is nothing extraordinary about Chris Rowan. Each day he wakes to the same faces, has the same breakfast, the same commute, the same sort of homes he tries to rent out to unsuspecting tenants.

There is nothing extraordinary about Chris Rowan. That is apart from the black dog that haunts his nightmares and an unexpected encounter with a long forgotten demon from his past. A nudge that will send Chris on his own downward spiral, from which there may be no escape.

There is nothing extraordinary about Chris Rowan...

www.blkdogpublishing.com

Printed in Great Britain
by Amazon